EVIL IN THE BADLANDS

EVIL IN THE BADLANDS

ACADEMY OF NECESSARY MAGIC™ BOOK FIVE

MARTHA CARR

MICHAEL ANDERLE

LMBPN Publishing
PMB 196, 2540 South Maryland Pkwy
Las Vegas, NV 89109

Version 1.00, May 2021
eBook ISBN: 978-1-64971-793-1
Print ISBN: 978-1-64971-794-8

From Martha

To everyone who still believes in magic and all the possibilities that holds.
To all the readers who make this entire ride so much fun.
To Louie, Jackie, and so many wonderful friends who remind me all the time of what really matters and how wonderful life can be in any given moment.

From Michael

To Family, Friends and
Those Who Love
To Read.
May We All Enjoy Grace
To Live The Life We Are
Called.

THE EVIL IN THE BADLANDS TEAM

JIT Readers

Dave Hicks
Dorothy Lloyd
Zacc Pelter
Diane L. Smith

If I missed anyone, please let me know!

Editor

Skyhunter Editing Team

CHAPTER ONE

"I tell you what, kid. Whoever came up with puttin' one of these things in every overpriced coffee shop in the country oughtta take a serious look at their sanity."

Amanda Coulier snorted and glanced sidelong at her bounty-hunter guardian from the passenger seat of his red Jeep. "You don't like Starbucks?"

"Hell. It ain't 'bout the name, and you know it." Johnny Walker sniffed and turned off the engine. "It's 'bout makin' folks drive all the way out to Marco Island just to drop their kid off at the train the rest of the world don't understand is a train."

"Oh, I get it." The fourteen-year-old shifter girl unbuckled her seatbelt and opened the passenger-side door. "You don't like having to drive me into an actual city."

Johnny got out of the car before she could close her door in his face, and it took all she had not to burst out laughing at his attempt to look wise and pissed off at the same time. "Naw, it ain't that simple. Though I should've just driven you out to the school and had you picked up there. If you need gettin' somewhere, kid, I'm here to get you there. I just ain't fixin' to turn into a damn teenager-chauffeur 'cause your redhead friend reckons she don't have to do any of the work herself is all."

Amanda grabbed her fully packed duffel bag from the back of the Jeep and grinned at the dwarf. "Don't worry, Johnny. In a year and a half, I'll be able to drive myself."

"Wait, what?"

"Then you won't have to *chauffeur* me anywhere." She joined him on the sidewalk in front of the Starbucks and patted his shoulder. "I can't wait to take Sheila out for a day. All by myself."

Johnny made a comically startled choking sound and blustered after her toward the front door. "Listen here, kid. No one drives Sheila but me. You know that."

"Hmm. What about the truck?"

"No." A little *ding* greeted them when he opened the door and held it for her.

"Well, then I guess you'll have to *buy* me a car. I have to drive *something*."

They stepped into the Starbucks, and Johnny scowled at his ward's profile. "Buy you a car? You ain't even learned *how* to drive yet. Why are we talkin' 'bout this right now? You tryin' to rope me into somethin'?"

She turned to fix him with a brilliant grin from ear to ear, widening her eyes and batting her eyelashes.

He leaned away from her, wrinkling his nose. "What're you doin'?"

"Reminding you how cute and sweet I am."

"Kid, this ain't the time to—"

"And asking if you'll buy me a coffee."

Johnny barked out a laugh. "Every damn time I drop you off for a couple of months, you come up with a dozen different ways to pull the rug out from under me at the last second. Where was all that *cute and sweet* over the summer, huh?"

"It's relatively new. Is it working?"

He looked her up and down with a low chuckle. "Nope."

Amanda's exaggerated grin instantly disappeared. "Fine. I'll work on it."

"Honestly, kid, you'll get a lot more out of tryin' to manipulate a fella if you go straight for the throat first. Use the gifts you got, huh? Bein' all cute and sweet just ain't for you."

"Wow." She stared at the menu sign hanging above the order counter and tugged the strap of her duffel bag over one shoulder. "Way to make an insecure teenage girl feel good about herself."

"Huh?" Johnny froze. "I ain't... Hell, it's got nothin' to do with..." He cleared his throat. "You ain't said a thing 'bout bein' insecure, kid. Can't for the life of me figure out why you would be, but... I mean, if you reckon you need to get somethin' off your chest before I go—"

"There is one thing, actually."

"All right."

Amanda turned to look at him and let out a heavy sigh. "Grande white-mocha latte with an extra shot of vanilla."

"You..." Johnny blinked furiously, then snorted and shook his head. "Straight for the throat. Now I'm eatin' my own damn words."

The girl's wide grin returned, but this time it was completely genuine. "I mean, it's not like that phrase only applies to teeth and claws, right?"

"Uh-huh." He playfully punched her in the shoulder and huffed out a laugh. "All this time bein' a bounty hunter and goin' after the worst of the worst, and I reckon *you'll* end up bein' the one magical to put me in an early grave."

"Aw, come on. You're already super old."

"I got plenty of years in me yet, kid." Johnny pointed at her. "Watch it."

"Yeah, totally. After coffee?"

"I ain't patronizin' a place I don't enjoy bein' at." The bounty hunter nodded toward the hallway leading toward the bathrooms in the back corner of the store. "And I reckon y'all got a tight schedule to keep."

Amanda followed his gaze and saw the red-haired Fiona Damascus stepping out of the hallway. The shifter woman smirked at them and leaned against the corner of the hall's entrance before folding her arms. "It's not *that* tight of a schedule. It's basically an orientation. I think."

"Uh-huh. Reckon it's a little more complex than walking onto that school campus and sufferin' through one of your principal's never-endin' speeches."

The shifter girl laughed and playfully rolled her eyes. "I definitely don't miss those."

"Well, *this* meetin's professional. Does you no good to be late."

"I thought the definition of professional was that you get *paid* for something—"

"Get outta here." Chuckling, he bumped his shoulder against hers to nudge her toward Fiona. "See you in a couple of months, kid."

Without warning, she turned and threw her arms around him for a tight hug, her duffel bag thumping against them both. "I'll let you buy me that coffee next time."

"Next time." Johnny shook his head. "You watch yourself. Don't do anythin' I wouldn't."

As she headed across the coffee shop toward Fiona, Amanda couldn't help but laugh before calling over her shoulder, "You know that's basically a green light to do whatever I want, right?"

"Now, hold on—"

"Bye, Johnny. Thanks for the ride!" She gave him an enthusiastic wave, then finally reached her shifter mentor and stopped outside the hall. "Any chance *you* want a coffee right now?"

"Hi to you too, kid." Fiona jerked her head up at Johnny in a quick nod of acknowledgment. The dwarf glanced suspiciously around the Starbucks, then spun and stormed back outside, grumbling the whole way. "Is that what you were trying to weasel out of him? A coffee?"

"It's not weaseling if he literally told me to get what I want by going for the throat."

The shifter woman glanced down at her mentee and raised an eyebrow.

"Okay, metaphorically. Obviously, he was wrong."

"Obviously." Setting a hand on the shifter girl's shoulder, Fiona chuckled and shook her head. "We don't have time to stand in that endless line now anyway. We got a train to catch."

"Endless… Oh, come *on*." Amanda gestured with an open hand toward the line that had suddenly grown ridiculously long just over the last three minutes. "I could've been standing at the counter by now."

"Cut your losses, kid. I'll get you your caffeine fix next time."

"Really?"

"Probably not." Fiona tugged the shifter girl after her toward the door at the end of the hall marked Supplies. She looked briefly back at the hallway, then opened the door and ushered Amanda inside.

The fake supplies closet fell intensely silent.

"You ready for this, kid?"

"What, you mean my first day as a fourteen-year-old intern hunting down mutated magical beasts for the Coalition of Shifters?" Amanda cleared her throat. "Why wouldn't I be?"

Fiona laughed. "I meant the train ride, but that's cool."

"Oh. Wait, I—"

Before she could get out anything else, her mentor cranked down on the large brass lever that dropped the supply closet down through the floor of the Starbucks like the Tower of Terror ride. Amanda's guts leapt up into her throat, and she gasped for another breath right before the dangerously descending elevator came to a complete stop with a shudder.

"Um..." She swallowed. "I guess I probably wasn't ready for that part. Again."

"You survived." Fiona winked at her. "That should make today a piece of cake for you, right?"

The elevator doors opened with a *hiss* to reveal the inside of the empty train car waiting for them. The shifters took their seats on the plush red upholstery, and Amanda dumped her duffel bag onto the floor at her feet. "Do you know what I'll be doing? Today, I mean."

"Hmm." Fiona studied the elevator doors closing first without a hitch, followed by the gilded exterior doors of the train car itself. She didn't say a word.

"Uh...Fiona?" Amanda had to snap her fingers in front of her mentor's face to catch her attention again. "Hello?"

"Hmm?" The shifter woman turned toward her again with wide eyes and blinked quickly. "What was that?"

"I asked if you knew what's gonna happen today, but... What was *that?*"

"Oh. Ha. Just give me a..." Fiona passed her hand back and forth through the air between herself and the closed doors.

Oh, jeeze. She's checking for invisible teenage witches.

Folding her arms and slumping back against the upholstered and cushioned back of the train car's bench, Amanda watched her mentor's strange ritual with a smirk. "She's not here, Fiona. I promise."

"Who?" The shifter woman leaned in the opposite direction to swipe her hand across the other side of the train car.

"I know you know what I'm talking about."

Apparently, that level of vagueness snapped Fiona out of her concentration, and she sat quickly back down on the seat again with a tight smile. "Your aggravatingly skilled witch friend slipped past both of us last time, and it didn't go well for any of us. I'm just being thorough."

"Yeah, but Summer doused herself in perfume last time. I'm pretty sure we'd smell her again."

"Oh, of course." The shifter woman frowned at the corner of the train car where the ceiling met the sliding glass privacy doors and tapped a finger against her lips. "Unfortunately, my frustration the last time I saw that girl was enough to prompt a...slip of the tongue."

"Huh?"

Fiona met her mentee's gaze and raised her eyebrows. "I told her exactly how to avoid being *sniffed out* during a hypothetical excursion under that ridiculous illusion of hers. Didn't I? Unless I'm misremembering the entire thing..."

Amanda forced back a laugh. "Baking soda, right?"

The shifter woman puffed out a massive sigh and nodded slowly. "Baking soda. I have no idea what I was thinking."

"Well, Summer Flannerty is *definitely* not here right now. Honestly, I'm glad you told her."

"Oh, really? Because I can't help but feel like the other shoe's about to drop. A shoe with purple hair and a bad attitude I can neither see nor smell."

With a snort, Amanda stood to pull the sliding glass doors shut. "We're alone. So you can stop being paranoid."

"This isn't paranoia, kid. This is due diligence. You have no idea what I had to do to clean up after your friend's little invisibility stunt." She glanced at Amanda and shrugged. "Which I obviously don't blame you for."

"Thanks."

"Neither does the Coalition, for that matter. I mean, they *did* at first, but I took care of it."

Amanda nodded. "Also thanks."

"Yeah, no sweat." Finally convinced they were alone, Fiona settled back into the seat and drew a deep breath. "Okay, now tell me why."

"Why I just thanked you, or..."

"Why you're glad I run my mouth when I'm angry instead of throwing tiny witches through walls."

"Oh." Amanda choked back another laugh. "It means I'm getting good at catching tiny witches who know exactly how not to get caught by shifters."

"For crying out loud. She took my suggestion to heart?"

"Yep. The day after you told her the answer to all her problems. Hey, don't worry. I can always tell when she's around. She does this weird thing where she holds her breath for way too long. Then it sounds like she's laughing when she starts breathing again. Like, in a whisper. Totally recognizable."

Fiona looked her up and down and chuckled. "At least you've figured all that out on your own."

"Doesn't mean Summer's very happy about it. She doesn't know I found her tell, so don't say anything."

"Trust me, kid. If I don't see that particular friend of yours ever again, it'll be too soon."

The overhead lights in the train car flickered, then the robotic female voice came through the speakers in the ceiling. *"This train will be departing in five minutes."*

"Oh, good." Fiona grinned. "We made it in plenty of time. Nice to have a few extra minutes to prepare yourself for shooting across the country underground at the speed of...well, magic, huh?"

Amanda raised an eyebrow and slowly shook her head. "We totally had time to get that coffee."

"You're fourteen, kid. Your veins are filled to the brim with renewable energy from the time you open your eyes in the morning to the second you pass out. You don't need coffee."

The shifter girl snorted. "Who *needs* coffee?"

"I..." Fiona glanced at the ceiling again and pursed her lips. "Fair point."

"You still haven't answered my question."

"Hmm?"

Amanda spread her arms. "First day on the job."

"I wouldn't start calling it a job just yet, kid."

"Okay, fine. Internship. Volunteer work. Extracurricular consulting. Whatever."

The shifter woman barked out a laugh. "That was a good one."

"Fiona."

"Okay, okay. So as far as I know—"

"This train will be departing in two minutes."

"What?" Amanda scowled at the speakers above them. "The robot lady literally just said five minutes, like, thirty seconds ago."

"Huh." Fiona looked completely clueless as she scanned their compartment. "Well, I guess we're running out of time, then."

"You can answer my question. At least give me a little heads up about what to expect when we get to The Pylon."

"Oh, we don't have anywhere near enough time for that now." The shifter woman ran a hand through her buoyant red curls and kept staring at the speakers in the ceiling. "Besides, we're not going to The Pylon today, kid. That was kind of a one-time deal we all blew to pieces."

"Okay, so—"

"This train is now departing. Please remain seated until you have reached your final destination. Thank you."

"Then where are we going?" Amanda blurted quickly.

Fiona grinned but didn't have time to answer before the Starbucks train lurched away from its station in Marco Island and shot toward its next stop at a speed faster than any living being was supposed to withstand.

Amanda was pressed back against her seat by the sudden takeoff and gritted her teeth against the force.

At least it's a magical train, so I won't get my guts splattered all over the seats. Is that why they're red?

CHAPTER TWO

They ground to a halt at four different stops along the Starbucks train's route. New magical passengers trailed in through the opening doors all along the train, including those leading into the car Amanda and Fiona shared. Fortunately, no one tried to enter the compartment with them. That didn't help the shifter girl's stomach.

After the fourth stop, she groaned and thumped her head back against the seat cushion before closing her eyes. "This is worse than carsickness."

"Huh. You get carsick?" Fiona watched the new passengers go between them to board the train, occasionally nodding at those who bothered to spare her a glance and nod first.

"No." Amanda groaned. "Which makes it worse. I don't think I can handle another stop."

"Good thing this is our stop, then." Fiona stood and headed for the sliding doors of the train leading out into the current station. "Come on, kid. I'd hate to have to come after you via train chase. Not the fun kind on horses or motorcycles, either. I mean one train chasing another. Let's go."

She grabbed the underside of the girl's arm and helped her to her feet.

Swallowing thickly, Amanda groaned again and barely held her stomach together when she stooped to grab the strap of her duffel bag. The luggage dragged across the ground behind her, then they were out of the Starbucks train and walking down a long, narrow tunnel with dim lighting and weird geometric patterns carved into the walls.

"Where are we?"

"Underneath the Starbucks in..." Fiona glanced at her watch. "Lakewood, Colorado. I think."

"Your watch doubles as a compass?"

"No. Funny, though." The shifter woman stopped walking and searched both ends of the hallway before grabbing Amanda's arm again. "It's always fun to see if I can time this right."

"I have no idea what you're talking about." *And if I think too hard, I'm definitely gonna puke.*

Footsteps came toward them from the other end of the hall, and Fiona grinned. "You will when you learn how to do this."

The jarring tingle of intensely strong magic racing through Amanda made her forget her nausea for all of two seconds, because the sensation of being ripped apart and pulled in two different directions drowned out everything else.

Then they were standing in the center of a vast field spanning a warm, sunny valley. Towering rocky mountain peaks surrounded them. Amanda staggered forward under the abrupt relief and surprise of being teleported by her mentor. The duffel bag *thumped* to the ground at her feet, and she fought back the urge to vomit right there.

"Whoa." Fiona gave her a sheepish smile. "You weren't kidding about the trainsickness, huh?"

"Teleporting's obviously not a fix for that."

"You'll be okay." The shifter woman patted Amanda on the back, then turned in a slow circle to take in their surroundings.

MARTHA CARR & MICHAEL ANDERLE

"It's been a long time since I've been out here, kid. Mm. Smell that mountain breeze."

"Also not helping." When she was finally sure she wouldn't be sick, Amanda forced herself to take deep breaths before taking in their surroundings. "Okay, *now* where are we?"

"Deep in the Rocky Mountains, kid."

"What?"

"Oh, come on. It's not that weird. We rode a train faster than light. And *you* are about to start your first day as a Coalition initiate."

"Don't you mean intern?"

Fiona shrugged. "Same thing in your case. Keep up."

The redhead shifter shoved both hands in her pockets and took off in a leisurely stride across the field.

Shaking her head, Amanda swung her duffel bag onto her shoulder again and shuffled after her through the grass studded with brilliant wildflowers. *I don't think I can handle teleporting again either. It's not like we have a choice. There's nothing else out here.*

"How are you with tight spaces, kid?"

"What?"

"Just kidding." Fiona reached out with one hand and slowly swung it back and forth as she slowed her pace as if she was trying to navigate a room in the dark instead of walking across an open valley in broad daylight. "Okay. It's gotta be right here, somewhere…"

The air rippled with opalescent light where her fingers had brushed through the enchantment. When they did, Amanda caught the thick scent of the valley's magic.

What the heck is that? Black pepper and...sunscreen?

"Well, look at that." Fiona chuckled. "Here we go, kid. Like I said, keep up."

Amanda stared at her mentor walking right into the shimmering light one second and disappearing from view the next.

Great. Illusions in the middle of the mountains, and I have no idea what to be ready for. A slow smile spread across the girl's lips. *That means this is gonna be fun.*

The black pepper smell grew overwhelmingly strong when she stepped through the shimmering light. Then she found herself standing not in an empty, open field but inside a white, sterile-looking hallway. The overhead lights gleaming off clean white tiles and pristinely polished stainless-steel surfaces made the inside of whatever this place was a lot brighter than being out under the sun.

Amanda scrunched up her face and blinked against the glare bouncing toward her from all directions.

"Come on, kid," Fiona muttered. "I think I can hear your welcoming committee."

The hallway took a sharp right. Then they stepped into a large circular room with a giant domed ceiling stretching from one side of the floor to the other in a massive bubble. Amanda thought she was looking up at a roof made entirely of windows until she saw the first flicker of light and what looked a little like static race across the building material. Then the panels forming the walls took on their clear, glassy reflection again as if nothing had happened.

Huh. I bet they keep the place all sunny-looking like this even if snow covers it or something.

Tables and chairs formed clusters around the large room, some of them stacked with books, others with computers or tools and equipment. Most of the seats were empty except for those at the closest table when Amanda and Fiona finally exited the hallway.

Half a dozen shifters had gathered to huddle over a document laid out on the table. None of them paid any attention to the newcomers until Fiona finally decided to clear her throat. The sound echoed incredibly loudly across the dome.

A shifter woman with close-cut dark hair whipped her head up, and her eyes widened. "Fiona. And…Amelia, right?"

13

"Amanda." The girl raised her hand for a small wave. "Hey."

"Yes. Right. You just... Hold on." The woman lifted a finger for them to wait, then returned to the group of huddled shifters. Then she stabbed that finger down in four different places on the document and muttered in a low, conspiratorial voice, "We can't even begin to entertain this idea until the information is one hundred percent verified. Understand? This isn't Hide and Seek on the playground, okay? Make sure they know exactly where the next flare *will* be, then—"

"If they're sure," interjected a pale shifter man with a constant twitch in his left eye, "they'll want to go after this one right away."

"I said one hundred percent, Jeremiah. The only way to test that is to let the next flare produce itself as predicted. If they're right, we know the algorithm works. Then we wait for the next one and stop it *then*. I shouldn't have to explain the basic mechanics of testing for an accurate projection when we're this close to..."

The woman's voice lowered even more, and Amanda didn't bother trying to listen in on the conversation. She was too busy staring at the walls, which occasionally flickered with the silhouette of a bird passing overhead or a large insect flittering around in the meadow outside.

If we're even in *a meadow at all.*

She leaned toward Fiona and whispered, "Who's that?"

"One of the top magical biologists on this planet, kid." The shifter woman smirked. "Melody's been—"

"*Dr. Caniss.*" The woman with short dark hair whispering orders at the table pointed right at Fiona without looking up from the forms. "It's always been Dr. Caniss, Fiona. I'm tired of correcting you."

"My bad." Fiona lifted both hands in surrender despite the biologist not having looked up at her once. Then she leaned toward Amanda and muttered, "She's brilliant. Which is why she's running this operation with the brand-new beasts and critters and whatnot. There's just not much room left in that huge brain of hers for normal social interaction—"

"There isn't enough room in this facility for your obnoxious comments," Dr. Caniss spat back. "Monica, I want a full report of this team's whereabouts on my desk in two hours, got it? If they insist on holding back information because they think this is ready to go, feel free to insist I'm perfectly happy not to pay them for going against my orders, and more importantly, protocol."

"Got it."

"Jeremiah, keep a close eye on the algorithms. If anything changes, let me know. And for the love of science, if any of those tracking markers close on the target by more than *ten* feet, we're shutting this thing down, understand? I'm not taking the fall for a magical Chernobyl induced by idiocy and a lack of common sense. Get to work."

The other shifters around the table—all of them in regular clothing, except for Dr. Caniss in a white lab coat—stood together and pushed their chairs in under the table. The smallest shifter woman, who couldn't have been older than her early twenties, gathered up the documents spread across the table and stacked them neatly in her hands. As the others turned away and headed to their prospective areas around the dome and the branching hallways extending from the circular walls, she licked her lips and nodded. "Do you want these on your desk?"

"Scanned into the system first, Lucy." Dr. Caniss still propped herself up with both hands on the table and loomed over it, staring at the glinting stainless-steel surface. "Then yes. On my desk. With a matcha latte and a double scoop of spirulina. Thank you."

Lucy nodded, glanced at Fiona and Amanda, but didn't say a word or give any other indication that she'd noticed their arrival before she scurried off to do her job.

"What the heck is matcha?" Amanda whispered.

"Beats me." Fiona shrugged. "If the doctor's drinking it, it's most likely as healthy as it is disgusting."

Dr. Caniss inhaled a long, deep breath through her nose, then finally straightened to look at her guests for the first time. "If you'd like one, all you have to do is ask."

"No, thank you." Fiona chuckled. "If—"

"You're the new intern." Dr. Caniss pointed at Amanda. "The girl from the Everglades."

"Um..." Amanda blinked and popped her lips as the biologist stared at her with wide eyes and no expression whatsoever. "Technically, I'm *from* New York. But yeah. The Everglades are home now, so I guess—"

"Parents, Bruce and Denise Coulier. Siblings, one. Identical twin Claire. All deceased."

"What?"

With a grimace, Fiona leaned down toward her mentee and muttered, "Roll with it, kid. She's processing. If I hadn't seen her bleed more than once, I'd say we're talking to the first real AI on either world."

Great. I'm here to work for a computer that looks like a shifter, and I'm not even getting paid for it.

Amanda stared right back at Dr. Caniss's dark-brown eyes and waited.

The biologist sucked in another sharp breath. "Kidnapped by the Boneblade gang in New York, put up for sale on the dark web pre-live auction at the Monsters Ball at Falcon Towers May of last year. Highest bidder, Lemonhead, AKA the Red Boar, AKA Chiron Fort. Freed by Johnny Walker, dwarf bounty hunter for the Federal Bureau of Investigation's Department of Monsters and Magicals, Bounty Hunter Division. Now his ward. And a student at the newly founded Academy of Necessary Magic in the *middle* of the Florida Everglades."

The shifter girl swallowed.

This is so creepy.

"That's, um… I mean, that's all pretty accurate—"

"Youngest student of this year's soon-to-be junior class at fourteen. Fifteen on December thirtieth. Passed years one and two with above average and still highly mediocre grades at a three-point-seven-eight GPA, when translated to traditional scoring systems."

"Wait, *highly mediocre?*" Amanda huffed out a laugh and glanced at Fiona. "I don't think—"

"Vandalized a seven-hundred-and-fifty-three-year-old soul tomb to unleash a vengeful spirit before quelling said force again by correcting whatever minor miscalculation you made. Broke school protocol to sneak into the Everglades kemana and sabotaged a high-level operation executed by one Adalynn Jade, Saithe."

"Okay." The girl folded her arms. "Sabotage is kind of a strong word. I had no idea—"

"Observed, investigated, and actively engaged Subject UM-43562 on school grounds before current data was available for analysis or interpretation."

"Huh?"

"Skillsets include unarmed close-range combat, rudimentary stealth, semi-advanced gardening and horticulture experience with at least four different species of highly volatile magical fauna, and defensively herding a small singular of…" Dr. Caniss's eyelids fluttered briefly, and Amanda didn't have any trouble at all imagining a stuttering click of the woman's internal gears clicking into place. When Caniss's eyelids stopped fluttering, she stared straight at Amanda again. "Wild boar."

"Wow." Taking a deep breath, Amanda turned her head slightly to eye the biologist sideways. *Either she'll let me talk now, or I'm about to get my future read for me too.*

"Well." Fiona raised her eyebrows and chuckled. "I guess that about sums it up, so now—"

"And…*and…*" Dr. Caniss thrust an index finger into the air, either to quiet her guests or to help her remember the final piece. Maybe both. "The youngest shifter currently on record to both grow Fatethistle and brew the activation tincture for successful integration of Saithe initiation alchemy to access and empower personal latent abilities. Magically speaking." As the woman lowered her finger, one corner of her mouth twitched in satisfied amusement. "Have I left anything out?"

Amanda frowned and couldn't think of anything better to say than, "Just my name."

Caniss snorted and turned her scrutinizing gaze onto Fiona. "You've clearly passed down some of your more irritating qualities to this disciple of yours."

"That word comes with way too many undertones, doc. Let's go with *student*, huh?"

As if Fiona hadn't said a thing, the biologist added, "I don't appreciate the cynicism."

"Hey, don't look at me." Fiona gestured toward Amanda, who slowly lowered her duffel bag to the floor because now her shoulder ached from holding it for so long. "She'd already mastered a smart mouth and a serious attitude on her own before we met."

Amanda looked up at her mentor and whispered, "What?"

"I give her full credit for everything else too." The redheaded woman shrugged. "I'm only the facilitator."

"Well, I hope she knows this isn't daycare."

"I'm sure she's well aware, doctor."

"Because I've never had the time for strong wills and argumentative natures. Certainly not yours, and I don't intend to suffer the same from your...student."

Fiona nodded. "She's ready."

"Yeah, and she's standing right here," Amanda cut in. She hadn't meant to yell, but her voice echoed around the dome as if she'd shouted it from the top of the Grand Canyon.

Both shifter women looked at her with wide eyes.

I don't know what I expected, but it wasn't this.

"I don't tolerate untamed emotions and unrestrained outbursts in this facility," Dr. Caniss said quickly. "You only get one warning."

"Sorry," Amanda muttered. "I'm ready to get started."

"See?" Fiona folded her arms and grinned. "I told you she has the right attitude. Brings it with her into everything she does."

"Yes, well, without practical application and an understanding of the correct procedures, not to mention the ability to carry them out as directed, the right attitude is as useful to me as a pair of vestigial gills." Caniss eyed Amanda up and down, then turned away from the table and her guests to storm across the massive dome. "Keep up, Amanda. If you gawk too long without paying attention, I won't come looking for you. Everyone else here is too busy to play babysitter."

Slinging the strap of her duffel bag over her shoulder again, Amanda took off after the insanely antisocial biologist and tried to keep herself from staring at everything they passed on the way.

Fiona fell in line beside her and chuckled as she playfully elbowed the girl in the side. "See? She *does* know your name."

"Yeah, apparently that's the least important thing about me."

"Nah. Don't let it get to you, kid. The doc has a love affair with facts and data. Names don't really factor into it. Now that I think about it, feelings don't either. So keep being yourself, and you'll be fine."

"Seriously?" Amanda huffed out a laugh and shook her head as Caniss reached one of the branching halls and stopped to type a security code into the panel beside the sliding door. "Because I'm pretty sure being myself here is gonna get me kicked out."

"Not even a little, kid. Being yourself is what got you here in the first place. It's why Dr. Robot up there requested you for this. By name."

Dr. Caniss didn't bother to turn around and ensure her guests followed her before she disappeared into the hallway behind the open door.

"I thought the Coalition board wanted me."

"Oh, they do. Still, they wouldn't have agreed to that nightmare of a first meeting if the doc hadn't pled your case. Ad nauseam. Or so I've been told." They entered the hallway, and the echo of Caniss's brisk footsteps trailed toward them as the edge of her white lab coat flitted around the corner down another intersecting corridor. "She wants you here. For good reason, too."

"Okay..." A loud metallic *bang* came from behind the wall on their right. Amanda stepped away from it and puffed out a sigh. "Whatever it takes, right?"

"That's it." Fiona's grin faded before she leaned toward her mentee one more time and lowered her voice into a real whisper. "Just maybe don't mention the board while you're here, huh? Like, ever."

CHAPTER THREE

Dr. Caniss led them both down an incomprehensible series of turns and branching hallways, all without slowing or waiting for her guests or offering to explain a thing.

This place is a maze. Amanda turned to look over her shoulder and found nothing but the same bright white walls lined with stainless-steel doors. *Someone could probably get lost and die in here. I wonder if anyone has?*

Finally, the biologist stopped at two wide double doors, also stainless steel, and punched in a ridiculously long security code before the doors slid away from each other to either side. Instantly, the musky scent of fur, feces, and wildlife filled this end of the corridor. Joining the smell was a cacophony of screeches, chittering, chirping, grunting, and something that sounded like a chainsaw revving up.

Caniss stepped inside, and Amanda had no choice but to follow. Fiona entered the room with a chuckle right before the metal doors slid closed again.

The room was as big as the first dome they'd entered, only instead of tables, empty chairs, computer monitors, and tech gear, cages filled the space.

They ranged in all sizes—from the tiny cage hanging from a standing hook like an actual birdcage to the largest ones in the back bigger than Amanda's bedroom at home and almost the exact size as her Academy dorm room. Most were empty, but six of them held creatures Amanda didn't recognize in the slightest.

"Initial examination," Caniss dryly said as she turned to face her new intern. "When we receive new captures from out in the field—unknown magical creatures, to be exact—they come here first. For both observational and quarantine purposes."

"Quarantine?" Amanda couldn't stop staring at the giant purple rat the size of a full-grown hog in the far corner of the cage. With every breath the creature took, the fan of elongating spikes covering its back like a porcupine's quills spread out like a cloak, then drew back inward. "For these...animals, right? Not us?"

"That's ridiculous. We can't contract anything from these subjects. We contained them with a complicated series of magical and technological safeguards. Caring for their physiological needs and biological functions, however, is a task we must perform by hand."

Right on cue, a door at the back of the room opened, and a thin shifter man wearing long yellow commercial-grade rubber gloves and a gas mask entered. He hauled two empty five-gallon buckets in after him and set them both down on a cart along the wall.

"Bill's the resident zookeeper," Fiona muttered.

"Don't be obtuse." Caniss waved a dismissive hand toward the shifter, who was now taking off his gloves and mask. "Ignore him."

Bill chuckled as he set his gloves neatly down on a shelf, followed by his mask. When he turned to catch Amanda's gaze, he nodded once and winked before heading toward the desk in the back area cleared of cages to type away at a computer.

At least not everyone here is so dry and boring.

"Oh, sorry." Fiona elbowed the girl and grimaced in mock embarrassment. "Didn't mean to be *obtuse*."

"All incoming subjects get processed through this wing," Caniss continued as she slowly scanned the room, completely oblivious to the private joke. "Two-week containment period for initial observation. Of course, we separate subjects by examination rooms according to similarity in temperament and dietary requirements. Or this would, in fact, become a zoo. It's not. This is a high-security research facility. Don't forget that. Once we've cataloged initial data at the end of the containment period, we relocate the subjects to a sophisticated and meticulously monitored ecosystem simulation field, where we—"

"Are all of these mutated creatures?" Amanda interrupted, unable to keep her curiosity at bay.

"Mutated?" Caniss scowled at Fiona. "*Mutated*? Is that what you told her this is?"

Fiona shrugged under the interrogation.

"Or evolved. Whatever you wanna call it." Amanda approached the closest medium-sized cage, which held a three-foot-tall red and silver bird with a bony crown circling its head. Except the thing had three legs—all glowing silver—and two tails fluttering in a breeze that didn't exist. "Evolved from the Oriceran version, I mean."

"Oriceran versions." Caniss hissed out a sigh and shook her head. "You have an astounding lack of experiential—"

"Doc." Fiona smiled at the biologist and nodded toward Amanda as the girl leaned toward the cage for a closer look. "I still have to get her back to the Academy today. Classes start on Monday."

"Well, of *course*, we wouldn't want to stand in the way of such invaluable knowledge taught at that school." Caniss stared right back at the redhead woman and raised her eyebrows. "One shudders at the thought."

The bird in the cage cocked its head and fixed Amanda with

one beady black eye. It shuffled toward her, ruffling its glimmering feathers, and a swirl of silver light bloomed within its eye before it opened its beak and croaked.

She pulled back with an unsure laugh and pointed at the creature. "That sounded like a frog."

"I think it likes you," Fiona said.

"*She* is advising you to stand back and give her space," Caniss snapped. "Most likely."

The bird cocked its head in the other direction and turned sideways, its tail feathers now fluttering out like the streamers on a windsock toward the shifter girl.

"Step away from there, girl. Unless you'd like to spend the entire train ride back to Florida covered in hungry slime."

"In what?"

"An excretion produced to attract a surprisingly large variety of amphibious species when the Harkliss hunts for prey. At least, the Harkliss as we know it." The biologist nodded at the bird's cage. "That one is a…divergent species."

"Meaning evolved, right?" Amanda smiled when the bird dipped its head toward her, then turned again to start preening itself.

"If that's the elementary definition you want to provide yourself, then fine." Caniss pressed her lips together and studied the shifter girl with distaste.

When Amanda saw the woman's expression, she backed away from the cage again with large steps. *She doesn't* look *like she wants me here at all.*

"It may be evolution," Caniss continued flatly, "or it may be something else entirely. These new species we've cataloged so far could have come from Oriceran if we wanted to stretch science into the realm of imagination and fantasy. The possibility is still unconfirmed, but there are plenty in the magical world who insist divergent species—even non-sentient and wild—somehow found their way through the gates from that planet onto this one. Like rats scrambling onto a ship before it sets sail for new lands."

"But there's...not a ship that goes between here and Oriceran, right?"

"Of course not. However, most of the world, magicals included, haven't fully learned how to utilize their capacity for rational thinking. The idea that these creatures who so closely resemble what we know of Oriceran life having stumbled through the gates to make a new home for themselves here is outrageous and juvenile." Caniss folded her arms. "Still, your discovery of Subject UM-43562 last fall has given us more than enough reason to believe these species are diverging from their original composition—both genetically and magically—right here on Earth. And quickly."

"Subject UM-43562." Amanda shook her head.

"The screechy mermaid cousins," Fiona muttered.

Caniss thumped the side of her fist against an empty cage. The startled creatures in the observation room shuffled around at the noise, jumping or rustling or fluttering away with small sounds of objection. "I will *not* suffer the use of such ridiculous monikers at the facility. If we don't have a scientifically accurate name for these creatures, they will be referred to by their assigned subject numbers. Is that clear?"

Amanda blinked quickly and stared at the woman. "Yeah, got it."

"I wasn't talking to you."

With a small chuckle, Fiona raised both hands again and nodded. "Understood, Dr. Caniss. My apologies."

After glancing back and forth between her guests, Caniss drew a deep breath and shook her head as if she was clearing the whole thing out of her memory altogether. "Now. Where were we?"

"Evolved creatures," Amanda offered. "I don't see why I'm

here in a lab. I mean, I thought the Coalition wanted me here to actually, like...find more creatures and—"

"And what?"

"I don't know. Bring them here, I guess."

"Hmm." Caniss turned to eye Bill, still sitting behind the desk. He looked up at her, raised his eyebrows, then returned his attention to his work with a shrug. "Come with me."

Amanda hurried after the doctor, tossing the evolved red bird another winning smile, and they left the initial examination room. The doors closed behind them with a hiss, and Fiona ran a hand through her red curls with a sigh.

"What do you think so far, kid?"

"Um..." The girl huffed out a quiet laugh. "I'll have to get back to you on that one."

"Yep. Keep your eyes open, huh?"

"What's that supposed to mean?"

The shifter woman shrugged. "Exactly what it sounds like. Eyes open. Pay attention. Until you have the privacy *not* to, of course."

"I'll thank both of you not to waste all our time by chit-chatting in the hall," Caniss called as she stopped in front of yet another door.

Whoa. She sounds like Principal Glasket. I thought this internship was supposed to be fun, not school in a weird shifter lab in the mountains.

"In here, Amanda." The doctor opened the door—this one with an actual doorknob—and gestured for the girl to enter.

"I'll take your bag, kid." Fiona slid the duffel bag off her mentee's shoulder before Amanda had a chance to decline the offer.

"I'm on a tight schedule this morning," Caniss said. "We all are. So please."

"Okay..." Amanda slowly headed down the hall, looking up

into the biologist's disconcerting brown eyes as she slipped past the woman and into the room.

It was a normal room, furnished with a low circular table, two chairs, a cushy-looking beige loveseat with a throw blanket tossed over the back, and a water cooler in the far corner.

"Subject UM-17552."

"What?"

"The divergent Harkliss that's quite obviously *not* a Harkliss," Caniss explained, her lips tightening in the first twitches of a snarl. At least she managed to contain her frustration. "In two hours, I want to know everything there is to know about that creature's habits. Your...*mentor* will retrieve you when the allotted time is up. So get to work."

"Wait, what do you want me to—"

Dr. Caniss stepped briskly out of the room and closed the door behind her. A lock clicked into place, and only when she looked at the closed door did Amanda realize this side of it had no doorknob at all.

She stared at the blank metal door and cocked her head, listening intently to the muffled voices from the other side in the hall.

"You didn't say a thing about tricking her into solitary confinement so she'd show you what she can do," Fiona said.

"If the girl can't think on her feet and figure out a way around a few walls, Fiona, she'll be useless in the field. And in here."

"I don't think she wants to be *in here*."

"We all have to start somewhere. Find Lucy when it's over, and make sure she gets every last detail."

"Would you like another gag-me latte while I'm at it?"

There was a long pause, then Caniss said quite matter-of-factly, "Not from you."

The biologist's footsteps echoed down the hall again, this time away from Amanda's apparent holding cell. Fiona's soft chuckle followed.

"Fiona?" Amanda stepped back toward the closed door. "Is this, like, one of those puzzle rooms or something?"

"Ha. Wouldn't *that* be something?"

"No, seriously. There's no handle on this side of the door. I don't even know—"

A gentle tap came through the door, followed by Fiona's low voice sounding much closer now as if she'd almost pressed her mouth to the metal. "Like I said, kid. Just be yourself."

"Wait, hold on."

"Do what you do, and I'll be back in two hours."

"Hey, how am I supposed to watch that bird if I can't leave the room? Fiona? Hey!" Amanda slapped her palm against the door, but that didn't get her a response, either.

She spun with a snarl and scanned the room. If she ignored the fact that there was no way to get out of it, it would have been a cozy little private space to sit for a snack or to read a book.

I don't even have those here with me. How am I supposed to watch the bird if the crazy scientist lady locked me up in a room by myself?

Clenching her fists, she made a tight circle around the room, sniffing the air for a scent of anything not quite right and listening for any indication that she was supposed to be looking for something specific. There were neither.

This has to be a test, right? It has *to be. Dr. Caniss wants me here. Fiona said it. Glasket basically said it last semester, and Johnny would never sign off on the Coalition kidnapping me for some kind of messed-up experiment.*

That last thought made her pause. Amanda didn't honestly think she was here to be experimented on or tortured. Not by shifters, at least, and those were the only magicals here. However, experimentation and torture had been on her mind last semester before she'd discovered the truth about the evolved mermaids who'd tried to make the swamp around the Academy their new home.

She backtracked toward the loveseat and sat on the soft cushions.

Be me and do what I do, huh? That's *the test. Observe the bird for two hours without leaving the room.*

The same way she'd found the mermaid creatures in that giant cage out in the swamp.

Good thing she'd been practicing her magic and calling out the ghost-wolf all summer long. She'd expected to have to use it at some point working with the Coalition.

I thought I'd be doing this out in a forest on a desert or something, not locked up in a research lab.

CHAPTER FOUR

Amanda drew a deep breath, closed her eyes, and let herself sink into the loveseat of her weird little test prison when she exhaled.

It's the same as every other time. Forget having no doors or windows. It doesn't matter.

She called up her shifter magic, which responded almost instantly. The tingling pulse of energy coursing through her was almost like right before a shift, but not quite. Still, she'd practiced enough to know the difference. She cracked one eye open just to make sure.

There it was—the ghostly white wolf had emerged from her body and now padded around the locked room as if being caged here wasn't a problem.

We're here like all the other creatures. You'd think a bunch of shifters would completely get rid of cages.

"Okay, wolf." Amanda opened both her eyes all the way and studied her ghost-wolf as it investigated the enclosed space. "Let's do this."

They didn't have to look at each other to bring her awareness into the incorporeal lupine form of her magic. As soon as she thought of seeing through her wolf's eyes, she was there. The locked room seemed a lot bigger and more spacious from that angle, but it didn't matter where her physical body was.

Because we're going through the walls. As we've done a million times before.

Amanda and her wolf together took a running head start toward the locked door. She saw a puff of white mist before she would have otherwise hit the wall, but they went straight through. The white wolf skittered across the hall, then lifted her nose to sniff the air.

Yeah, I know which way we came. Just gotta follow it back to those double doors.

It only took them three minutes to find those high-security steel doors, and Amanda didn't waste any time worrying about whether or not anyone would see her. She knew they would.

That's probably the whole point.

With the initial jolt of moving through physical objects now diminished, she and her ghost-wolf padded through the sealed double doors and re-entered the initial exam room.

There it was—the red and silver Harkliss—or not quite a Harkliss—standing in its cage and still preening its feathers. Amanda moved slowly toward the enclosure and stopped four feet away.

So this is it? Sit here for two hours and watch the bird?

A loud *clang* came from the desk in the back of the room. The mutated Harkliss let out a croaking squawk and spread its wings halfway in distress. Then a low chuckle filled the air.

"Well, look at that. Didn't take you much time now, did it?"

What? Amanda froze, scanning the room. *Is that the zookeeper guy?*

Slow footsteps approached her, and there was Bill, the skinny shifter who'd been cleaning out the "observation cages."

"Here's the deal. If you don't mess with my job, I won't mess with yours. Sound good?"

I literally can't talk to you, Bill. Don't you know that?

The shifter man lifted the smaller plastic bucket in his hand and reached into it before pulling out a glowing purple cube.

The mutated Harkliss let out a scream like a cougar on the prowl, jolting Amanda out of the connection with her ghost-wolf as Bill tossed the purple cube into the creature's cage.

She gasped and sat bolt-upright on the loveseat in the locked room.

"Are you kidding me? I get scared out of my magic by a growling *bird?*"

None of it made sense, but at least she knew now to be on her guard.

Fine. I'll go back in, and I won't be so scared of a three-legged bird in a cage.

Balling her fists beside her on the cushion, she willed out her ghost-wolf one more time. Her awareness practically surged out of her body after it, then they raced through the door again, down the hall, and back into the exam room.

Bill was now on the opposite side of the room, tossing reduced size glowing cubes to the smaller creatures stuck here for observation.

Looks like they've been here long enough to know when it's time to eat.

Amanda padded toward the birdcage again, glanced at Bill—who chuckled and moved along down the cages, focused on feeding the animals—then sat back on her haunches. She couldn't feel the cold tile floor beneath her, but she could smell the Harkliss.

Cinnamon and peppers. That's not as bad as it sounds.

Bill sniffed the air, then turned to face her. "Whoops. I'd step back a bit if I were you."

She stayed right where she was. *I'm not getting distracted again. Only here to watch this bird and remember everything so I can report on this super-weird test. I think.*

The mutated Harkliss shuddered where it stood, its glimmering wings slightly lifting before it pranced from one of its three feet to the next.

"I know it looks like a dance," Bill added, "but it's actually—"

The Harkliss fully extended both wings and opened its beak to let out a startling loud hiss. A burst of silver light erupted from its body and spread in all directions like rippling water.

A very powerful ripple propelled by intensely strong magic. It blew Amanda and her ghost-wolf back across the floor by two inches before she was knocked out of the connection again and the exam room disappeared.

"Oh, come on!" She pounded a fist into the cushion beside her and scowled at the locked door.

Fine. I'll do what I have to do and *listen to Bill's advice. Why couldn't they get* him *to watch the thing?*

Three more times over the next fifteen minutes, Amanda reconnected with her ghost-wolf and hurried back toward the exam room to do what Dr. Caniss told her to accomplish. The first time, Bill had finished feeding the creatures and focused on sweeping up the floor instead. He eyed the wolf made of white smoke and magic when she stepped back through the closed door and chuckled. "Don't say I didn't warn you, kid."

Each time she sat to observe, the mutated Harkliss blasted Amanda out of the connection with her magic, only in new ways that didn't have the same telltale signal as the shuddering three-footed dance and raised wings.

On her fourth journey of being shoved back into her own body on the loveseat, Amanda growled and leapt to her feet.

That bird's just trying *to piss me off!*

She paced around the room a few times, trying to quell her frustration because she was on the verge of forgetting her ghost-wolf altogether and going for a full-on shift. When she'd finally calmed down, she decided to lay down on the loveseat and spread out.

Maybe I need to be more comfortable. If I can smell the Harkliss, I bet it can smell me. So stay calm, easygoing, quiet. Just like a regular wolf, okay?

Merging with her magic happened instantly, and the trip back into the room full of cages felt almost instantaneous. She and her wolf skidded into the containment room and backed instantly away from the Harkliss's enclosure.

The five other creatures screeched and howled and growled, snuffling around the bottoms of their cages and bumping up against the bars. One of them—a pastel-blue fluffball that looked like a cross between a Pomeranian and a rabbit but with a monkey's long limbs and tail—let out a stuttering cackle and tossed a glowing bolt of silver-blue light at Amanda and her ghost-wolf. She leapt away from the puffball's cage with a snarl— or what would have been a snarl if her magic made a sound.

The creature's magical projectile hit the tile floor, and the other animals went crazy in their cages, all of them staring at Amanda.

Then she realized Bill was gone.

It was only her—and her ghost-wolf—in here with six mutated magical critters who either knew she was trying to get something done in here or plain didn't like her.

I'm pretty sure I'm not a fan of these guys, either. Still, I'm here. I'm staying.

She padded toward an open space five feet from the Harkliss's cage and sat on her haunches again. The smell of cinnamon and peppers filled her heightened senses again, but she stayed right where she was.

Can't scare me off with a little magical burst. It won't hurt me. I'm not even here.

The second she had that thought, the three-foot-tall bird started up its shuffling dance again. It turned away from the back of the cage toward Amanda, its wings spreading slowly outward and higher along its glimmering feathered back. It stopped when it fully faced her, then stepped as close as it could get to the bars and cocked its head.

Yeah, sure. We'll have a staring contest. For over an hour. I'll tell Dr. Caniss you stand there like a dumb—

The Harkliss let out a warbling cry that sounded like a full-grown man screaming at the top of his lungs. The muscles in its neck trembled, its feathers ruffled and fluttered as if in an intense wind, and the other creatures in the cages kicked up a brand-new round of screeching, hissing, hooting, and grunting.

Oh, come on. Like this is some kind of fight?

Amanda would have laughed if she'd had a voice.

She didn't have time to think much more about it because when the weirdly man-like cry cut off, the creature beat both wings against the cage with a rattling *clang*.

For a second, Amanda thought the creature had hurt itself. Its brilliant red and silver wings erupted in red smoke that surged through the bars of the cage. However, the smoke didn't dissipate or filter into the air. Instead, it drew *through* the bars, coalescing on the other side into the same shape as the Harkliss in the cage —wings outstretched, beak open all the way, eyes wide with the rear leg lifted half an inch off the floor.

What the heck is this? Amanda and her ghost-wolf stood and stepped backward, overwhelmed by the cloying sweetness of that cinnamon-pepper smell.

The frozen Harkliss of red smoke unfroze and let out an agonizingly loud screech. It shook itself from head to toe, beating its wings heavily. Small tufts of red smoke peeled away from the creature's magical projection of itself and floated toward the ceiling. Then the smoke-bird turned its head to fix a churning red eye on the white ghost-wolf three feet away.

Amanda glanced at the bird's actual body still frozen in place against the cage bars, then studied the twitching red-smoke version outside the cage and walking awkwardly toward her with long but jerky strides.

Crap. It is a fight. If I found this room, I bet this weird smoke-bird could locate me too. Like, the real me.

The smoke-Harkliss jerked its long neck toward her and snapped its beak together with a sharp *click*. The puffball monkey-thing shrieked and threw another glob of glowing blue light. The giant rat-hog with quills bugled and stood on its hind legs to bring both tiny front paws crashing down against the bars of its cage.

For a better view, huh? Amanda and her ghost-wolf circled the open space with the red smoke-bird as the magical creatures went wild over the standoff. *I can't believe I'm doing this. At least it'll make for an interesting report later.*

The smoke-bird spread its wings wide and high and raced toward her across the tile floor. She didn't have to think about how to respond. The instincts of her magic and her wolf combined took over completely, and she flew through the air toward the territorial bird that didn't have a body.

The only thing Amanda was aware of was how much it surprised her to finally hear her ghost-wolf's voice—a low, terrifying snarl as they crashed into the smoke-bird, pinned it to the floor, and clamped their jaws around the squawking creature's neck. The smoke-bird struggled uselessly for all of five seconds. Amanda and her ghost-wolf weren't biting hard—not that anyone could get hurt in a skirmish that took place outside physical bodies. Still, they were somehow heavy and fierce enough to subdue all the fight right out of the mutated Harkliss' magical projection.

The smoke-bird angled its head enough to look the white ghost-wolf in the eye, let out a final diminished *squawk*, then disappeared in a puff of red.

The crazed animals in cages stopped their excited racket

immediately. The quilled rat-hog thumped back down on all fours with a grunt and curled up in the corner of its cage.

Amanda snorted and shook her head, trying to get the sudden vinegary sting out of her senses.

A low croon came from the Harkliss' cage, where the creature had now regained physical movement and awareness. It settled down, tucking its wings tightly against its chest, and strutted back and forth across the cage before kneeling and practically sinking into a mountain of silver and red feathers.

When it stopped moving, only its face was visible above a puffed-out pile of plumage.

Amanda and her ghost-wolf sat on their haunches again and stared right back at the defeated creature staring at them.

Well, now I know I can fight outside my body too. That was...weird. A flood of bursting energy and warmth that made her want to race right out of this entire facility and sprint through the woods filled her. If she'd been in her body and shifted, that probably was what she would've done. She still recognized the feeling as her wolf's overwhelming pride at what they'd done together.

Yeah, everything in my life is weird. This was awesome!

CHAPTER FIVE

The rest of her allotted two hours went by in the blink of an eye, then Amanda heard Fiona's voice calling her simultaneously from very far away and close enough to touch.

Time's up, I guess.

Instantly, she was back in her body with her ghost-wolf returned to its place—wherever magicals kept their magic, even shifters. She opened her eyes and saw Fiona standing inside the open doorway with a smirk.

"Did you have fun?"

Amanda snorted and stretched out her legs on the loveseat. "After I figured out how to quit getting blown back into this room, yeah. You won't believe what happened in there—"

"Save it for the debriefing, kid. Okay? We have to meet Little Miss Assistant in..." Fiona glanced at her watch. "Right now. So get up and get a move on."

After scrambling to her feet, Amanda hurried across the room to join her mentor, grinning from ear to ear. "That was crazy."

"Oh? I take it you had fun lounging around for two hours?"

"Come on, Fiona. We both know I wasn't taking a nap. By the way, that evolved Harkliss is psycho."

The redheaded woman laughed. "That's what I like to hear."

They didn't see Dr. Caniss again before their time at her facility was over. The meeting with Lucy was dull and uneventful despite how excited Amanda was to tell the doctor's assistant about everything discovered—both about herself and about the divergent species of Harkliss they had locked up in that cage. When she finished relaying the entire story, which Lucy had recorded on a small device, Amanda grinned at the assistant and leaned forward in her chair. "So now I get to go monster hunting, right?"

Lucy scribbled something on a piece of paper, then set both that and the audio recorder aside. "Not quite yet."

"Wait, what?"

Fiona sat in the chair beside her mentee, arms folded as she stared at the far wall of the small office without any reaction.

"Fiona. You told me this was like an orientation for the new—"

"Dr. Caniss wants to assess the full extent of what you can do. Today's session was only the beginning."

"Session?" Amanda let out a bitter laugh. "I had a magic battle from a completely different room with a *bird in a cage*. What else do you guys need to see?"

Lucy gave her a deadpan stare. "Once we know how you fit into this operation with your given skillset, then we'll put you on assignment. If Dr. Caniss thinks you're ready."

"But—"

"That's it. Thank you." The assistant stood and nodded at Fiona before gesturing toward the door. "Ms. Damascus, I'm sure you know the way out."

"Oh, come on."

"I do," Fiona replied. "Thanks for your time, Lucy. We'll be back soon."

Amanda didn't have any more time to protest or try to argue against the decision already made. Her mentor whisked her out of her chair and out of the assistant's office. Once they were in the hall, Fiona plopped Amanda's duffel bag into the girl's arms and gestured down the hallway. "Time to go, kid."

"Really? You brought me all the way out here so I could sit in a room for two hours, fight a smoke-bird, then just leave?"

The shifter woman smirked. "It was an excellent story. Good work today."

"I thought I was joining the Coalition to fight *monsters*!"

"You are. You have." Fiona turned down a branching hallway that was dimly lit and moved away from the main collection of rooms and labs and whatever else was here in this weird invisible shifter-scientist dome. "The doc has her way of going about things."

"The Coalition already *knows* what I can do." Amanda readjusted the strap of her duffel bag and hurried to catch up. "That's why you brought me here in the first place, right? Otherwise, they wouldn't have even—"

"Listen, kid. I'm only the messenger with this, okay? The decision-making part's out of my hands. Besides, you have to get back to the Academy to start your junior year."

"It's Friday."

"And?"

"Classes don't start for another three days. If you only brought me out here for a couple of hours to take a tour of, like, three rooms and work with my magic for two hours, we could've done that somewhere else."

"Ah, but Dr. Caniss isn't *somewhere else*, is she?" They reached the end of the hall, which didn't have a door or any kind of panel that Amanda could see. "School's important, kid."

"Really? Because Caniss sure didn't seem to think so."

"Well, that shifter has been through more schooling than I can fathom at this point. I'm pretty sure she has at least three Ph.D.'s.

So your job now is to focus on school. Go to classes. Keep practicing your magic. You'll be back here next weekend."

"Really?"

Fiona nodded. "Every weekend until something else pops up, yeah. So let's get you to school."

The shifter woman walked right through the wall at the end of the hall and disappeared.

Amanda sighed. *Oh, good. Illusions that look like actual walls.*

She followed her mentor and found herself stepping back out into the sunny meadow in the center of the valley—blue skies overhead, birds chirping, wildflowers all around.

Fiona took a deep breath of the fresh mountain air and grinned. "TGIF, right?"

"Not really—"

Moving in a blur, Fiona grabbed the girl's wrist and teleported them out of the Colorado Rockies.

Amanda gasped and stumbled forward down the dark hallway that looked exactly like the one from which they'd stepped off the train. A low rumble grew steadily louder and closer as she fought to regain her balance. Then the grating shriek of metal on metal came from the far end of the hall, followed by a flash of yellow light and a small, final elevator *ding.*

She blinked at the end of the hall. "We're back at the train station, aren't we?"

"Hey, good work." Fiona headed toward the double doors opening at the end of the hall to let out three other magicals stepping off the Starbucks train at their final destination. "It's been a while since I've been so on time with this thing. If we hurry, I bet we can get an even better cabin."

"Okay, let me get this straight." Amanda frowned at the huge half-Kilomea stomping down the hall toward them. The guy was so tall that he had to duck and bend partially forward to keep from scraping his head against the hallway's ceiling. Fiona slipped past him like a ghost, and Amanda pressed her back flat against the wall to let the giant magical pass before catching up with her mentor. "You're a shifter with magic."

"I'm a lot more than that, but yes."

"You can…" A witch in tight workout clothes stepped off the train, towing her bags behind her with a levitation spell. Amanda lowered her voice and hurried into the open cabin after Fiona. "You can teleport."

"You don't have to whisper, kid. It's not exactly a secret."

"Really?"

Fiona studied the train cabin where they stood, then slowly looked down at her mentee with a smirk. "Fine. Maybe all of it is still a secret from the rest of the world. Nobody's gonna believe you anyway."

"Well, there's nobody here, so let me finish." Amanda started to sit on the red upholstered seats but stopped when the shifter woman poked her head through the open doors on the other side of the cabin and looked up and down the aisle. "Hey—"

"Definitely time for a better cabin. Come on."

With a sigh, Amanda tightened her grip on her duffel bag and hurried after Fiona. The bag knocked against the doorframe and almost jerked her backward before she whipped it around the corner and headed down the narrow train aisle. "Are you gonna let me finish what I'm trying to say, or are we gonna run up and down the train the whole time so you can avoid answering questions?"

Fiona laughed. "Now *that* I'd like to see. If we were out here while this particular train was moving, I'd be dropping off a pile of magical guts at the Academy instead of a smart, curious, stubborn, mostly talented shifter girl."

"Mostly talented?"

"I'm trying not to give you a big head, kid." The woman stopped at another set of open cabin doors on the opposite side of the aisle and grinned. "Oh, nice. A cushy room all to ourselves."

We had *a room to ourselves.*

Trying not to start screaming on the Starbucks train, Amanda darted into the open cabin and stopped. "Whoa."

"Right?" Fiona chuckled. "Look at this. Two beds. A nice couch bolted to the floor. Private bathroom, kitchenette, bookshelf." She slid her fingers through the metal-mesh cabinet doors closed and locked in front of the bookshelf. "Safety first, right? Nobody wants their library flying all over the place on the move."

"I feel like this probably belongs to somebody else."

"Yeah. Us." Fiona flopped down on one of the made-up twin beds—also bolted to the floor—and chuckled as she bounced on the mattress. "It's a first-come, first-serve kinda deal, kid. To be perfectly honest, this is my first time on the first-come list."

"Why would anyone need a cabin like this on a train that crosses the country in less than ten minutes?"

"Good question." Fiona lay back on the bed and folded her arms behind her head. "The answer, of course, is because this train doesn't always go that fast. It's a seasonal thing."

"That doesn't make any sense."

"Sure it does. Have a seat."

Amanda dropped her duffel bag onto the floor with a *thump*, then sat on the couch and stared at her mentor.

Fiona laughed. "Oh, come on. Why are you so upset, huh? You got your intro to one of the most brilliant shifter minds today. Actually, I'd be willing to put good money on Dr. Caniss being in the top five all-time genius-y geniuses on *both* planets. Plus, you get to ride back to your school as an upperclassman in style. With me."

"I meditated for two hours instead of doing what I thought was gonna be the biggest move for me as a bounty hunter, and you're lying in bed on a train."

With a snort, the shifter woman pushed herself up to eye her mentee. "Okay, what's going on?"

"Nothing."

"Listen, even if you weren't an open book, kid, I can tell when

43

someone's carrying way too much on their shoulders. You're in that category today. Did something else happen?"

Amanda sighed heavily and shook her head. "I thought this was gonna be a big break for me, you know? I spent my whole life until I was twelve having to shift in secret only with my family and trying to fit into this weird box my parents wouldn't let up about."

Fiona's carefree smile faded. "To protect you. You know that."

"Yeah, sure. But it didn't protect them." The girl slumped back against the couch. "Then Johnny found me, and that was great. That was finally... I don't know. Somewhere I felt like I belonged. He didn't tell me not to shift or run around the swamp. I mean, yeah, he has other dumb rules, but at least he didn't try to make me be something I'm not."

"That's a lot of backstory for what you're leading up to."

"It's not backstory. It's all part of the same dumb problem."

Pushing herself fully upright to sit at the edge of the bed, Fiona tilted her head and looked the girl up and down. "Which is?"

"That I don't do things like everyone else."

"Oh. That's not a problem, kid. That's one of your better attributes, honestly." The woman snorted. "Seriously. Doing things the way everyone else does them is a surefire way to live a boring, everyday life. Predictable. Stable. Safe. Non-life-threatening. Maybe enjoyable, but hey. Different strokes, right?"

Amanda blinked slowly and scowled at the woman. "You're not helping."

"Don't tell me you want *normal*, Amanda. I know that's the last thing I want out of my life, and I'm pretty sure you're right there with me."

"No, I don't want normal. I'm just... I'm sick of being told I'm different and special and *skilled*, or whatever, but not being able to do anything with it. First the Academy, which was fine. I got through freshman year without everyone thinking I was a freak.

Mostly. Then that whole weird 'paying off my debts' thing with Adalynn was a huge waste of time."

"Aw, come on." Fiona chuckled and pulled her legs up onto the bed to cross them beneath her. "That's how we met."

"Yeah. Then *you* had me doing all kinds of useless stuff with practicing my magic—"

"Ah, yes." The woman snorted. "I did enjoy wasting your time for an entire school year."

"You know what I mean."

"I also know you needed the practice. Not to mention direction and a goal to focus on while you were trying so hard to focus on anything else *but* school."

"That's not what I was trying to do."

"Hey, I get it. I'm the same way. If I don't have some kind of distraction, I go looking for it. That's the way we are. Most shifters too, honestly, but I'm pretty sure it applies extra to you and me. Plus, you live with a dwarf and his Light Elf partner who really don't give a damn about the rules at all. At least not when those rules stand in the way of them doing their job." Amanda closed her eyes with a heavy sigh, and Fiona studied her a moment longer before adding, "I get it. You were raised to keep your head down and not make any noise. It didn't work. Now you have more support and encouragement at your fingertips than you knew was possible, and you want to show everyone you're capable of bigger and better things."

Amanda's eyes flew open. "Exactly. So why is it so hard to get the chance?"

Nodding slowly, Fiona stared at the floor and pursed her lips, trying to hide a smile. "It's normal, kid. Trust me."

"No, it's not. *I'm* not. I shouldn't have to sit back and wait for everyone else to make decisions for me when I *know* what I can do."

"Okay, you have a point there. You're not a regular kid or girl or shifter. Fair. Still, no matter how unique your situation is, and it *is*, everything you feel is totally normal."

"That… That doesn't even make sense."

"Sure it does." Fiona winked at her. "It's called being fourteen."

Amanda slumped back against the couch with a groan and stared at the cabin ceiling. "It has nothing to do with how old I am."

"Nope. Just everything to do with your hormones. Growing pains, kid. At least you're a girl."

"What?"

"It takes a lot longer for guys to wrap their heads around stuff like this. Not to mention how old the average male is when he *finally* finishes going through puberty—"

"Ew. Okay. Just stop."

Fiona laughed and flopped back down on the bed. "What, you're not interested in hormones and boys?"

"No. I'm interested in using my magic and hunting monsters and graduating from the Academy at the top of the class so I can finally make a decision for myself for once."

"You're doing great, kid. Keep going. Only two more years, right?"

Amanda didn't say anything.

The last two years took forever. How are the next two gonna be any different?

Their fancy new cabin fell completely silent, then the overhead lights flickered, and the robotic female voice came over the sound system.

"This train will be departing in five minutes."

"Great," Amanda muttered. "Which means we have two."

"Not this time around." Fiona stretched her arms out by her sides as far as they would go, her hands dangling over the sides of the bed. "Well, at least once we get closer to Florida."

"Huh?"

"The Marco Island stop's finally on the map. Kids boarding

the Starbucks train to get to school. Let me tell you, whoever runs this lightning bolt underground made a good choice when they decided to slow train rides down when the thing is full of adolescent magicals who don't know how to follow directions."

Amanda sat up to frown at the woman. "I have no idea what that means."

"Kids going to school. Magical kids on a magical train. You think any of them are wise enough *not* to run around on this thing when it's moving at top speeds?"

"You mean we're taking this train back to Florida at *normal* speed?"

"I mean, normal for the Starbucks train, sure. Should be back right after dinnertime is my guess. Maybe an hour or two later. So I'm really, *really* glad we claimed this little spot for ourselves. Comes with a lock on the doors and everything."

"Great."

I don't wanna be on a train full of kids right before I spend all semester on a campus full of kids. This was supposed to be my *day before school starts.*

When the robot-lady returned to give them their two-minute warning before departure, Fiona rolled onto her side and propped her head up with one hand. "So what were you trying to ask me?"

Amanda pulled her legs up onto the couch and leaned back against the armrest. "What do you mean?"

"When we first stepped on the train, kid. You said you wanted to get something right. I'm assuming you had one of your usual sarcastic questions so you could put two and two together in your head and also try to catch the other magical off-guard by phrasing it in a way that points the finger back at them. Well, *me*, specifically."

The girl wrinkled her nose. "I don't know what you—"

"I'm a shifter with magic, and I teleport. That's where you started."

"Oh, right." Amanda scanned their cushy train cabin and shrugged. "I don't get why you can't teleport us right outside the school grounds."

"Ah." Fiona gestured at herself with her free hand moving from head to toe. "There's only so much I can do, kid. Even a shifter's magic has limits."

It was hard enough not to make a face at Fiona's weirdly suggestive presentation of herself, but when the shifter woman wiggled her eyebrows and broke into a wide grin, Amanda burst out laughing.

CHAPTER SIX

The train didn't take off at its literal break-neck speed this time, and Amanda got to enjoy the spacious private cabin for almost an hour. The stocked kitchenette held snacks—popcorn, cookies, pretzels, sample-sized cartons of ice cream, chips, and six different kinds of soda.

"Ooh!" Amanda grabbed a bottle of Juicy Tune and turned toward her mentor with a grin. "You want one?"

"What's that?"

"Juicy Tune." She tilted the bottle slowly from side to side.

"I'll have to take a hard pass on that one." Fiona shook her head as she popped open a bag of potato chips. "I don't know why they call it *juice*. It's practically flavored sugar."

"It's not juice, it's—wait a minute. You've never had this before?"

"Nope. Feel free to have another *for* me, though."

With a laugh, Amanda twisted off the bottlecap with the sharp *hiss* of releasing air, then a yodel in a deep baritone voice emerged from the bottle before she raised it to her lips and chugged down the sugary, magical orange soda.

Fiona stared at her. "Did I hear—"

Amanda lowered the bottle with a satisfied sigh, and the yodeling filled the cabin again before she screwed on the lid.

"Okay, admittedly, now you've caught my interest."

"What about all the sugar, though?"

"I'm not gonna *drink* it. I'm gonna sit here and watch what happens to *you*."

The Juicy Tune's intense fizz worked quickly, and Amanda thumped a fist against her chest before letting out an enormous belch. Sparkling orange bubbles flew from her mouth, and the yodeling took on a weird two-toned quality of the magical baritone voice and hers. As the bubbles popped, the yodeling continued in fits and bursts.

When it was over, Amanda raised an eyebrow at her mentor, who stared at her with wide eyes.

She looks like she watched someone cut my head off.

The thought made her crack up laughing, and she collapsed back onto the couch.

"That was... Hold on." Fiona stood and went to the minifridge. "I don't get it."

"It makes you sing. Kinda." Amanda wiped a tear from the corner of her eye and opened the bottle again for another drink.

"Why the hell haven't I seen this stuff before?"

"Beats me. They're all over the kemana. In the vending machines. Oh, yeah. And at the candy store."

"SweetPops?"

"Yeah, that one."

"No wonder. I don't do sugar or vending machines, but I can't *believe* I've been missing out on this." Fiona snagged a bottle from the fridge, twisted off the lid with a *crack* and a *hiss*, then slowly removed it to hear the specific brand of music. Nothing happened. "Aw, come on. It's magical soda, and I got the only dud—"

A growling roar exploded from the bottle and made the woman jump. Fizzy orange Juicy Tune sloshed all over her hand

and the cabin floor, sending hundreds of tiny glittering bubbles into the air, all of them joining the bottle in the same head-banging growl.

Amanda burst out laughing and hugged herself around the middle.

Fiona stared at the dripping bottle. "This isn't singing. This isn't even *music*."

"Tell that to Johnny!" Amanda shrieked before falling into another fit of laughter.

"Oh, yeah? He's into death-metal?" With a sidelong glance at the bottle, Fiona shrugged, then knocked the Juicy Tune back and chugged half of it in one breath.

Amanda stopped laughing. "Um..."

"Wow. That's actually pretty good."

"I don't think you're supposed to—"

Fiona's burp echoed with her voice and dozens of echoing death-metal screams in a wordless tune. "Huh. That's—"

She belched again, then again, and tried to swallow another in the chaos of growling voices chanting some unknown magical song. "You—"

More orange bubbles spewed from her mouth, Amanda laughed so hard she could barely breathe, and Fiona fumbled in a panic to screw the lid back onto the bottle.

"This isn't—" Her next giant burp lasted four seconds, and the cabin had started to take on a shimmering orange glow.

The woman slammed the half-empty bottle down on the table and clapped a hand over her mouth.

Amanda almost fell off the couch and gasped as she struggled to catch herself. "Oh, man. I wish you could see your face right now!"

"I'm—" Fiona blinked when no more bubbles emerged from her mouth, then let out a massive sigh. "I'm fine. *You*, on the other hand..." She pointed at her abandoned bottle of orange soda. "You like that stuff?"

"It tastes good, it's full of sugar, and it cracks me up. Yeah. I like it."

"I don't remember being into this stuff when I was your age."

"Probably 'cause it didn't exist back then."

"Hey." Fiona spun with a chuckle. "I'm not *that* old."

"Oh, yeah? Then how old are you?"

"Old enough." The redhead woman returned to her seat on the bed and snatched up the bag of potato chips. "And too old for death-metal soda."

The next time the regular-speed train stopped, the aisle outside their private cabin quickly filled with voices. Kids voices.

Amanda wrinkled her nose and sank lower on the couch although no one was looking for her.

"What's the matter, huh?" Fiona swapped out the book she'd only skimmed for a new one from the caged bookshelf. "You embarrassed to be seen with me or something?"

"No." She glanced at the cabin doors. "There's a reason I don't stay at the Academy over breaks and during the summer with the rest of my class."

"Like the fact that you have a home to go to?"

Amanda rolled her eyes. "I could stay at the school if I wanted. I don't."

"Yeah, I get it. Alone time's important. With all those raging hormones crammed into one—"

"Will you stop with the hormones already?"

Fiona laughed and opened her newest book. "I'm just saying. Don't worry, kid. I'll stay right here. Won't do anything to embarrass you. Promise."

"Yeah, thanks."

The laughing, chattering voices grew louder and closer, and Amanda stared at the door in hopes that none of the other students on their way to whichever school they attended would see her there.

Then they'd ask more questions. Who's the redhead? Why do you get a fancy cabin all to yourself? Don't you live in the Everglades? Let us all in and share everything you got.

No one seemed to notice the doors into the private cabin or the fact that there *were* private cabins set up like hotel suites.

When the train took off again from the station, she started to feel a little bad about wanting to hide from everyone.

I guess I've already been trying to hide for a while anyway. It's not like I have anything to hide this time. Except for my magic, and I am not doing anything with that on this train.

Fiona was completely absorbed in her book, and after the first twenty minutes, the rocking of the train going at the magical version of normal speeds started to put Amanda to sleep.

Then the shouting started.

It was only a crowd of excited kid voices at first, but then the sound grew into practically a roar of half-cheering, half-angry shouts.

"Sounds like hormones to me," Fiona muttered.

Amanda wrinkled her nose and stood to check through the frosted windows of the cabin's double doors. "No, I think that's a fight."

"Oh. Fun."

She listened at the door a while longer. Then there was a sharp *pop* from the aisle, a communal exclamation of surprise, and a rise of taunting laughter mixed with the pounding of feet.

That doesn't sound good.

"Is there anyone on this train who, like, breaks up fights or something?"

"Not as far as I know." Fiona peered over the top of her book, then returned to her reading. "It's not like you're a prisoner in here or anything. I'm only the chaperone today. If you wanna go play mediator, by all means, have at it."

Another *pop* came from farther up the train, followed by panicked shouts and the *thump* and scuffle of at least two kids locked in either a wrestling match or a fistfight.

Nope. I'm not about to be the shifter girl who breaks up fights. Or tries to. It's only a bunch of freshmen and sophomores freaking out about a new school year—

"You want me to blow this whole train off its tracks, or what?" a girl shouted.

Amanda froze. "No way…"

"Yes, way." Fiona chuckled. "I promise. I won't even go out there and try to stop you from making a—"

"I'll be right back." The girl jerked open the sliding double doors and stepped into the aisle. Then she quickly closed the doors again and stared up the path at the knot of magical kids gathered five or six compartments down and blocking the way through.

They pushed and jostled each other back and forth, everyone trying to get a better look at the scene playing out inside one of the other cabins across the hall.

"I said back off!" the same girl shouted.

"Oh, come on. Like you don't think I can call your bluff." The kid who'd spoken—and he had to be a kid, or else this entire incident was super messed up—had a voice like an adult man. Still, Amanda could hear him snickering inside the cabin in question.

"It's not a bluff," the girl growled. "Get out."

Amanda quickened her pace up the aisle because now she knew exactly who the girl was.

Can't expect Summer not to make a scene on a train, can I?

"Let us in," the adult-voiced kid demanded. "You got room in here for at least four more—"

"You *had* your cabin, dumbass. I was here first."

"Yeah, but it smells like old socks and SpaghettiOs." Some of the other kids laughed at that and shouted jeering calls toward a cabin farther ahead—presumably the one that smelled bad.

The crowd of kids surged forward toward the open cabin where the fight had broken out, but those smashed up against the doorframe pushed back, unwilling to be shoved inside with the angry girl tossing around threats like it was her job.

"Or we could pull you outta there, huh?"

"I'd like to see you try."

"Hey!" Amanda finally reached the dozen kids jammed up in the aisle. "There are, like, a hundred cabins on this train. Go get another one."

The laughter and shoving died, and everyone turned to look at the shifter girl standing there.

From inside the open cabin came a muttered, "Damnit. Come on…"

The huge Crystal kid with the overly mature voice leaned away from the doorframe—which he gripped with both hands as if he owned the place—and looked Amanda up and down. "Who made you the train police?"

"The idiot who doesn't know when to give up before he gets his hands blown off," she snapped back. "You have no idea who you're talking to, do you?"

"What, this emo witch?" He snickered and glanced inside the cabin again. "She looks pretty pathetic to me."

A bitter laugh came from the cabin. "You wanna test out that theory, you moron?"

Amanda briefly closed her eyes and drew a deep breath. *That's not the way to get somebody to calm down.*

"Leave her alone, okay? Seriously." She pointed up the aisle, where the crowd of onlookers had already started to disburse. "Go find a different cabin."

"Sounds like you know this witch." The Crystal boy sneered and cocked his head. "You her bodyguard or something?"

"Don't be stupid."

A tall elf girl beside the Crystal peered around his arm and looked into the cabin. "Oh my God."

"What's wrong with you?" the Crystal muttered.

"That's the girl. The one who got kicked out of the School of Necessary Magic two years ago."

"What?" the kid laughed and turned toward the cabin. "So why are you on the school train, huh?"

Amanda could very clearly imagine Summer's warning scowl when the witch muttered, "That's none of your goddamn business. Now get the hell out of my face."

"Not until you tell me what you're doing here." The Crystal cocked his head with a smirk. "I heard nobody gets back into a school once they're out."

"Hey, except for that new school," the elf girl said, then burst into a high-pitched giggle and covered her mouth. "Is *that* where you're going?"

"Get out," Summer growled.

"Wait, the school for rejects? That's that juvie place, right?"

"Okay." Amanda stalked toward the cabin again now that the younger kids had started to clear away. "Do you need help walking away? 'Cause I have no problem giving you a hand."

"You better listen to her, iceface." Summer snickered in the cabin. "She's not messing around."

"Yeah, and she's tinier than you. Nice try, whoever you are." The Crystal looked Amanda up and down and scoffed. "I'm not giving up this nice little room—"

"I was here first!" A streak of red light burst from the open cabin and struck him in the center of his chest.

He roared in surprise and staggered backward across the aisle. "Did you seriously start a magic fight with me?"

"Bring it, asshole."

"No." Amanda leapt forward to try getting between the kid and a pissed-off Summer Flannerty inside the cabin. "You don't wanna—"

"Piss off." The kid reached toward Amanda in an attempt to shove her away from him, thinking nothing of the small, skinny girl who looked like she couldn't possibly have taken a giant Crystal boy with a grown man's voice on her own.

Amanda snarled, caught his wrist in both hands before he'd touched her, and yanked him toward her. The Crystal yelped in surprise as he staggered away from the door. Amanda stepped quickly aside, swept her foot under his, and let the huge kid's momentum take him down. He crashed to his knees. When Amanda jerked his arm back up behind him and pressed her knee against his back enough to get her point across, the kid screamed, and his oh-so-adult voice finally broke in a shriek.

Summer barked out an exaggerated laugh. "That sounds better."

"Do I have to *keep* helping you," Amanda snarled as she dipped her head toward the kid's ear, "or do you think you can find your way back to your spot by yourself now?"

"Oh my God, let him go!" the elf girl screeched. "You're gonna break his arm!"

"Not yet. If he's stupid enough to try touching me again, I won't feel bad about dislocating a shoulder."

"Jesus, get off me," the Crystal shrieked, his voice breaking again. "I didn't even touch you!"

"You're not going to." She stepped away from him and released his arm.

The Crystal leapt to his feet, cradling his sore arm against his chest, and spun to glare at her. "You're so screwed—"

"Really?" Amanda stepped forward and growled. Judging by the kid's widening eyes and the color draining his face, he'd seen her eyes flash silver as the tingle of her shifter magic flooded through her. She held it back.

"You're a *shifter*?"

"And that was a warning." She pointed up the aisle past the elf girl, who stared at her in surprise and terror and was already slowly backing up down the hall. "Go ahead. I won't chase you or anything."

"You're a psycho." The Crystal brushed past her, then scowled into the open cabin. "Both of you are psychos. No wonder you can't get into a real school."

"Hey, shifter girl. Does that sound like he's asking for round two?"

"Screw you." The kid hurried down the hall toward a different cabin, still cradling his arm and jerking away from the elf girl who fawned all over him to make sure he was okay.

Dozens of heads poked out of the other open cabin doors lining the aisle. The other kids stared after the Crystal bully and his elf accomplice until both kids disappeared into another cabin and slammed the door shut. Then they all turned to stare at Amanda.

She spread her arms and shrugged. "Yeah. I'm the ANM shifter girl, okay? Anybody got a problem with that?"

A tiny wizard with strawberry-blond hair and freckles covering every inch of his face broke into a huge grin. "Cool."

"Yeah, that's where we're going too," the kid sticking his head out above Freckles' added. "Freshmen. Hey, is that where you learned how to break his arm—"

"Save it for Combat Training," Amanda muttered as she headed toward Summer's cabin. "You'll learn everything you never wanted to know about it there."

"Combat training? That's *awesome*!"

"Hey, what about—"

Amanda turned to pull the double doors together with a loud *bang*, and the curious questions from the Academy's new freshmen dampened. Then she turned and fixed Summer with a deadpan stare. "You could've found a different cabin."

"And take it lying down? I don't think so, shifter girl." Summer folded her arms where she sat on the red-upholstered bench and smirked. "Plus, you put on a hell of a show."

"I was trying to help you not get your ass kicked."

"Please. I could've taken him."

"It sounded like you already tried." Amanda glanced at the small silver cylinder in her friend's hand. "You wouldn't actually blow up the Starbucks train, right?"

"I mean, I *could*." The witch lifted the cylinder and wiggled it back and forth. "Not with this, though. Loud bang but no boom."

"Right." Taking the opposite bench, the shifter girl studied her friend and huffed out a laugh. "Nice hair."

"Yeah, you like it?" Summer gestured at her hair, which had grown out since her mohawk last semester. It was now a short pixie cut she'd dyed in rainbow colors this time. "Honestly, I wanted to shave my whole head, but it's kinda hard to dye scalp."

"No, it's cool. I like it."

"Great."

CHAPTER SEVEN

It took Amanda less than a minute of sitting in silence across from Summer to realize something was wrong. "You okay?"

"That premature voicebox didn't hurt me if that's what you're wondering."

"No, I mean… You kinda look like you've been crying."

The witch scoffed. "Me? Cry? No way. I don't do that."

"Summer, your eyes are all red."

"Yeah, well, lots of things do that to your eyes, don't they?" The girl sniffed and leaned back against the cushioned bench. "I'm fine."

"Wanna talk about it?"

"Wanna tell me why you're riding the dumbass Starbucks train when you live, like, twenty minutes away from the school?"

"Sure." Amanda's smiled slowly. "Turns out you didn't ruin my chances with the Coalition after all."

"That's where you're coming from?"

"Not the stop *we* got off on last year. I kinda maybe…went to a secret shifter lab and got experimented on."

"What?" Summer straightened, and her red-rimmed eyes widened.

"Kidding. Mostly." Amanda shook her head. "First day as a Coalition intern, and they locked me in a room for two hours."

Summer snorted. "The stuff that comes outta your mouth sometimes, shifter girl. I swear."

"Yeah, you too. What about you? Why are you on the train today and not like...I don't know. Last week or something."

"That's, uh..." Summer sniffed and stared at her lap, blinking furiously. "Yeah, that might be part of the problem. If I *had* a problem, I mean."

"What happened?"

"Doesn't matter."

"Wait a minute. You don't have a problem, and you haven't been crying, so go ahead and tell me what it would hypothetically be, huh?"

The witch scratched the side of her head and wouldn't look up at her friend. "Just more bullshit at home.

"I'm sorry."

"Don't be. It's no big deal."

"Okay, well, if you wanna talk about it—"

"You know what, Amanda? I don't. Like, I *really* don't. So feel free to drop it."

Amanda nodded. *Must be a pretty big deal if she used my name.*

"Sure. Hey, so I know you were defending your territory and everything in here. Like, on principle." They both chuckled wryly, and Amanda stuck her thumb out toward the cabin doors. "We have this crazy huge cabin a little ways back. It has a bed and a kitchen and a shower and stuff. Wanna come check it out?"

"We?"

"Oh, yeah. Fiona's with me."

"No thanks." Summer rolled her eyes. "I'm not feeling a fun cabin share with Big Red, okay? She hates my guts."

"Like that's ever bothered you before."

The witch shook her head.

"Okay, fine. *I'm* going back there. Someone loaded it with snacks."

"For real?"

Amanda stood with a grin and opened the cabin doors. "Yep. Plus a bunch of Juicy Tune and—"

"I'm starving, shifter girl. Lead the way." Summer leapt to her feet and grabbed her single rolling suitcase and her backpack to head after her friend. "Then I'll be too busy eating to talk to your babysitter."

"She's not my babysitter." They walked down the aisle toward the private cabin, ignoring the stares from the younger kids on their way to magic school for the year. "And she doesn't hate your guts."

"Oh, yeah? 'Cause you two spend so much time talking about *me*, right?"

"Actually..." Amanda paused outside the closed doors and leaned toward the witch to whisper, "She was a *little* paranoid on the train this morning. Because of you and your illusion last time."

Summer grinned and perked up immediately. "Really? I made that much of an impression?"

"A big one."

"Hell yeah."

Amanda slid open the doors, and the girls found Fiona propped up on the bed with yet another open book in her lap. She looked back and forth between the students and sighed. "Company. Wonderful."

Summer tossed her bags onto the floor inside the doors and headed straight for the kitchenette. "Don't worry, Red. I'm only here for the grub."

"Red?" Fiona tried not to smile as Summer rummaged through the cabinet and pulled out bag after bag of potato chips and cookies and crackers. "You have a thing about nicknames, don't you?"

"You know, right now, I have a thing about food and not talking. Thanks." After closing the door, Summer stalked across the cabin and flopped down on the couch. A bag of Cheetos popped open in her hands, quickly followed by the rustle of the bag and the obnoxiously loud *crunch* as she dug in.

Amanda climbed onto the other bed and crossed her legs. "Toss me those cookies."

"Yep." More snack bags flew across the room, and Summer shoved food into her face as she studied their compartment. "What's a cabin like this cost, huh?"

Fiona chuckled. "Actually, it's—"

"First-come, first-serve," Amanda finished instead.

"You mean, like, free?" Summer jiggled the now-empty bag to slide the rest of the crumbs into her open mouth, then crumpled up the noisy package and tossed it at the trashcan. It missed, but she didn't get up. "Cool. Then I can eat as much as I want, right?"

"It's all junk food," Fiona said. "Not exactly—"

"Gourmet?" The witch ripped open a bag of crackers this time and shrugged. "That's exactly why it's so good."

Amanda pulled a cookie out of the tiny travel-sized package and took a bite. Fiona met her gaze with wide eyes, then nodded toward Summer and raised an eyebrow.

The shifter girl shrugged. *I have no idea what's going on with her. I'm pretty sure I'm about to find out soon, though. I hope it doesn't get us both into more trouble we don't need like every other time.*

When the Starbucks train finally made it to the Marco Island stop, the students heading for the Academy of Necessary Magic filed out through the open cabin doors and into a long hallway converging at a wide staircase leading up toward the surface. The stairwell echoed with all the new freshmen's and sophomores' excited chatter, and Amanda, Summer, and Fiona brought up the rear.

At the top of the staircase, a garage-style door opened into the bright light of the early August evening. The heat and humidity blasted down the stairs. Then all the kids swarmed outside into the parking lot behind the actual Starbucks.

"All right, all right, now, kiddies," Shep Frederick called, waving them all forward. "Y'all bring your bags this way, now, and we'll get y'all loaded up to head on out."

"Wow." Amanda stopped and stared at the van behind the Academy's resident wizard driver. "I can't wait to see how everyone fits into that thing altogether. That'll be fun to watch."

"Fun to be a part of too," Fiona added and set a hand on her mentee's shoulder. "Because you'll be riding it."

"What?"

Summer laughed. "What's wrong, shifter girl? The magic school bus isn't good enough for you?"

"No, I thought… I mean, Fiona, you're right here. Can't you—"

"No can do, kid." The shifter woman walked backward away from them and spread her arms. "I got work to do."

"It'll take you, like, five seconds."

"Sure. Then I'll get requests from every student at your school to start popping them in and out on command. Not exactly my cup of tea. I'll see you Saturday morning, though." She pointed at Amanda and winked. "Don't forget."

"Yeah, okay."

With a smile and a nod, the redhead shifter woman spun and walked briskly from the parking lot before disappearing around the corner of the building.

Summer brought the last handful of potato chips to her mouth and crunched down noisily on them. "What exactly does she do again?"

"She works with the Coalition."

"Yeah, but like...doing *what?*"

Amanda opened her mouth to reply, then frowned and had to think about it. "You know, I don't actually know."

"Don't sweat it, shifter girl. She probably has a whole group of other shifter kids she's trying to help find their magic or whatever. You're still the best. Hey, maybe they'll start paying you to grow more of that glowy shifter plant for them—"

"Hey, can we *not* talk about all that stuff right where everyone can hear it?" Amanda scanned the underclassmen, though none of them were paying attention to the private conversation. Instead, the kids crowded around Shep's van painted with the Florida Gators' mascot on the side in green and gold as the wizard levitated their luggage into the back.

"No one's paying attention." Summer licked the chip crumbs off her fingers. "Seriously. Look at them. All wide-eyed and impressed by a freaking *van.*"

"Still. Not a conversation I want to have while we're standing here waiting to load up, okay?"

"Sure. How 'bout once we get *inside* the van?"

Amanda shot her friend a deadpan stare, and Summer cracked up.

Her laughter snuffed out immediately when Shep approached them with a huge, gap-toothed grin. "Well lookie here. If it ain't the dynamic duo itself."

Summer wrinkled her nose. "What?"

Amanda laughed. "Hey, Mr. Frederick."

"Hey, yerself, Miss Coulier. Now, I saw that fire-headed friend of yours walkin' away down the street, so I reckon somethin' called her away?"

"Yep. Pretty much a given at this point."

"Uh-huh." The wizard chuckled and pointed at Summer. "I was wonderin' when you'd make it down here, Miss Flannerty. Got me a little worried when I didn't see you here the last few weeks. Glad to see you found your way, even a little later'n regular."

"Yeah, well." Summer shrugged and scuffed a shoe across the asphalt. "Things are different this year, I guess."

"Oh, sure. Y'all're at the top of the food chain now, huh?" Shep giggled, then shushed himself and looked over his shoulder at the sophomores climbing into the van single file and freshmen standing there and staring at them in mute awe. "Whoops. Shh. Don't let any of *them* hear me callin' y'all that. We're all in this at the Academy together, ain't we?"

"I guess."

He grinned at them both, eyes glinting and the wrinkles around them deepening as he looked back and forth from one girl to the next. "Welp. I'll take y'all's bags."

"No, that's okay. I'll—"

Shep pointed at Amanda's duffel bag, and it lit up with pale yellow light before sliding off her shoulder and heading toward the back of the van. Summer's suitcase followed, but fortunately, she didn't have to fight to keep her backpack.

With a wink, Shep floated their luggage through the air. "Get a move on into that there van, huh? Then we'll be on our way."

"Okay. Thanks." Amanda forced back a laugh as the driver hobbled away with their things. "This is so weird."

Summer looked around the otherwise empty parking lot. "What, magic out in the open?"

"No. I mean, yeah, that's odd. I mean this. Off the train and into the Academy van."

"Aw, come on, shifter girl." Summer bumped her shoulder against Amanda's and headed toward the vehicle. "This isn't even *close* to the weirdest thing you've done. Now you get to see how the other side lives."

"The other side?"

"Yeah." The witch turned and spread her arms as she walked backward. "You know, the kids who don't have bounty-hunter parents that founded the school, don't live in the Everglades, and aren't shifters."

"Summer, that's not the *other side*. That's everyone but me."

"Same thing."

With a snort, Amanda followed her friend to the open back door of the van. "So we just...what? Climb in?"

"Yeah. Try not to fall down the stairs."

"The *stairs?*"

"Jeeze, shifter girl. It's like you're doing this for the first time all over again. Come on."

"It's my first time in the magical school van that fits over fifty kids, yeah."

When she stepped up into the vehicle, she had to pause to take it all in. *Oh, man. It's like a double-decker bus under the van.*

"Hurry on up, now, Miss Coulier." Shep approached her from behind and reached for the door. "If you're feelin' up to it, I'd appreciate a quick reminder to the young'un's down there not to fiddle with the resizer, huh?"

"What's that, exactly?"

He twirled his finger in a circle. "Big glowin' red circle looks like a target. Now, I realize my mistake in basically makin' a big red button says, 'Do not touch.' 'Cause everyone knows kids can't stop themselves from pushin' it anyhow. But if they push too much, everyone down there in that sittin' area's like to find themselves squashed into teenage pancakes. Know what I'm sayin'?"

"Yeah. Yeah, I'll let them know."

"You're one of a kind, Miss Coulier." He winked at her and clicked his tongue. "Get on down there and enjoy the ride. We'll be at the school in no time."

Shep slid the door closed, and Amanda stood there at the top of the staircase inside the van, looking down at Summer standing ten feet beneath her. The kids sitting in the four real passenger seats at the top of the stairs smirked at her.

"What, are you scared?" a sophomore boy asked.

She scoffed. "No. You probably should be, though."

"Why?"

"Start of a new year with Petrov." She chuckled as she headed down the stairs. "Just remember *nothing* is what it looks like."

"Huh? Wait, hold on. Hey. What's that supposed to mean?"

"All right, y'all." Shep's voice boomed through a sound system reaching down to the long, narrow area seating most of the Academy's freshmen and sophomore classes. "Buckle up, and don't touch nothin' that don't look like it oughtta be touched. Here we go."

The engine rumbled to life, and Amanda quickly took an empty bus seat next to Summer.

"Don't touch anything?" asked a freshman girl in pink sweatpants and a shirt that had "I'm A Star" written across the front over a glittering smiley-face star. "What does that even mean?"

Amanda frowned at the girl's shirt, then pointed at the red glowing target on the wall at the back of the room. "That. Don't touch that."

The van lurched forward. Then they raced out of the Starbucks parking lot, out of Marco Island, and toward the Everglades' magical Academy.

Summer kept staring at the other girl's shirt with an amused frown. "There's a five-year-old girl in my parents' neighborhood. Two doors down. I think she has that same shirt."

Amanda choked back a laugh and shook her head.

CHAPTER EIGHT

"So…how about now?" Amanda asked as the van bumped back and forth over whatever road Shep drove them down.

Summer shot her a sidelong glance. "For what?"

"For telling me what's been going on with you."

"Nice try, shifter girl." The witch nodded at the other students sitting across the aisle from them. Most of them were staring at her rainbow hair. "I'm not going down that rabbit hole while everyone's staring at you."

"Me?" Amanda barked out a laugh. "I'm pretty sure it's your hair. Again."

"Huh." Summer leaned back in her seat and returned the stares aimed her way. "Is there something on my face?"

The same tiny, freckled boy smirked but looked quickly away.

"I haven't seen you upset like that before," Amanda muttered. "That's all."

"I'm fine. Seriously. Probably better this way anyway."

"What way?"

Summer bit her bottom lip and shook her head. "Remember that dumb amulet last year?"

"The one that broke out of the box you kept in my..." Amanda cleared her throat. "That I was hiding for you?"

"Yeah, that one." The witch puffed out a sigh through loose lips and dropped her head back against the seat. "Obviously, it got back home before I did."

"Your mom wasn't too happy about it, huh?"

"Like I said, I'm not even sure Marianne's my real mom. Yeah. She was pissed. Plus..." When Summer looked up and saw more freshmen staring at her again, she spread her arms. "Hey, maybe take a picture. It'll last longer."

They all looked away and went back to their other conversations with friends.

"Seriously. We have magic, go to a magic school, we're riding in a giant room inside and under or wherever it is on a magic bus, and it's my *hair* these idiots can't stop staring at?"

"I thought you didn't care about what anyone else thinks."

Summer rolled her eyes. "I don't. I also don't like being stared at when I'm trying to have a *private conversation*."

A group of freshmen burst out laughing.

"See? I don't get it."

Amanda shook her head at the younger kids, who smirked but fell silent, only casting occasional glances up at the only two upperclassmen in the van. "You know, you could whisper it."

"Yeah, as fun as it sounds to play whisper-and-giggly-little-secrets, I don't think so."

"I'm the only one who'd be able to hear you. And you obviously have to get something off your chest."

"Ha. Yeah. My whole life."

Scrunching up her nose, Amanda shrugged and stared at the floor. "Well, I'm here."

"Uh-huh." The van went over a particularly large bump, which sent two freshmen flying from their seats to a rise of exploding laughter.

Summer stared at the kids scrambling to get off the floor and whispered, "They're getting a divorce."

Amanda looked at her friend with wide eyes. "You meant for me to hear that, right?"

"What do *you* think, shifter girl? I said it, didn't I?"

"Your parents?"

The witch dipped her chin in a quick nod. "Apparently, I'm the—"

The van screeched to a halt with a roar of crunching gravel, then Shep's voice came over the speakers again. "Here we are, ladies and gents. Y'all come on up in an orderly fashion, now. Don't make me come down there to sort y'all out."

His high-pitched giggle cut off halfway through, then the light from outside spilled into the van and down the staircase toward the magically enlarged sitting area.

The students stood quickly and headed for the foot of the staircase, jostling each other and laughing as they tried to get there before their friends.

Amanda and Summer didn't move, and the shifter girl studied her friend's profile with a sympathetic frown. "You're the what?"

"Problem." Summer scratched her rainbow hair vigorously, puffed out a sigh, then dragged both hands down her cheeks. "Whatever. They can suck it, right?"

"Wait, your parents said you're the reason they're splitting up?"

"For everyone to hear, shifter girl? Really?" The witch stood and stormed toward the stairs.

"Okay, well, first, I didn't mean to piss you off. Second, you shout out my business all the time."

"No, I don't."

"Summer—"

"Forget I even said anything, okay? It's fine."

"Hey." Amanda grabbed the other girl's arm to get her to slow down, then let her go when Summer glared at her. "I'm sorry."

"We're cool. Don't worry about it."

"No, I meant about your parents. That sucks. I'm sorry you have to deal with that."

"Yeah, well, maybe I won't have to deal with it from now on."

"What does that mean?"

Summer headed up the stairs again. "It means I'm fine. That's it."

As the last one out up the stairs, Amanda watched Summer leap out of the van, then the witch disappeared. *No wonder she's so pissed off all the time. She probably saw this coming a long time ago, and now it's happening.*

Amanda finally ducked through the open van door and hopped out onto the grass. This year's students getting ready to start a brand-new semester at the Academy already flooded the campus. The freshmen milled around like lost little puppies, staying in close groups of friends they either already knew or had made on the train. The other upperclassmen took up most of the main field, tossing spells around and shooting fireworks into the sky.

One such firework went sideways and launched toward the oncoming freshmen, making half of them duck and the other half run away screaming.

Summer barked out a laugh. "Look at that. They're all out there showing off like they own the place."

"I mean, they do *live* here."

"We all do, shifter girl."

"All year 'round."

"Meh." Summer waved her off and headed toward the central field. "So what do you think? Will we end up being as stuck up as last year's seniors?"

"You mean running around and showing off like we own the place?"

"Real funny, shifter girl."

As Shep got to work unloading all the luggage from the van to take to the dorms, the girls headed across the central field. A few other upperclassmen shouted greetings or nodded at them, but most were busy messing around on their last Friday of freedom before the semester officially started.

Amanda sniffed the air and grinned. "I think we made it back in time to grab some food."

"You're still hungry after all those train snacks?"

"You're not?"

Summer shrugged. "Yeah, okay. I could eat some real food."

They took off for the outdoor cafeteria, where a handful of students still sat around at the picnic table beneath the pavilion. The buffet tables hadn't been broken down yet from dinner, and there was plenty of chicken salad, potatoes, green beans, and mac 'n cheese left to feed a hungry shifter girl and her witch friend.

Halfway through their silent meal, Summer finally looked up and cocked her head. "What?"

Amanda blinked quickly. "Nothing."

"So why are you staring at me?"

"I'm not."

"Look, I can *feel* it, okay? Like a bunch of ants crawling all over my skin. Just spit it out, huh?"

"Ants." Amanda smirked.

"That funny?"

"It's a pretty good description. Kind of like what I feel with *my* magic too."

Summer snorted. "I seriously hope you're not gonna send your ghost-wolf at me if you stare too long. I've had enough run-ins with that thing already."

"Okay, so if I promise *not* to beat you up with my ghost-wolf if you talk to me about what's going on at home, will it work?"

The witch crammed a huge bite of chicken salad into her mouth and stared at her friend without blinking. "You know, for someone who likes to keep her secrets, you're going about this the wrong way."

"Come on, Summer. It's not like you've never threatened *me* to open up about something."

"Is that what you're doing right now? Threatening me?"

Amanda slowly placed both hands on either side of her plate on the picnic table and called her magic just a little. White mist swirled away from her hands, and two ghostly white paws emerged from them to hover over the table as she leaned forward. "Is it working?"

Summer eyed the display and chuckled. "I don't know. Maybe. That's insanely cool, though."

The shifter girl pulled back on her magic and laughed. "Yeah. You won't believe what I had to do with it this morning."

"Try me."

"You first."

The witch rolled her eyes. "I fell right into that one, didn't I?"

"Hey, we don't have to talk about anything if you don't want to. But it kinda seemed like you wanted to on the ride here, so I figured I'd remind you. Forcefully."

"Ha. Remind me that I hate talking about this crap? Yeah."

"No. Remind you that I'm here. If you want to talk about it."

They stared at each other, then Summer crammed more food into her mouth and talked around it. "I don't know. Not much else to say. My 'parents,' if that's what they even are, can't handle being together and dealing with *me* at the same time anymore. So I guess that's it."

Amanda offered her friend a sympathetic frown. "Did they actually say that?"

When the young witch looked up at her with wide eyes, she didn't have to answer but did anyway. "Marianne did. Like, right to my face. No clue what Michael thinks, but he always lets her walk all over him anyway. He didn't stick around to talk to me about it."

Jeeze, she's going through a lot.

There was so much in there to unpack that the only thing

Amanda could think to ask after that was, "When did you start calling them by their first names?"

"Ha! *That's* what you wanna know?"

"It's a little weird."

"Hey, do you call *your* stand-in parents Mommy and Daddy? No. Neither do I."

"Wait." Amanda cocked her head. "So you *are* adopted?"

"I didn't say that."

"Then why—"

"Coulier!" Jackson shouted from the other end of the cafeteria, waving both arms like mad. Walking with him were the rest of Amanda's close friends, Grace and Alex. Jackson elbowed Grace in the ribs and looked ridiculously pleased with himself. "See? I told you she'd be here."

Grace playfully rolled her eyes, then the trio reached the table and slid into their seats. Alex sat next to Summer and stared at her short rainbow-dyed hair. "I miss the mohawk."

"Well shit, Woody. If I knew you'd be so upset about it, I still wouldn't have cared."

The Wood Elf cracked a smile at her and shook his head.

"How was your summer?" Grace asked. "Anything fun?"

"Just another normal summer, I guess." Amanda shrugged. "Hunting, hanging out in the swamp, waiting to start this thing with the Coalition."

"How'd that go?" Jackson asked.

"Not...exactly the way I expected."

"You did start it, right?" Grace leaned over the table toward the shifter girl and widened her eyes. "When do you start hunting monsters?"

"I have no idea."

Jackson frowned. "That's dumb. Didn't Glasket say they wanted you at the end of last year?"

"Yeah. All I did was tour a research facility. Where they keep mutated creatures or whatever. Maybe I'll start doing something useful soon, so we'll see."

"What about you, Summer?" Grace smiled at the other witch and briefly glanced at the rainbow on her head.

"Yeah, how was your summer, Summer?" Jackson snickered. "That's funny."

"Oh, *man*." She grinned at him. "I've never heard that one before, Romeo. You're really on a roll this year, huh?"

The wizard frowned. "It *is* funny."

"He's asking how you are to catch up," Grace added. "No reason to get all uptight about it."

"Thanks for the translation, Blondie. If I wanted to get all uptight about it, that's *my* business."

"Whoa." Jackson ran a hand through his disheveled dirty-blond hair. "Hey, I didn't mean to start anything."

"No, but *she* did."

Grace huffed out a bitter laugh. "Me? You're the one who can't even be nice for one whole day."

"Well, maybe I wouldn't get so pissed off if you guys didn't keep nagging me with questions and making jokes about my stupid summer!" Summer stood and quickly swung her leg over the picnic bench to get away. "Screw this."

"Hey. Summer, wait." Amanda started to stand.

"Don't," the short-haired witch growled as she stormed away from the outdoor cafeteria and toward the dorms.

"What's her problem, huh?" Grace shook her head. "All we did was ask her about her summer. You know, 'cause she gets to *go home* for three months."

"Two and a half," Alex muttered.

"What?"

"Technically, it's two and a half months for summer break."

"You know what I mean."

Amanda watched Summer disappear around the end of the

kitchen building, then slowly sat again. "I think that's her problem."

"What, two and a half months instead of three?" Jackson snorted. "More time out of school is never a bad thing."

"No, I mean the going home part." Amanda scooped some more food into her mouth and glanced at each of her friends. All three of them looked clueless, so she quickly swallowed her mouthful and tried to explain. "I think she's going through some pretty rough stuff at home."

"Okay." Grace folded her arms on the table. "That's not an excuse to be a jerk about everything."

Amanda wrinkled her nose at the other girl. "I don't disagree with you, but that's kind of hypocritical."

Grace laughed. "What? *I'm* not a jerk."

"I wasn't talking about you. Except for Summer and me, every single junior and senior this year is here because they don't have anywhere else to go. It was causing a bunch of problems for a bunch of other magicals. Some people might even consider living underground in L.A. 'pretty rough stuff at home.' I mean, that's why they started this school in the first place."

"Summer wasn't there with us," Grace muttered. "That doesn't apply to her."

"That doesn't matter." Amanda tore up the cold dinner roll on her plate piece by piece. "Look, I don't know what's going on with her, but I know it's not good. At home. With her parents. So many try to be a little nicer knowing all that."

"Amanda, I *was* nice. I asked about her summer—"

"Which was a sore spot. Obviously. And the minute she shut down, you asked what her problem was."

Grace grimaced. "You're right. I know."

Jackson turned toward the witch with wide eyes. "Wow. I didn't expect you to agree with her."

Alex snickered.

"Look, I'm not trying to be a jerk." Grace glanced at the ceiling of the pavilion and let out a massive sigh. "She makes it so *hard* to not call her out on…whatever she's trying to do with all the jokes and the dumb nicknames."

"I'm cool with Woody," Alex muttered as he stared at Amanda's plate. "You want the rest of your beans?"

"Here." She slid the plate across the table toward him and returned to the conversation. "We all have our issues, right?"

The Wood Elf snorted as he dug into the rest of her late dinner. "Speak for yourself."

"Oh, yeah." Jackson punched him in the arm. "Because it's totally normal to get all slap-happy about Petrov losing it on us last semester and throwing a fit in Combat Training."

"Yeah, that was pretty awesome."

Amanda and Grace exchanged a confused look, and the blonde witch rolled her eyes before mouthing, "Boys."

"Okay, and that only proves my point," Amanda added with a laugh. "We *all* have our issues. So maybe if you tried asking Summer sometime if she's okay and *mean* it when you ask—"

"How am I supposed to do that?" Grace gestured toward the end of the outdoor cafeteria. "She walks off whenever she wants. She'd only laugh at me anyway and make some stupid joke. She wouldn't even take me seriously."

"Then keep trying." Amanda shrugged. "Give her a reason to take you seriously. I mean, we can all be friends. It's not that hard."

"Amanda, we have no idea what her deal is."

"You didn't know what *my* deal was freshman year, either. You didn't stop being my friends just because I wouldn't tell you right away."

Alex chuckled. "No, we had to wait 'til you called the spirits of your dead family on Halloween and almost let an angry ghost destroy the school." Everyone stared at him, and he shoveled more food into his mouth before he realized it. "What? Too soon?"

Amanda barked out a laugh. "I guess not."

"Fine." Grace tucked her hair behind her ears, then lifted both hands in concession. "I'll work on it, okay? Like, I'll try to ignore all the things about her that drive me crazy, 'cause I know... I mean, she's not *that* bad."

Jackson cracked up laughing.

"What's so funny?"

The wizard shook his head and couldn't quite catch his breath.

"Did you swallow some kind of laughing bean or something?" Grace shoved him in the shoulder. "*What?*"

"Oh, man. Sorry. I just... Whew." Jackson looked at Amanda and raised his eyebrows. "They'd get along pretty okay if they stopped blaming each other for everything."

Amanda snorted. "Yeah, that's kinda the point."

"I don't *blame* her..." Grace rolled her eyes, froze, then leaned away from the table. "Wow. Maybe I do."

"Only took you two years," Alex muttered.

"Okay, moving on." The witch pointed at Amanda. "I wanna hear about your shifter intern thing."

"You really don't. It's not that great yet. I mean, I did get to use my magic to fight a Harkliss bird's spirit. I think."

"Wait, you *what?*" Jackson slapped his hands down on the table. "That's so *cool!*"

"Now you have to tell us everything," Grace added. "'Cause that sounds pretty great to me."

So Amanda told her friends about the odd Coalition research facility in the middle of the Rockies—about Dr. Caniss and Lucy and Bill and her two-hour "test" that led to absolutely nothing—but the whole time, she was still thinking about Summer.

If her mom told her the divorce was her fault, no wonder she's so angry all the time. She doesn't even have someone like Johnny or Lisa to go to. She's all on her own.

CHAPTER NINE

After settling into her dorm room for the night and unpacking all her things—including her school-prohibited contraband of the cell phone, signal box, and small utility knife Johnny had given her—Amanda found herself completely unable to sleep. Only some of that came from the fact that she wasn't tired yet.

The main reason, though, was because someone had decided to throw a giant party out in the central field.

Last Friday of the summer, right? Maybe I should start moving back onto campus early after breaks.

The sound of laughter and dozens of conversations drifted through her closed window, mixed with incredibly loud music pounding away. Maybe the other girls in the dorm couldn't hear the noise, but a teenage shifter definitely could.

Fine. I'll go check it out.

First, she stopped at Summer's room two doors down across the hall and knocked gently. "Summer? You in there?"

The witch didn't respond, but Amanda heard the rustle of movement on the bed.

"I'm going out to the field. Sounds like a party. You wanna come?"

Again, no answer.

"Okay, well… Find me if you want." She waited a few more seconds, but Summer Flannerty was apparently not in the mood for a party.

Weird. I get it though. She needs space.

So Amanda slipped out of the otherwise quiet girls' dorm and headed out into the field. It was after 10:30 p.m., which would become Lights Out for this year's freshmen, but none of that mattered on the last Friday of freedom before classes started.

Someone had built a large bonfire in the middle of the central field. Most of the kids gathered around it were upperclassmen, and only a few sophomore stragglers had joined the fun. Amanda counted only six freshmen brave enough to come outside at night and try to party with the kids who knew the Academy inside and out, but no one told them to get lost.

"Hey, Amanda!" Anabelle turned away from the bonfire to head toward her. "I didn't know you were here already."

"Yeah, I came in a little early this year." She grinned at the dwarf girl and pointed at the bonfire. "Is this a regular thing?"

"It is now. I think the seniors started it last year. You know, party for the upperclassmen, right? Now it's our turn."

"It's not only upperclassmen, though."

"Yeah, I know. The freshmen look pretty terrified, right?"

"We probably did too."

Anabelle laughed. "Come on. Everyone's out here. Grab a seat."

Gazing around the firelit main field, Amanda drew a deep breath of the balmy night air and followed the dwarf girl toward the bonfire. *It's not even cold enough for a fire. What's the point?*

"Coulier!" Jackson grinned at her when she reached the pocket of juniors around the fire. "You finally get to see *the upperclassman blaze.*"

Anabelle sat next to Grace, and both girls rolled their eyes. Farther away from the bonfire, Alex and Tommy Brunsen played catch with a ball of blue light that randomly sparked and shocked whoever didn't throw it back quickly enough. Tommy snorted. "Dude, that name's never gonna stick."

"Yeah, and it makes us sound like we're all getting high," Alex added as he tossed the blue light back.

Tommy caught it and stared at the Wood Elf. "Wait, do you have anything?"

"Nope."

"Huh. I wonder if Pete managed to—ah!" Tommy chucked the blue light back at Alex and shook his hand after the jolt of energy had crackled up to it. "Dangit."

"You guys can't be serious about trying to find *drugs* right now," Grace said. "That's the dumbest thing I've ever heard you say."

"I was only asking." Tommy caught the orb and sent it right back. "Besides, I heard something about Pete bringing back an entire case of HardPull the last time he went to the kemana. No idea how he smuggled it in, but if he still has some…"

Grace perked up, stared at the fire, and shrugged. "I mean, if he's sharing, I wouldn't say *no*."

"Yeah." Jackson snorted. "'Cause he's all about sharing for free."

"Well, I don't have anything to trade."

"I bet he'd give you some if you did his homework for him," Alex muttered.

"*What*? No." Grace folded her arms. "Nothing's worth *that*. He can do his homework."

"I might take him up on that," Anabelle said.

Grace's jaw dropped. "You would not."

"Maybe. I like HardPull."

"Okay, stop." The girls laughed, and Grace leaned forward to wrap her arms around her bent knees before looking at Amanda. "Where's Summer?"

"I think she's still in her room. Told her I'd be out here, though."

"She knows about this," Jackson added. "I mean, she was here last year when the upperclassmen did this. I bet she thinks it's boring."

Amanda looked into the high flame of the bonfire and noticed the complete lack of wood to fuel the fire. "So who mastered a giant bonfire spell?"

"Kurt." Jackson pointed at the group of this year's seniors sitting dangerously close to the flames. "I'm pretty sure it takes, like, three people to make it this big, though."

"Huh. It's not even burning the grass."

Grace scoffed. "Like Glasket would let us do this if it set the field on fire. Hey, did anyone read up on what we're learning in Alchemy this year?"

Everyone stared at the blonde witch with blank expressions.

"Oh, come on. Advanced Alchemy. Nobody else cares?"

"We haven't even started class yet." Jackson ran a hand through his hair. "Can't you wait a few days before you start breaking apart the lesson plan?"

"I'm just saying. I think it's exciting. We finally get to learn something advanced."

"Yeah, well, keep your excitement—"

A high-pitched whine came from the other side of the field, followed by a glittering ball of yellow light spiraling straight up into the air. When the light reached the top of its spiral, it exploded with dozens of *pops* and sent glittering yellow birds flying all over the field.

The conversation in the central field momentarily died, then a massive wave of cheering and whistling took its place.

"Who's doing that?" Grace leapt to her feet. Everyone else was standing too, as two more spiraling lights shot up into the air. "I can't see where they're coming from."

"Looks like right outside the main building." Amanda ducked

when the next two magical fireworks exploded and rained down blue flowers and multi-colored spiraling disks.

"Yeah, but nobody is standing there." Grace walked around the bonfire to get a better view. "That doesn't make sense. If someone's casting a spell for these—" Two more fireworks exploded. One of them cast a shower of sparks down around the central field like a dome, and the other sent google-eyed smiley faces raining down with the last of the birds and flowers. Cartoonish laughter came from the faces. Grace rolled her eyes. "The spells would be coming from whoever's casting it. And there's no one there."

"Hey, relax." Jackson nudged her with his elbow. "It's a party. Enjoy the show."

"Not when it doesn't make any sense at all."

The other upperclassmen cheered and stayed where they were. No one else was bothered by the mysteries behind the bodiless caster.

The next explosion was the loudest yet, and instead of playful fireworks, it launched a giant, glowing red middle finger into the air. The students burst out laughing, and the very last crackling firework unleashed a string of blocky letters into the night sky above the middle finger: "Summer, bitches!"

"Oh my God." Amanda put a hand to her head and stared at the bright-yellow letters slowly floating toward the ground. "No."

"Wait a minute." Grace whirled around to face her. "Did she..."

"I have no idea."

"It's the last day of summer," Alex said through his laughter. "Obviously."

"Or she left a calling card for the last summer party," Jackson added. "Which is pretty awesome."

More fireworks launched into the sky from seemingly nowhere outside the central field. Someone cranked up the music, and the light show blasts kept getting louder and louder.

The last one was deafening and released a glittering magical version of a mushroom cloud from a real explosion. When it cracked through the air, the students jumped away and clapped their hands over their ears.

Amanda grimaced against the ringing in her ears. When the glittering specks of light faded, the entire central field had fallen silent except for the pumping of the bass—probably coming from Pete's portable stereo—and the crackle of the bonfire.

Because now Principal Glasket and Ms. Calsgrave were rounding the side of the main building from the faculty housing behind it. Neither of them looked particularly happy.

"Great." Grace rolled her eyes. "Now we won't even be able to throw this party next year as seniors."

"Maybe they wanted to join us?" Anabelle suggested, but she didn't sound convinced of it.

Grace stared at the dwarf girl and shook her head.

Two more fireworks launched into the air, and Glasket pointed at them. A streak of white light shot from her finger, separated in two to engulf both fireworks, and the sparks fizzled out before they could explode. A collective groan rose from the students.

Ms. Calsgrave opened her hands toward the space where the light show had originated. A purple wall of light emerged from her hands and washed across the grass with a light breeze. It cleared before it reached the students around the bonfire, but in its wake, it left a single humanoid-shaped pocket of shimmering light. Then the light winked out, and Summer Flannerty stood there halfway between the central field and the main building.

She looked down at her hands, then groaned and spun. "Oh, come on. Do you know how long it took me to get that illusion completely right?"

Glasket opened her mouth to respond, but the upperclassmen burst out laughing, throwing out cheers and whistles.

Summer turned back toward the bonfire with a wide grin and spread her arms for a theatric bow.

Amanda stared at her friend with wide eyes and shook her head. *That's how she deals with hard crap at home. Sure, Summer. Bring all the illegal fireworks you can find or make and start the year off with a bang.*

The thought made her snort.

"All right, everyone, quiet down!" Glasket shouted. "Please!"

Two students had picked up chanting Summer's name, but it didn't catch, and they eventually fell silent with the rest of the kids out in the field.

"Miss Flannerty, a word, please?" Glasket nodded toward the front of the main building.

"Why? It's the end-of-summer party. That's still a thing."

"With a magically contained bonfire and student-selected music, sure." Glasket scanned the group of students and raised her voice. "Which might in fact be a little louder than we agreed, Mr. Cross." A group of junior boys burst out laughing, and the music turned down a notch. "It doesn't include unapproved fireworks displays, Miss Flannerty."

"Hey, it's only a little fun. Nobody got hurt."

"That's not the point." Glasket nodded at the main building again, but Summer didn't move. The principal sighed and stepped toward her instead. "I don't want to give this year's freshmen the impression they can blow things up whenever they want."

Summer barked out a laugh and folded her arms. "Seriously? 'Cause I showed up at this school with that impression already."

Glasket raised an eyebrow and leaned toward the girl to whisper something.

Over the sound of the music and the conversations that had picked back up again, Amanda couldn't hear a thing the principal was saying. But she saw Summer's back straighten and her hands clench into fists at her sides.

Don't do anything stupid, Summer. Please.

The short-haired witch surprised her, though, when she stepped away from Glasket and nodded. The principal nodded too, then turned to head for the faculty building again.

Calsgrave watched her leave, then pointed at Summer and shot her a crooked smile. "I'm not saying I condone the disruption, but good work on that illusion. I almost didn't expect to find you there when I undid it. Almost."

Summer shrugged. "I guess I'll take the compliment."

"Good. Enjoy the rest of your night, Miss Flannerty." Then the Illusions teacher walked away, leaving Summer standing there with her fists still clenched.

Grace huffed out a laugh. "Did she get a compliment for that?"

"I think so." Amanda broke into a grin. "I mean, she *has* gotten good at it."

"And she's using it to break all the rules with illegal fireworks."

"Not *all* the rules," Jackson muttered. He stepped away from Grace when she shot him a warning look and shrugged. "What? It's only a few fireworks. That was awesome."

"Wow. No one cares about the rules, huh?"

Amanda shot the blonde witch a sidelong glance and couldn't help but laugh. "I mean, we're supposed to break the rules sometimes, right?"

"Not all of them all the time. Watch. Now Summer's gonna come over here and get cheered again because she…" Grace scanned the field and the front of the main building, then turned with a frown. "Wait. Where is she?"

Summer was gone.

"Maybe she made herself invisible again," Alex suggested. "I mean, if *I* could cast that illusion as well as she does, I'd probably be invisible all the time."

Anabelle giggled. "That could be either really cool or totally creepy."

The Wood Elf smirked at her. "You'd never know. 'Cause I'd be invisible."

Amanda went back to the end-of-summer party with her friends, trying to enjoy their last Friday of relative freedom before classes. Still, she couldn't stop looking around for Summer.

I hope this was a one-time thing and she got it out of her system. Otherwise, this semester's gonna have way too much going on if she keeps working out her feelings with a bunch of explosives.

CHAPTER TEN

The next morning after breakfast, Amanda headed to the greenhouse to check on her plants from last semester. She'd set up the watering system to take care of the plants in the troughs while she was gone for the summer, but what she really wanted to check were the Fatethistle plants she hoped were still growing in her secret cellar under the green metal cabinet.

When she hopped down into the hidey-hole, she found the purple glow of the fast-track plant she'd grown at abnormal speed still flourishing and healthy. The other two plants were almost as large and equally healthy, the tiny ash-gray flowers starting to bud amidst the clusters of violet-colored leaves.

Well, that's a relief. Now I have three rare and highly illegal mature plants growing here, and I have no idea what to do with them.

She brushed her fingers along the tiny purple leaves, which shuddered and glowed at her touch.

Maybe the Coalition will take them. I don't need them anymore.

Thinking about how to broach the subject with Fiona eventually, Amanda climbed back out of the hole, dropped the trapdoor back into place, and shoved the heavy, squealing metal cabinet back over it to keep it hidden. The second she stepped away from the cabinet, someone knocked on the door.

"Miss Coulier?"

She spun to face the door and let out a slow sigh when she saw that she had closed it all the way. "Yeah?"

"It's Dean Glasket. May I come in?"

"Uh, sure." Amanda hurried across the room to open the door for her principal. "You have a key, right?"

"I do." Glasket stepped into the greenhouse with her hands clasped in front of her. "However, I understand how much this place means to you. I'm not in the habit of barging in on students when they're taking a few quiet, private minutes for themselves."

"Oh. Well, thanks." She frowned at the principal. "Is everything okay?"

"As far as I know. I came to ask you the same thing about the plants in here. Is everything accounted for and still doing well?"

"Yep. As far as I know."

Glasket chuckled and pulled a folded piece of paper and two small brown packets of seeds from the pocket of her slacks. "Good to hear. This is a list with specific instructions for two more plants you'll be growing this semester. With a few seeds to get you started. You'll be harvesting them as well before winter break, when they're ready."

"Okay." Amanda took the seed packets and paper but didn't bother to unfold the latter.

"Of course, I don't expect you to get started on these until your first class period spent in here. So don't think I'm trying to give you extra work outside of what you already do." The principal nodded at the list. "Those two were specifically requested by our friends in the Coalition. Until they're fully mature, they asked me to inform you that you'll be harvesting the Blindman's Bane, Shiverbloom, and Fool's Supper plants as much as you can before next weekend and taking them with you on your next trip off-campus with Ms. Damascus."

"Sure. I can do that."

"Wonderful. If you think of anything you might need for your work in here, let me know."

"Okay." Amanda set the folded list and seeds on the work-bench at the end of the center trough and stared at Glasket. The principal stood perfectly still as she studied the five long gardening troughs stretching the length of the greenhouse and filled with healthy plants.

Why is she standing there? There's no way she saw me moving that cabinet back.

"Well, I was about to leave anyway, so…"

"Oh, of course. I did have a few more questions for you if you don't mind."

Amanda raised her eyebrows as the principal turned toward her.

Glasket licked her lips in contemplation, glanced at the ceiling, then met her student's gaze. "Has Miss Flannerty opened up to you at all about what she's going through right now? Maybe mentioned any…difficulties in her personal life?"

With a small chuckle, Amanda shook her head. "I don't know if you've noticed, but Summer's not really the kind of person who *opens up*."

The corner of Glasket's mouth twitched in a small smile. "Yes, Miss Coulier. I've noticed. I also know how close the two of you are, both when you're focusing on school *and* when you're sniffing out trouble wherever you can find it."

Amanda folded her arms. "I didn't know about the fireworks."

"I'm not talking about the fireworks. That's over and done with." Glasket drew a deep breath and one more slow scan of the greenhouse before adding, "I only wanted to know if she'd told you anything. Sometimes, it's easier to process and understand difficult situations when we have a friend to help us through it."

She's trying to figure out what's going on. Summer would kill me if I spilled her secret to the principal.

The girl shook her head. "I don't really know anything. You could try asking *her*."

"Hmm. Yes." Glasket frowned, but it quickly disappeared under a courteous smile before she nodded. "Thank you, Miss Coulier. Enjoy the rest of your weekend. I'm looking forward to seeing how well these new plants come along over the semester."

"Shouldn't be a problem."

"I know." The principal headed toward the door and paused to look back over her shoulder. "That's why we're bringing these to *you*." Then she opened the door, stepped into the hall, and closed it behind her. Her clicking footsteps echoed along the tile floors and faded down the corridor.

Amanda puffed out a sigh and ran a hand through her hair.

That was close. And weird. Why is she so interested in Summer all of a sudden?

She glanced at the seeds and Glasket's list, then shook her head. Those could wait until her first greenhouse period during Illusions class.

Right now, she wanted to leave the greenhouse and pretend Glasket hadn't tried prying Summer's secrets out of the shifter girl who was probably her only real friend.

She didn't have a chance over the rest of the weekend to talk to Summer about the weird meeting with their principal. The witch was either running around with her invisibility illusion on at all times or had decided to lock herself up in her dorm room. However, when Amanda knocked on the door of Room 233C to see if there was a good time to talk, she got no reply at all.

When Monday finally rolled around for the first day of classes, though, Summer was there in the central field with the rest of the student body for Glasket's opening announcements to the entire school.

At the end of it, Glasket grinned at the students from her place on the stage, where one of LeFor's floating microphones bobbed beside her head. "So another warm welcome to this year's freshman class. Now it's time to start."

Each of the teachers launched their colored sparks into the air and shouted for the class that would start the day with them to gather. Ralthorn sprayed purple sparks from the tip of her finger and waited silently for the junior class to join her in front of the main building.

"At least *those* announcements didn't have any creepy references to monsters and a Monster Squad and being on high alert for danger," Summer muttered as they headed toward the History of Oriceran teacher.

Amanda smirked. "Yeah, it's nice to have all that behind us."

"Well, it's not really behind *you*, is it, shifter girl? You get all the excitement when you leave the swamp to go fight mutated monsters with your shifter friends."

"It's not really like that."

"Why not?"

Amanda shrugged. "Apparently, I have to *prove* what I can do before I start hunting anything."

"For real?" Summer scoffed. "That's the dumbest thing I've ever heard. You already proved yourself. Isn't that why they wanted you?"

"Yeah, that's exactly what *I* said."

The junior class gathered quickly in front of Ralthorn. The history teacher quickly blinked as she took in all the faces she already knew, then tucked her hair behind her ear and spun for the main building's front doors. "Keep up. You know the drill."

The juniors filed inside and followed her down the branching hallways toward her classroom.

Amanda kept shooting Summer sidelong glances, biting the inside of her cheek. *She's acting like nothing happened. As if she didn't disappear all weekend.*

"Okay, say it already," Summer muttered. "I told you I could feel you staring at me."

"I'm just...wondering if everything's okay."

"Yeah. Totally. We get to start a brand-new year in Snore class. What's not to be happy about?"

With a snort, Amanda shook her head. "I mean with you. I didn't see you all weekend."

Summer shrugged and ruffled her rainbow hair. "I needed some time to myself. Like, completely. Don't tell me the shifter girl who sneaks out in the middle of the night to go wolf around in the swamp doesn't get that."

"Ha. No, I totally get it."

"Cool. Thanks for, you know, not trying to hunt me down or anything. All good now. Everything Summer Flannerty is totally normal."

"Uh-huh."

"I mean normal for me. Obviously not everyone else. 'Cause that would be, like, just shoot me now, you know?"

"You're the last person I'd ever say was normal, Summer."

The witch laughed and thumped Amanda's arm with the back of her hand. "Give yourself more credit. There's no universe where *you're* normal, either."

"I'm okay with that."

"Yeah, me too."

The class settled into their seats for what they were all sure would be another one of Ralthorn's droning and sleep-inducing lectures on Oriceran history, plants, animals, and events that mostly didn't apply to their lives. Instead, the teacher pointed at the air beside her, and the glittering magical blackboard she liked to use appeared in the air with her scrawling handwriting across the top in glowing pink light.

"Juniors." Ralthorn smiled tightly at them. "You've made it through the rigors of old-world history over the last two years. You know about Oriceran's past and some of Earth's now too.

This year, we're taking it a step further and breaching the nuanced and highly complicated subject of current magical affairs and politics."

Jasmine thumped her hand on her desk, then shot it straight up into the air.

"Yes, Miss McVar?"

"What do current affairs and politics have to do with bounty hunter school?"

"I…" Ralthorn cocked her head.

"Yeah," Evan shouted from the back. "Or history. Aren't junior and senior year supposed to be about getting us ready for our actual jobs after we graduate?"

The teacher drew a deep breath through her nose. "Yes, Mr. Hutchinson. That's what we'll be covering during your junior year."

"Why?" Corey folded his large, hairy arms.

"Because there's more to being a bounty hunter than barging in to blow things up and fight criminals."

"Wait, there is?"

"If you'll let me continue, Mr. Baker, I'm sure you'll understand how it all fits together. Which is the point of school in the first place. Seeing as you've been here for two years already, I have no issue saying that the next student who interrupts my class with questions that I will answer later will start their junior year in Dean Glasket's office. Understand?"

The class fell silent, and Ralthorn grinned. "Thank you."

Summer leaned toward Amanda's desk and raised her eyebrows. "You think she's always been less of a pushover with upperclassmen, or you think two years of teaching us is finally starting to wear her down?"

Amanda shook her head and tried not to laugh.

"Shh." Behind them, Grace nodded toward Ralthorn writing more magical notes on the floating blackboard. "I want to hear this."

"Of course you do." Summer rolled her eyes.

"First," Ralthorn said when she finished writing, "I'll go over what we'll be covering this semester. We've made a bit of a time jump, so if there's anything else you'd like to cover between the beginning of the twentieth century and now, I have a list of additional resources for anyone interested. Feel free to cover those topics on your own time."

Grace shot her hand into the air.

"Miss Porter?"

"Will we get extra credit for doing that?"

Ralthorn blinked and cleared her throat. "Not that you need it, but I don't believe extra credit is necessary at this point. I'm hoping at least one student from this school will acquire a deeper interest in magical history. Moving on." She pointed at the floating blackboard, and the first line pulsed once with a brighter light. "As you know, magicals have been on Earth for tens of thousands of years, crossing through the gates between this planet and Oriceran during the alignment period while those gates are open. Only quite recently, from a historical perspective, has the human world on Earth known about magicals, Oriceran, and magic at all. The reveal of magic almost thirty-three years ago now changed everything.

"There were a few key players in this reveal, and you may even recognize the names if you pay attention. Leira Berens was one of the first—"

"Who?" Tommy asked.

Ralthorn raised an eyebrow. "Are you that excited to spend the next two hours with Dean Glasket, Mr. Brunson?"

"No. I don't remember who that is."

The teacher stared at him and let out a heavy, exasperated sigh.

Anabelle turned in her desk to glare at Tommy. "She helped start this school. With Johnny Walker and James Brownstone. You were here for that."

"Oh. Right. The elf."

"Thank you, Miss Lamar," Ralthorn said. "Yes. Leira Berens has a proven track record of getting in at the beginning of many things to help them move along. One of her most notable achievements around the time magicals and magic revealed themselves to the human world was a sort of contractual alliance with the FBI. That sparked the first years of—"

"The Department," Amanda blurted with a huge grin.

Summer stared at her and shook her head with a "what are you doing" frown.

"Of...Monsters and Magicals," Amanda added. "Because she's a bounty hunter."

"Yes, Miss Coulier. Thank you." Ralthorn gestured dejectedly toward the blackboard. "Which is what I was about to say. So we'll dive into how that federal department is structured, how government officials have worked with magical bounty hunters over the last few decades, and what all of you can expect after graduating if you do in fact decide to pursue that line of work. Generally speaking, of course. No, I can't answer specific questions about *how* to get those jobs or help you compare the different kinds. That will be part of your curriculum next year.

"You may, however, be able to ask those questions of a special guest we might be hosting here next semester for a sort of pre-graduation address. For the outgoing seniors, obviously, but I highly recommend you attend that particular assembly. You'll probably get a lot more information from it than you think."

"Who is it?" Brandon asked.

"As of right now, Mr. Everly, it's unconfirmed. So I can't drop any names until we know for sure. The guest speakers we've approached about this will all be highly entertaining and infor-mative, I promise. Now, beyond the FBI, there are several other government agencies, as well as US military branches, who have opened their doors to working directly with magicals. Yes, specifically bounty hunters in many cases—"

"Except for the CIA, right?"

Ralthorn stared at Amanda.

"Um...sorry." The girl shook her head and puffed out a sigh. "I get it. I'll go to up to Glasket's office—"

"Where did you hear that bit of information, Miss Coulier?"

"What, about the CIA?"

Ralthorn frowned. "Yes."

"I just, you know...heard it in passing."

"Hmm." The teacher turned and shuffled through the stack of papers on her desk.

Summer snickered. "You can't let it go with the whole 'I know more 'cause I live with bounty hunters' thing, can you?"

"I'm not *trying* to be a know-it-all," Amanda whispered back. "I'm just...excited about this part, I guess."

Two desks down from hers, Jackson laughed and quickly covered it up with a forced cough. "You're excited about history?"

"I mean, it's not history if it's happening right now, is it?"

Grace partially stood to lean over her desk toward Amanda. "Technically, it's—"

"That's enough, thank you." Ralthorn turned, and everyone resumed their seats and closed their mouths. "Miss Coulier is correct. The CIA does not currently contract magical individuals. Which is quite a shame. That's none of our concern, however, and it certainly doesn't apply to you right now. Maybe when you graduate, that particular agency will have pulled their heads out of their—"

She stopped and stared with wide eyes at the back of the classroom. A flush of color rose in the witch's cheeks, and she cleared her throat. "Maybe they'll change their minds."

Tommy and Evan snickered in the back of the class. "She should've just said it. It's not like we can't fill in the blank."

"Hey, Corey. Mad Libs time. How 'bout a noun?"

The half-Kilomea kid folded his arms and didn't look away from the teacher as he muttered, "Knuckle sandwich."

"Get their heads out of their knuckle sandwich. Nice." The boys at the back of the room exploded with subdued laughter until Ralthorn cleared her throat.

"I realize I misspoke and just barely caught myself, boys. I also know it's nothing you haven't heard before, so *please*. Drop it."

The rest of the class had a good laugh, and Ralthorn let herself smile a little before returning to the semester's overview.

For the first time since coming to the Academy, Amanda sat up straight at her desk and paid rapt attention to everything Ms. Ralthorn said.

Finally. We're getting some actual knowledge about what we'll be doing when we graduate. I'm not gonna miss any of it.

CHAPTER ELEVEN

Advanced Alchemy with Mrs. Zimmer was next. The second the blaring alarm bell rang to signal the end of their first-period class, Grace was out of her seat and flying down the hall before the other classrooms had even emptied.

"Whoa." Jackson stared as the rest of the juniors stepped into the hall, and Grace disappeared around the corner toward the end of the east wing. "She wasn't kidding about being excited for this one."

Summer snorted. "They could call a class Advanced BS, and she'd still be all over it."

"Do you guys know what we're supposed to be doing this year in Alchemy?" Amanda asked as she and her friends navigated the quickly flooding hallways.

"Why would we know that?" Alex gestured down the hall where Grace had disappeared. "Our student encyclopedia ran away."

The boys laughed, and Summer wrinkled her nose. "We'll still be reminded over and over of what we're *supposed* to be doing for that class. So it's not like we need to know ahead of time. Kinda useful, actually."

Alex and Jackson stopped laughing and stared at her. "Was that an actual compliment?"

Summer shrugged. "Maybe. Don't go telling Blondie that, though. She'll think I'm making fun of her."

"And...you're not?" Jackson leaned away from her, looking her up and down like she'd just sprouted wings. "Like, for real?"

The witch clicked her tongue and picked up the pace to get ahead of them.

He scratched his head and frowned after her. "Weird."

"Better watch out," Alex muttered. "The next thing you know, Summer and Grace are gonna be best friends."

Jackson groaned.

"Why's that such a bad thing?" Amanda laughed.

"Seriously, Coulier?"

"Yeah. I mean, they've tolerated each other for two years. They might as well be friends now."

"See, but you're not playing this out to the end." He pointed at her. "If those two go all BFF, we're screwed."

"That makes no sense."

"Sure it does," Alex muttered, also frowning down the hallway despite both Grace and Summer having disappeared around the corner. "It means they won't keep fighting each other."

"That's a good thing."

"You'd like to *think* that, wouldn't you?" Jackson spread his arms. "That's not how it works. They'll need somebody else to fill the spot."

"The spot?"

"Yeah. Of who they're gonna pick on. Who do you think they're gonna start looking at when they finish trying to pick each other apart?"

"Nobody." Amanda shook her head. "I have no idea where you're going with this."

"Us, Amanda." Alex tapped his chest, then punched Jackson in the shoulder. "That's who's gonna fill that spot if they end up actually liking each other and doing girl things. Us."

"Yeah, then it's even *worse* because it'll be double-powered."

She barked out a laugh and readjusted the straps of her backpack. "Where do you guys come up with this stuff?"

Alex shrugged. "It's the truth."

"Yep. That's how girls are. The only thing that makes sense about it is that it doesn't."

"Doesn't what?"

"Make sense."

"Okay. Whatever. If Summer and Grace finally end up being friends, like real friends, it can only make things easier and more fun for all of us. So whatever you're afraid of—"

"We *told* you what we're afraid of, Coulier." Jackson swung an arm over her shoulders as they slowed in front of Mrs. Zimmer's classroom. "If you don't do anything to stop it, you might as well be in on the whole thing with them."

Amanda snorted and shrugged out from under his arm. "Nice try."

"Hey, look." Alex pointed at a piece of paper taped to the closed door. "We get a different room this year."

She read the quick note scrawled in Zimmer's neat handwriting.

Juniors and Seniors, Advanced Alchemy One and Two are in the east wing in Room 134A. Now you have no excuse to be late.

"Aw, man." Jackson clicked his tongue. "I wanted to pretend to get lost."

"Go for it, dude." Alex clapped a hand on his shoulder and gave the wizard a little shake. "It's not gonna work."

"Yeah, well, we're not all super-excited about Alchemy. Or in love with Zimmer."

"Shut up." Alex took off down the hall.

"Hey, some of us can't even *do* Alchemy. I almost blew my face off last semester."

Amanda bumped her shoulder against Jackson's and nodded down the hall. "You can partner with me if you want. I can't exactly pull my magic out of thin air for Alchemy. You know, the whole secret-shifter-magic thing. I know how it works, though."

"Wait, you..." Jackson swallowed thickly, then hurried to catch up with her. "You wanna partner with me? Like, during class?"

"Uh...yeah." She shot him a confused smile. "If you want some extra help. That's all."

"I mean, sure, but... I didn't... That's not..." A deep red flush bloomed up the sides of his neck and to the tips of his ears.

Amanda quickly looked away.

What's his deal?

"Only for Alchemy, Jackson. It's not like you have to sit next to me for everything."

"Yeah, no. I mean, I would, but—I mean, I want to. Or not that I *want* to, but I don't *not* want to because why would that even be a problem?" A nervous laugh escaped him, and he shrank into his hunched shoulders before turning slowly toward her with a grimace. "Forget everything I just said, okay?"

Amanda pressed her lips together and nodded. "I didn't hear a thing."

"Great."

They were the last to step into Zimmer's advanced class for the upperclassmen. Fortunately, they weren't late enough to warrant getting called out by the Light Elf teacher.

"How nice of you to join us. Please take your seats. You all have had enough training at this point that I'm not messing around with detailed how-tos anymore. Not this year."

Zimmer tossed her long brown braid over her shoulder, walked behind her desk, and stopped to face her students again. "This semester specifically, you'll be learning about which types of magic are the most useful to alchemize for a variety of different scenarios. Then you'll collect and transmute those various types of magic into something useful."

"Like what?" Brandon touched his ice-encrusted hair.

Zimmer smirked. "Yes, like Crystal magic, Mr. Everly. Magic from anyone else sitting here in this classroom, but also from plants, Oriceran minerals, and occasionally magical creatures. Don't worry. None of you will have to hunt for these things. Now, you may wonder *why* you need a specific type of magic to combat whatever you might find yourself against, and the answer is quite simple. Certain forms of magic will cancel out others. For instance, Miss Flannerty gave us an excellent example of that Friday night."

Summer sat up straight in her chair and glanced up at the teacher. "I did what?"

"Oh, good. You *were* paying attention." Zimmer rested her hands on the desk and drummed her fingers. "Miss Flannerty gave us an excellent demonstration of a completed and fully sealed invisibility illusion. Ms. Calsgrave had the opposing-magic antidote for that—"

Grace shot her hand into the air but didn't bother waiting for the teacher to call on her. "Ms. Calsgrave used an actual spell for that, though. Not alchemy."

"True. But just like not everyone can cast the illusion Miss Flannerty seems to have mastered, not everyone can cast magic like Ms. Calsgrave's to reveal it. That's where alchemy comes in handy, especially for anyone with a job that requires quick thinking and not necessarily enough time to go through one's entire repertoire of spells to find a solution."

"Like a bounty hunter job?" Tommy asked.

"Yes, Mr. Brunsen. That *is* why you're all here. So it's incredibly helpful to know how to combat an adversary's magic with anything and everything necessary. If you can't cast the spells yourself, you can always alchemize a different type of magic to the same effect."

"Oh, yeah." Amanda perked up in her seat at the long black table and nodded. "Yeah, I get it. I watched… Well, I saw somebody fight off a Logree's insanely flammable ink, I guess you'd call it, with alchemized Crystal magic loaded into the tip of a crossbow bolt."

The entire class fell silent again although some of the students snickered this time or coughed to cover up their laughter.

She ignored all of them and shrugged, shooting Zimmer a crooked smile. "You know, because shooting explosives at it only made things worse."

The Light Elf teacher pressed a hand against her lips in amusement and nodded. "Yes, that's exactly what I'm talking about, Miss Coulier. Alchemizing opposing magic to combat a particular magical problem. I have to say I'm impressed."

"Yeah, sorry."

Summer cracked up laughing, even though Amanda had immediately realized the Alchemy teacher wasn't coming down on her for getting something wrong.

"Wait…" She leaned forward and frowned at Zimmer. "You're impressed?"

"Absolutely. Looks like everything you learned last year is starting to pay off now that you can put the pieces together on your own. Well done." Zimmer pursed her lips to try hiding a smile, but the effect made her look like she was trying so hard not to scratch an insane itch right under her nose. "Although I can't say I have any idea what a Logree is or why you were shooting flammable creatures with alchemized crossbow bolts—"

"No, *I* didn't do it." Amanda couldn't help a small laugh. "I was only there to watch. And it's an Oriceran squid. I think."

"A squid." Evan folded his arms and snorted. "That doesn't even make sense."

"Well, I saw it, okay?" Amanda turned in her seat and shot him a warning look. "And they *talk*."

The kid wrinkled his nose and leaned away from her.

"Okay, story time's over." Zimmer clapped to regain everyone's attention. "So today, I'll pass out lists of the six major types of existing magic. As far as we know. The four elemental types, obviously, plus destruction and healing magics. *Your* job is to take a look at the different subsets within each major type and try to figure out which other form of magic they might cancel out if you alchemized one or the other to use at your discretion. No, Mr. Hutchinson, you can't say all Water magic cancels out all Fire magic and leave it at that. It's not that simple."

The teacher grabbed a large stack of papers and tossed them into the air over her desk. With a flick of her hand, the pages evened out and floated down toward the rows of tables in front of every student.

"Wait..." Evan stared at the paper fluttering toward him before he snatched it from the air. "You mean you could've magically handed us whatever we needed for two whole years, and you're only starting to do it now?"

"Perks of being an upperclassman, Mr. Hutchinson." Zimmer pointed at him. "I want you spending more time *in* your seats than out of them. So get to work."

Amanda pulled a pen from her backpack and glanced up at Zimmer as the Light Elf took her seat behind the desk. For a brief moment, their gazes met, and Zimmer's mouth twitched into one of her not-quite smiles as she gave Amanda a curt nod. The interaction went unnoticed by everyone else—Zimmer pretty much constantly looked like she was satisfied with giving her students a stern lecture and exact directions anyway—but Amanda couldn't help a small smile of her own.

Yeah. She's impressed. Because finally, everything I learned from Johnny actually comes in useful this year.

106

CHAPTER TWELVE

After lunch, Amanda headed out to the greenhouse while the rest of the juniors went to Calsgrave's classroom for Advanced Illusions.

I couldn't even handle regular Illusions. Really glad I have this place instead.

She went to the worktable at the end of the center trough first, where she finally unfolded the list Glasket had given her and looked it over. DarkSkull and Angler's Root were direct orders from whoever the principal was in contact with inside the Coalition of Shifters. When Amanda took out the *Magical's Guide to Magical Greenery* to look them up, she found only the new plants' magical properties but no descriptions or instructions for how to grow them successfully.

Yeah, that's because I have two more plants in the dangerous and deadly category.

With a snort, Amanda closed the hard-backed *Magical's Guide to Magical Greenery* with a loud *clap* and went to retrieve her warded gloves and enhanced magical-gardening shears from the metal cabinet. Glasket's list had also come with an estimated amount of how much of each currently blooming plant she was supposed to harvest and drop off with the Coalition the next time she met them.

Wrinkling her nose, she grabbed an empty five-gallon bucket and started with the Underweaver plants.

Might as well get the most dangerous stuff out of the way first. Plus, I'm gonna have to make a lot more room in here if I'm supposed to grow everything for everyone. Maybe I can convince Glasket to get a few extra troughs built. Or a bigger greenhouse.

The Underweaver leaves shimmered as she approached, but fortunately, the subduing effects of the Anchorbloom plant growing right beside it canceled out the flesh-eating side effects of growing Underweaver in the first place. Even with her warded gloves that had already proven protective enough against the deadly plants, Amanda worked slowly to trim away the mature leaves and flowers before tossing them into the bucket. Half the time she held her breath, and she only got close enough to be able to reach the harvested stalks with both arms stretched as far as they would go in front of her.

That took her most of the class period, and she already knew she didn't need to check on the Fatethistle plants in her secret cellar. Still, when her mind turned to what she'd kept under the greenhouse since last semester, Amanda also ended up thinking about Summer's buzzing black box she'd hidden in there too until her mom's stolen amulet had finally escaped.

Grimacing, Amanda headed toward the next trough of plants to be harvested for the Coalition and started to feel bad.

It's not my fault she stole that thing, and it's not my fault it broke out of the box and buzzed back to her parents.

Bits of Shiverbloom came off in her gloved hands as she snipped them away before tossing them into a different bucket.

Maybe that's what happened to her over the summer. The amulet got home before she did, and her mom let her have it. Not exactly a reason for her parents to get divorced, but still.

The Shiverbloom in her hands shuddered when she brought

the shears too close to a blooming flower that wasn't quite ready to be cut. Amanda quickly stepped away, swallowed, and sighed.

I should've let her keep that box in the cellar. Then again, she should've told me what it was in the first place. Not that hard.

The next time she reached for another immature blossom, the plant shook violently. A soft *hiss* rose through the rustling of leaves, and Amanda instantly pulled her hands away.

"Focus, Amanda. And...sorry, plant."

The last thing I need is another greenhouse mishap because I'm feeling guilty about something that has nothing to do with me.

Over that week, the rest of their curriculum for each class over this year's first semester made itself clear. History and Alchemy were pretty straightforward. LeFor's Applied Tech first thing for juniors on alternating days was a little more convoluted.

"Now you know the basic mechanics of using the technology around you to make something work the way you want," the redhead teacher said. He shoved his glasses back up the bridge of his nose and squinted at the high square table where Tommy and Evan sat with two of their friends. "That doesn't necessarily mean anything you've created over the last two years deserved a patent or even a standing ovation, but at least you passed my classes. This year, you'll finally get to work on combining tech with magic. Which is honestly my favorite part."

"So you want us to make more floating mics?" Tony asked.

"No, Mr. Malone. I've improved those devices about as much as possible. I mean that everything you do in this class will go hand-in-hand with what you explore and create in Advanced Alchemy. Transforming someone else's magic—or some*thing* else's magic—into a workable reagent is one thing. Knowing how to use it and apply it to a working device is something completely different."

"Wait, wait. Hold on." Jackson slammed both hands down on his table. "Are you saying we're making *weapons*?"

"Mr. Pris, I don't ever want to hear that question again." LeFor sniffed and looked around the room. "Or anyone else here, got it? We do *not* build weapons. No. You're…creating a practical application for impractically alchemized magic. That's it."

Summer leaned toward Amanda at their table and muttered, "Sounds like someone thinks they're better than Mrs. Learn That Reagent."

Amanda tried not to laugh and returned her attention to LeFor's unnecessarily long explanation of *why* the Academy of Necessary Magic did not condone its students building weapons of any kind.

This is exactly what Johnny does with his stuff. Only he's way better at it and actually builds weapons. LeFor only makes fancy Louper gear.

"I'll tell you right now, so nobody has a hissy fit when the time comes, that your work with designing and building your magitech will only be the focus for the second half of every class while you're here. During the first half, you juniors get to look over and grade the poor excuses for what hurts me even to *call* technology made by this year's sophomores."

Half the glass groaned, and the other half looked completely clueless.

"Mr. LeFor?" Grace raised her hand.

"Miss Porter?"

"Are you telling us that we're going to be your teacher's assistants for the first half of class?"

"Yes. However, it's not for extra credit, and it won't get you a better grade in my class. You have to do it because I said so. That part starts next week. Until then, I want you guys to go through your textbook and figure out what you want to start working on first this semester. Groups of four this time, I think. That's plenty of extra brainpower that should make it easy enough to create something useful."

"But...Mr. LeFor?"

The red-haired wizard stared at Blake and raised his eyebrows. "This is me calling on you, Miss Lively. I'm looking right at you."

"Right. Sorry. Um...we only have one partner in Zimmer's class, and we're all working with different alchemy stuff. How are we supposed to fit that together into the *same* project here? You know, like if mixing the two has a bad reaction or something?"

LeFor chewed on the inside of his bottom lip and narrowed his eyes. "We haven't gotten that far yet. I'll make sure Mrs. Zimmer and I sit together and decide who absolutely should *not* work together in here with a bad combination of alchemy reagents."

"Aw, man..." Summer puffed out a sigh and propped her chin up in her hand. "This was finally gonna be a fun class, but nope."

The teacher gave her a warning glance and pointed at her as he walked across the workshop toward his desk. "I'm gonna pretend I didn't hear you say that, Miss Flannerty. If any of you don't already have a textbook, get one now from the shelf. I want books open, mouths shut, and eyes on the pages. By the end of the week, you should all have a good idea of what you want to build and combine it with whatever you...make in Alchemy. Get to it."

Amanda pulled her textbook out of her backpack and looked up across the room where Jackson sat with three other juniors at a separate table. "Hey, Grace."

"Yeah." The blonde witch thumped her textbook down onto the table and immediately opened it to scan the table of contents.

"What LeFor said... That means whoever we partnered with in Alchemy is gonna end up being our partner in this class too, right?"

"Yep. Why, is that a problem?"

Amanda quickly looked away from Jackson, mostly because

she didn't want Grace to see and also a little because he'd looked up at her at the same time. "I guess not."

I told him it was only for one class. How was I supposed to know this was gonna happen?

"Wait a minute." Grace looked across the room, then slapped her hand down on the open textbook and leaned toward Amanda to whisper fiercely. "You and Jackson, right?"

"Yeah. It's not a big deal."

Summer grinned at her and wiggled her eyebrows. "Looks like you got yourself suckered into that one, shifter girl."

"Shut up. I'm the one who offered."

"Exactly."

Finally, the juniors got to head out to the training building for Combat Training with Mr. Petrov, and no one had a clue what to expect. A lot of crestfallen faces and apprehensive grimaces met the teacher when the junior class entered the building, took off their shoes, and stepped onto the mats. Because Petrov stood there with his arms folded and feet set squarely apart, looking pleased with himself. Again.

"Just kill me now," Jackson muttered. "If we have to go through last semester all over again, I'm out."

"Right, dude." Alex shook his head. "Like you can say, 'Peace,' and leave class."

"I can leave the school, though."

"This is it, juniors," Petrov barked. "The year you finally get to try your hand at being something better than…what I've seen over the last two years. Mostly. So here's the thing. You'll only have an actual Combat training class once a month. This first one doesn't count because this is the 'rules and regulations' class."

Blake wrinkled her nose and stepped toward Amanda. "What's he talking about?"

"I have no idea."

"This is good stuff, kid. I promise." Petrov snapped his fingers, and a giant poster unraveled mid-air beside him. He pointed at the line at the top in bold red letters and nodded. "You get to play Bag the Bounty."

"Please, no more illusions," Jasmine whispered with wide eyes as she shook her head.

"It's a game. Obviously." Petrov scanned his students' clueless faces. "Four teams. That's how we'll split the class. Every month, your team as a whole only has one goal. Find and apprehend the target I give you at the beginning of each class. You have four weeks to get that done. If you succeed, you get points. If you fail, you don't get any points at all." He pointed at each bullet on the floating poster. "If anyone sees you apprehend said target, whose identity will only be known by me until you and your teammates can figure it out on your own, you lose points. Yes, I'm sure at least one team here will end the semester with negative points."

Blake slowly raised her hand.

"Lively."

"Um...who are the targets?"

The grin flashing across the teacher's face made the closest students around him take a step or two back. "Your classmates."

Summer barked out a laugh. "Wait, so you want us to team up against someone in here, and...what? Beat them up?"

"I said apprehend, Flannerty. If a beating happens to be a part of it, Nurse Aiken is already aware of the small likelihood of that happening."

"What if we find the target in the middle of class or whatever?" Evan asked. "Do we get to, like, jump them or something?"

Petrov's eye twitched. "Would you shoot your bounty in the middle of a crowded shopping mall in broad daylight? No. You'd figure out where they go, what their patterns are, and you'd find the best place to snag them. In secret. If I hear from any teachers or other students that they *saw* you acting out this game, you get negative points. Yes, even if you nail your target and retrieve the artifact."

"Does Dean Glasket know about this?" Grace asked.

Petrov snorted. "I'm not staging a coup, Porter. Of course, she knows."

"She's *okay* with it?"

"Listen, if it's ever your turn to be the target, I'll give you all the information you need about that if and when it happens. Until then, you don't get to know the whole plan, or what would be the point?"

"Um…not getting beaten up," Blake added.

"Come on, Lively. You won the medal last semester. There are only two—well, maybe one other student who could take you one-on-one. I know what you're really capable of underneath all that wide-eyed innocence. So. Bag the Bounty. You check in here with me the first week of every month to get your new assignment. I'm not giving out names. Only a description of an item each of the four targets will get before you get your assignments. Only your teammates will know if you're another team's target and vice-versa. So, four lucky kids each month get to play double-agent. Should be fun."

"What do we do if we catch the bad guy?" Brandon asked.

"Catch the—" Petrov sighed and pinched the bridge of his nose. "Sure. Look at it that way. If you catch the target, you snatch the artifact. Any team who comes back for the check-in with the artifact I sent them after gets their points. Only if no one sees them. And I do mean even by teachers, including me."

The class stood where they were, some of them staring at Petrov in anticipation of his next crazy idea while the others exchanged uncertain looks with each other.

"Oh, come on. This is good stuff. You know your basics with hand-to-hand combat, defensive and offensive, and you guys went nuts with the magical combat last year. This is a team-building exercise."

"You're pitting us against our classmates."

"No, I'm pitting teams against each other. When you're out there in the field, your chances of getting anything done are slim to none when you're alone. Work with a partner or even a whole team, and you can wrap your head around any obstacle thrown your way. Everybody has different skills. Time to use them." He pointed at the very last bullet item on the poster and cleared his throat. "Okay, so *two* objectives. Work to find and apprehend your target before retrieving the assigned artifact, and do whatever you can to keep the other team from finding *their* target. Who happens to be one of your teammates. Any questions?"

"What about the rules?" Tommy asked.

"They're right here, Brunson. I'm pointing at them."

"Yeah, but like...what's off-limits? You know, like how we find whoever we're looking for. Or how we take their artifact...thing."

Petrov's eyelids fluttered as he inhaled deeply through his nose. "No rules. Okay? You don't get disqualified, you don't get kicked out, and you don't have any rules to break. We're going off a point system here. Motivation."

"So what if we don't wanna find the target?"

"Well, that's up to you. In which case, I'd say you have a pretty crappy chance of getting any kind of good job after graduating. At least the kind this school was specifically set up to prepare you for, so I guess you'd be out of luck after wasting four years of your life." The bald teacher cleared his throat. "Also...the top-scoring team each semester passes my class this year with flying colors and won't have to take their finals."

A startling cheer rose through the junior class, making Petrov scowl.

"Should've led with *that*, Sarge," Summer called.

He pointed at her. "Don't call me that again, or I'll make sure your team doesn't get any points at all. I'm the one who makes nicknames around here, Flannerty."

Jackson snorted. "You sure about that?"

"That's enough useless talk. Time to break up the teams and—"

The students automatically started divvying themselves up into teams with their friends, but when Petrov snapped his fingers and sent a cracking *boom* through the training building, everyone stopped.

"No. *I'm* picking the teams. *You* get to learn how to work with what you have. Team One! Come gather by me."

He called names one by one, and the class of twenty-five juniors was broken up into four groups as evenly as possible. Amanda found herself on Team Three with Grace, Tommy Brunsen, Margaret Allgood, Corey Baker, and Katie Thompson.

Grace leaned toward her and muttered, "This'll be so easy. Just watch."

"What do you mean?"

The blonde witch grinned. "We have *you*."

Amanda rolled her eyes. "That doesn't mean I'm gonna do all the work myself."

"No, of course not. Totally." Grace shrugged and glanced sidelong at her friend. "I'd never let you take *all* the credit."

With the teams spread out across the mats, Petrov went to each of them in order and handed over a piece of paper for each group to read and look over so the others wouldn't overhear. When he got to Amanda's team, Grace seemed like the natural leader to hand over their assignment to. All six of them crowded around the blonde witch to read the paper over her shoulders:

Artifact: a silver keychain in the shape of a rose. Starting tomorrow, your first task is to find the other player with this artifact, then retrieve it before the next class meeting next month.

Your second task is to protect your team's artifact-keeper from Team One, should they discover he has said artifact.

Team Three's artifact-keeper this round is Corey Baker.

After eyeing each of Amanda's teammates in turn, Petrov muttered, "Any questions?"

"Yeah." Corey tried to raise his hand, but Grace grabbed the half-Kilomea's hairy forearm and shoved it back down. "Yeah," he whispered. "I don't have—"

"The *artifact-keeper*," Petrov said in a warning growl, "will find their assigned artifact for this round in their dorm room before Lights Out tonight. Didn't you hear me saying that to the other teams?"

"Um…I guess so."

"Keep your voice down, Baker. Or your team's gonna have a hard enough time carrying the weight for you." Petrov snatched the paper out of Grace's hand, and as he'd done with the other teams' assignment sheets, he ignited it in a ball of blue flames and let the charred pieces scatter down toward the mat before they disappeared completely. "Get to work."

Then he left them to follow the same procedure with Team Four, leaving the other groups alone to come up with their plan.

"How are we supposed to find who has the keychain?" Katie whispered.

"We look for it, obviously," Grace replied.

Tommy snorted. "Oh. Sure. Sneak into every other kid's room after Lights Out and go through their stuff."

Corey scratched his shaggy head. "Not mine."

"Duh, not yours." Tommy thumped the half-Kilomea in the arm. "You're on *our* team."

"There has to be a way for us to find these things," Grace added, folding her arms and frowning at the mat beneath them. "I bet the artifacts are enchanted. You know, give out some kind of signal during the day so that whoever's looking for it will find it. Right?"

"I mean, that's the only way we'd ever be able to find it, right?" Margaret shrugged. "Guess we'll have to wait until tomorrow to find out."

"Yeah, but we need a plan." Grace chopped one hand down

into her opposite palm. "Okay, here's what we'll do. Team meeting tomorrow after Alchemy and before lunch—"

"Whoa, whoa. Hey." Tommy snickered. "Who made *you* team captain?"

She shot him a deadpan stare. "Well, if you have any ideas for a plan, Tommy, now's the time to spit it out."

He looked at everyone else around their small group and shoved his hands in his pockets. "Yeah, I got nothing."

"Great. And I'm not *trying* to be team captain. Not like we even need one in the first place." Grace tucked her blonde bob behind one ear and nodded. "But here's what we'll do. Our arti-fact-keeper will bring the artifact they have with them to this meeting. Let's say behind the girls' dorm."

Tommy snickered and bobbed his head from side to side. "Hey, why not the *boys'* dorm—"

"Does it really matter?" Grace hissed.

"No. Jeeze."

She glared at him a moment longer, then glanced at everyone else on the team one by one. "So the artifact-keeper brings the one they have. We'll study *that*. If it has any enchantments, maybe we can deconstruct those enough to figure out how to find *our* artifact. Then the hunt's on. Got it?"

"Uh…I got a question," Corey muttered and slowly raised his hand.

Grace playfully rolled her eyes. "I'm not a teacher, Corey. Just ask."

Tommy punched the other boy in the arm, but the half-Kilomea didn't notice.

"Yeah, how do we know who's bringing the artifact to the meeting?"

Everyone stared at him. Then Katie and Margaret exchanged amused glances and snorted out laughter before quickly covering it up.

"Dude." Tommy shook his head. "No wonder you're the oldest kid in the class by like three years."

"Thanks."

Amanda patted Corey's shoulder and nodded. "If you find anything in your room that you've never seen before, bring that with you tomorrow, okay?"

"Sure." Corey sniffed and looked more confused than normal. "I guess."

"Okay…" Grace stared at the giant kid and puffed out a sigh. "So that's our plan. Tomorrow after Alchemy. Don't forget."

"Aye-aye, Captain!" Tommy gave her a goofy salute, and she slapped his hand away.

"Don't."

"Sir, yes, sir."

"Oh my God."

Pressing her lips together to hold back a laugh, Amanda nodded at Grace, and her friend gave her a wide-eyed, exasperated stare.

"All right!" Petrov boomed. "Everybody has their assignments, and every team knows who their keeper is for round one. Just so you don't forget in your excitement for honor, glory, and no final exam at the end of the year, I'm gonna tell you this one more time. *No one* can see you apprehending your target to retrieve the artifact they're carrying on them. And the artifact-keeper *has* to carry it on them *at all times*. I don't care what you have to do to remember. Put it by your toothbrush, lay it out with your underwear the night before, keep it in your pocket and wear the same pants for a month. Whatever it takes."

"Hey, yeah. Great idea!" Evan shouted from Team Two's corner before giving Tommy an air-high-five across the room.

"Ew…" Anabelle stepped away from Evan and looked him up and down. "The boys' dorm *has* a washer and dryer, right?"

Evan shrugged.

"I can't believe I heard all that," Petrov muttered as he pinched the bridge of his nose again. When he looked up and found the entire junior class staring at him, he pointed at the door and barked, "Get out. I don't want to see you in here again until our next meeting on the third week of September. Go."

The training room exploded with conversation as all four teams streamed toward their neat line of socks and shoes by the door before heading out onto the training field.

Amanda shoved her feet into her sneakers and caught up with Grace as they headed outside into the muggy late-morning heat. "Hey. That was awesome."

"What? I didn't do anything."

"No, you were yourself, and it was awesome."

Grace rolled her eyes. "Don't start calling me team captain too, okay?"

"Cross my heart." Amanda drew an X on her chest, and both girls laughed. "I'm serious, though. I never would've thought to look at *our* artifact so we could figure out how to find the one we're supposed to grab. How'd you come up with that?"

"It seemed like the best place to start. Pretty obvious, don't you think?"

"Only after you said it out loud." The girls grabbed their school bags from the grass along the training building's exterior wall and headed with the rest of the juniors toward the outdoor cafeteria for lunch. "We're totally gonna win."

"I don't know about *that*…" Grace eyed the students from the other teams in suspicion. "We don't know which team has the keychain."

"Yeah, but it'll be a piece of cake." Elbowing her friend in the side, Amanda grinned. "We have *you*."

The blonde witch snorted. "Yeah, okay. I'll take the credit."

CHAPTER THIRTEEN

The first week of classes blew by, and it seemed every conversation Amanda had with her friends was about how much more advanced and complicated their courses were this semester compared to the last two years.

"I mean, we *are* halfway through our school years," Jackson said as he crammed fried chicken into his mouth at dinner on Friday. "It's supposed to get harder, right?"

"I said *more complicated*," Grace corrected. "Not necessarily harder." She looked across the table at Summer, who slowly picked at her food with her fork and tossed flecks of breading across her plate. "What do you think, Summer? Are things harder this year?"

The other witch looked sharply up at Grace and scowled, her eyes red-rimmed but dry and her cheeks a little blotchy. "What's that supposed to mean, huh?"

"I don't know. I guess I'm asking how you're doing. Hey, if there's anything you need help with—"

After slapping her fork down onto her plate, Summer grabbed her backpack off the bench and stood. "Not from you."

"Whoa, hey. Wait. I just—"

"Yeah, I bet."

Everyone around the table stared after Summer as she stalked off toward the girls' dorm, and Grace's shoulders slumped. "Seriously? I was nice that time."

Amanda wrinkled her nose. "When I said to ask her how she's doing, I meant, like...you know. In private."

"Private?" The witch shook her head. "When am I ever gonna be alone with her in private?"

"That's the point."

"What?"

"Like, making an effort," Amanda said softly. "In case you couldn't tell, I'm pretty sure Summer doesn't want to talk about any of her problems out in the open where a bunch of people can hear."

"But she's totally fine talking about everyone *else's* problems in public."

"Grace..."

"Okay, okay. Fine. I know. I'm trying."

Amanda shoveled coleslaw into her mouth and nodded. "I know."

I'll talk to Summer later.

"Okay, everybody, listen up," LeFor called from the end of the nearly empty banquet table. "A little announcement for this year's Louper team. After Keith Pelson graduated last year, we have one slot open. If anyone wants to try out for the team, we're holding those tomorrow morning at six. There's a lot to cover before our first match in two weeks, so only do this if you're serious about it." He scanned the faces staring at him from the picnic tables and snorted. "If you're only stepping up to the plate because your parents promised a nice vacation as long as you tried out for a sports team, don't bother wasting all our time. I'll write you a note and say you did it."

A group of sophomores two tables down from Amanda's exploded in laughter. She found the short dwarf boy with glasses who'd tried out with her last year, and he made a face at all of them before pulling out his inhaler for a quick puff as his friends slapped him on the back.

"So that's it." LeFor's gaze settled on Amanda for a moment. "Tomorrow morning at six. Don't be late."

Then he grabbed a dinner roll off the banquet table and took it with him away from the cafeteria.

"Is it just me, Coulier, or did that look like he was talking right at you?"

Amanda shook her head. "Doesn't matter."

"Why not?" Grace asked. "I thought you liked to play."

"Not to mention that epic win you took last year," Jackson added as he punched Alex in the shoulder. "Right, dude?"

"Yeah. Epic." With the wizard distracted by his excitement, Alex looked up at Amanda and slid his hand toward Jackson's plate to take one of the four cookies stacked there.

She forced back a laugh and looked over her shoulder at LeFor disappearing across the central field. "I do like the game. I mean, it's fun. But until they change the gameplay so I can be a shifter in the game who uses *magic* in the game, there's no point."

Grace's eyes widened. "You can use it now? Your magic, I mean."

"Yeah." Amanda grinned. "I can. Or at least a lot more than I could last year, and it's awesome. Thing is, I don't think Louper's ready for a shifter girl sending out a ghost-wolf to take down opponents and actually have it *do* something, you know?"

"They will be if you show them you can do it," Alex muttered around the last mouthful of Jackson's cookie.

"Yeah, but I'm not..." She lowered her voice and leaned forward across the table. "I'm not technically supposed to tell anyone that I can do this. I mean, I haven't gotten the okay to move from practicing magic in private to using it for everyone to watch on live...Louper-view or whatever."

"Ha!" Jackson pointed at her. "Louper-view. That's a good one. You should trademark it or something."

"Trademark?" Grace raised an eyebrow at him.

"Yeah. So no one else can use it. Then you should totally play, Coulier."

"I don't think so. I mean, even if I did wanna keep pretending to be the only player on the team with no real magic, I don't think I could. I definitely can't make it to tryouts tomorrow. Fiona's coming by to get me, and she'll probably be here to get me Sunday too."

"Oh, that's *right*." Grace's face lit up with a wide grin. "Your meetings with the Coalition."

"Yeah, and maybe keep it down about that too, okay?" Amanda looked around the cafeteria, but of course, nobody was paying attention to their conversation. "Yeah. The whole intern thing."

"Hey." Alex shrugged and snuck his hand toward Jackson's plate again. "Hunting mutated monster creatures is way more exciting than Louper anyway."

"No, it's not—dude!" Jackson shoved the Wood Elf's hand away from his plate. "Get your own cookies. If I wanted any less than four, I would've…" He slowly counted the three remaining cookies and slid his plate away from Alex. "Unbelievable."

"You should pay attention."

"You should get your own food."

Alex snickered. "I did."

Amanda propped her chin on her fist and stared right at Grace. "So. Any progress on figuring out how to deconstruct the you-know-what?"

"The what?" Jackson asked as he tried cramming two whole cookies into his mouth at once.

Grace grimaced at him, then shook her head. "Yeah, actually. I mean, I only had two and a half hours to look at it today before you-know-who said he had to go try on his pants from last year."

Amanda barked out a laugh. "Seriously?"

"Yeah, I honestly don't know if he's gonna graduate."

"Wait, who are you talking about?" Jackson looked back and forth between them. "What pants? What thing?"

"It's a secret," Grace said.

Alex stood, shaking his head. "Chicks, man."

"I don't get it."

"Eat your cookies, Jackson." Grace shot him an overly sweet smile as she batted her eyelashes and stood from the table to collect her trash. "It has nothing to do with you."

"Then why are you talking about it in front of us? Hey, wait. Grace. Grace!"

She laughed as she headed toward the trashcan, then the wizard leaned over the table toward Amanda and spread his arms. "You gonna fill me in, Coulier?"

"Nope." She stood to grab her plate and the trash Summer had left behind.

"Well, why not?"

"'Cause we're gonna win." She wiggled her eyebrows at him and turned away, stifling a laugh when she heard him groan in frustration.

If anyone can figure out how to track down this artifact-keychain for Combat Training, it's Grace. Maybe she'll end up doing that *after graduation. For real cases.*

That night after Lights Out, Amanda glanced at the alarm clock on her bedside table and sighed.

Almost eleven. Everyone else has to be asleep. I'm not leaving Summer in there by herself another night. She needs to get out.

After quickly slipping into her shoes, she slowly opened her door and peered up and down the hall. The girls' dorm was unusually quiet, but it was late, and the Academy of Necessary

Magic had two whole years to work out the kinks in its curriculum. Most of the students were too tired even on a Friday night to throw teenage parties the first weekend of the semester.

Amanda moved silently down to Room 233C across the hall. She reached out to knock on the door but paused when she heard a sniffle and airy, muffled crying on the other side. She waited a few more seconds, then lightly knocked on the door. "Summer?"

A quick sniff, the rustle of movement, and a squeak of the mattress inside was the only reply.

"Hey, I know you're in there."

"So?" The witch's voice was thick and scratchy.

If this were anyone else, I'd leave them alone. Summer never left me alone though, and this is me returning the favor. She needs this.

"So…" Amanda pressed her mouth against the edge of the door where it met the doorframe. "You're gonna open the door and come with me."

"Nope." Summer sniffed again. "I'm good. Go bother someone else, shifter girl."

"I don't *like* bothering anyone else." She couldn't keep the laughter out of her voice. "You're my favorite."

"Are you *trying* to get your face smashed in?"

"Maybe."

There was another long pause, then the mattress squeaked again, and Summer's footsteps headed toward the door. The doorknob turned, and the witch cracked the door by three inches to glare out at her friend. "I'll do it."

"I know." Amanda squared her stance and folded her arms. "So do it."

"Get lost." The door started to swing shut again, and without thinking it through, Amanda caught it with one hand and forced it roughly back open again. Summer stumbled backward and spread her arms. "What the hell?"

"Sorry." After staring at the door with wide eyes, Amanda

swung it open all the way and lifted her hands in surrender. "I didn't actually mean to barge in and throw you across the room."

"Well, you did!" They stared at each other, then Summer let out a bitter laugh and quickly wiped the tears from her cheeks with the back of a hand. "What do you want?"

"To get you out of there. Just for like an hour."

"Not interested." Summer started to sit on her bed, but Amanda hurried toward her and grabbed the witch's hand to haul her to her feet. "Hey, did you hear me? I said I'm not—"

"Yeah, I don't really care if you want to or not, rainbow witch. This is what you need."

Summer snorted. "Did you just call me rainbow witch?"

"Yeah, it kinda came out." Amanda glanced down at her friend's feet—fortunately, Summer was still wearing her shoes—then tugged her across the room. "This is payback for all the times you forced me to do something I only kinda wanted to do but was too stuck in my head to commit."

"Ha!" Ruffling her multi-colored hair, Summer let Amanda drag her out into the hall. "That sounds like a thank you."

"Well, maybe it is." Amanda shut the door to her friend's room, then grabbed her hand again and tugged her down the hall. "Trust me. After this, you'll thank me too."

"Doubt it."

"Okay, maybe only in your mind. I'm cool with that."

"Whatever. I'm not holding hands with you, though." Summer jerked her hand away, and they both laughed. "What's the deal, shifter girl?"

"The deal is… It's… A surprise."

The witch groaned and rolled her eyes. "Listen, if you're trying to drag me out to some secret spot on campus where we can share a box of tissues and spill all our secrets to each other, tell me now. I'll hit you over the head and run."

"Trust me." Amanda opened the door to the back stairwell and made sure Summer was following her before heading down toward the first floor. "This is about as far away from mushy as it can get."

"Huh. Then I guess I'm a *little* curious."

As juniors, they didn't have to sneak out of the dorms, and the Academy had taken down the security enchantments after their first year. Amanda led her friend out the back door of the girls' dorm anyway, to make it seem like they were up to something.

Two sophomores passed them—a boy and a girl holding hands—and when they saw Amanda and Summer crossing the open space toward the outdoor cafeteria, their eyes widened, and they hurried away toward the back of the main building.

Summer scoffed. "Right. Like we give a shit."

Amanda shook her head. "I think they're less afraid of being caught together at night than being messed with by the shifter girl and the psycho witch."

"Aw... Psycho witch?" Summer plastered an exaggerated frown of heartfelt feeling on her face and placed her hand on her heart. "That's so sweet. Is that what everyone's saying about me?"

"Under their breath? Probably." They both laughed, and Amanda headed straight for the back door of the kitchens. When she stopped, she turned to grin at the witch and wiggled her eyebrows. "Ready?"

"For food? Jesus, shifter girl. We don't *all* have to eat at every hour of the day and night."

"Shut up. We're not here for snacks." Amanda faced the door again and knocked in the rhythm she'd been using for the last two years. "That'll probably be part of it anyway."

"Listen, I'm not trying to make any new friends or anything, okay? I don't need some kinda magical pie to make me all—"

The door opened swiftly, and Fred's massively bushy beard and wide grin greeted them. "There you are, girl! Perfect timing."

Summer stared at him with wide eyes. "Whoa."

"Come on in." Fred chuckled and stepped aside to let the girls enter. "We were just talking about you."

Once he closed the door behind them, he spun toward the raised stainless-steel table in the center of the room. "Carlos! Time to pay up!"

"Nuh-uh." The pixie with neon-orange hair sitting at the table shook his head and folded his arms. "She's not alone, man. It doesn't count."

"It totally counts. We didn't say anything about whether or not she came alone. It's still the first week, and you owe me fifty bucks."

Rolling his eyes, Carlos snapped his fingers, and a fifty-dollar bill materialized in his hand. Fred took a giant step toward the other pixie and snatched away the bill before stuffing it into the breast pocket of his button-down shirt.

Amanda burst out laughing. "Wait, you guys made *bets* on me?"

"Yeah. You." Carlos pointed at her. "Not you plus one."

Summer folded her arms in perfect mimicry of the orange-haired pixie and cocked her head. "Says the grown man with wings."

The kitchen fell silent, then Fred roared with laughter. Sitting in her rocking chair in the far corner, Gloria cackled and rocked even faster.

Carlos narrowed his eyes at Summer, then slowly slipped off the high stool and walked toward her. "You got a mouth on you, huh?"

"I bite too."

"For real?" He looked her up and down.

"Maybe. I guess you'll have to find out."

Carlos stepped closer and squinted as his gaze slowly roamed across Summer's face. He took in her rainbow-dyed hair, then lifted a finger and only halfway pointed it at her. "Okay, smartass."

"You watch that mouth, Carlos," Gloria warned.

He didn't break away from Summer's gaze, even when she snorted at him and shook her head. "I only have one question…"

"Hit me, glitterboy."

Fred barked out a laugh, clapped a meaty hand over his mouth, and looked at Amanda with wide eyes. She shrugged and shook her head, but now it looked like Summer Flannerty was squaring off toe-to-toe with the second-to-least friendly kitchen pixie at the Academy.

This was supposed to help. If she starts fighting the staff, we're both in serious trouble.

Carlos tilted his head comically far to the side and whispered, "What's your opinion of Boston Cream Pie?"

Summer scoffed. "Are you kidding? That crap's for people who can't make up their minds about desserts, so they go with the most disgusting option available."

"Ha!" Carlos stabbed his finger toward Fred. "*You!* Pay up."

"What?" Fred shook his head and chuckled. "Nope. That doesn't count."

"The hell it doesn't. If you win your bet with Amanda showing up right now, I win the Ixnay on the Ostonbay. It's crap."

"You can't be the only one who gets to bend the rules, Fred," Gloria added from her rocking chair.

The massive bearded pixie sighed, jammed his thick fingers into his breast pocket, and removed the wadded fifty again.

"That's right." Carlos pointed at it, and the bill zipped into his hand before disappearing in a cloud of orange smoke. "Now we're even. And hey." He pointed at Summer and stepped away. "I like you, Rainbow."

Fred scrunched up his face, opening and closing his hand to mock the other pixie's words, then grinned down at the girls.

"This is Summer," Amanda said. "Fred, Carlos, Gloria."

"Nice to meet you, honey." Gloria resumed her slow rocking and nodded.

"Uh…yeah." The young witch ruffled her hair. "Wait, so *these* are the kitchen pixies you've been sneaking out to see every night?"

"Ha!" Fred slapped his huge, muscular belly. "I sure hope we're the ones. Otherwise, girl, I might be a little offended. As far as I know, we're the *only* kitchen pixies." He winked at Summer, and she let out a low, uncertain giggle.

"You mean jealous." Carlos stabbed a finger at him. "Not offended."

"I meant what I said, you little sprite."

"Hey. I resent that."

"Can't fight what you are, sugar." Gloria chuckled in her rocking chair. "Trying to be anything else won't help you be more of what you are."

Everyone turned toward the blue-haired pixie woman with silent, confused stares.

She shrugged. "He's half-sprite—"

"Oh, come on, Gloria." Carlos rolled his eyes. "That's personal.

"I'm just saying."

Fred roared with laughter and pointed toward the counter beside the kitchen window. "How about some Boston Cream Pie—"

"No!" Summer and Carlos shouted it together, and the kitchen filled with laughter as Fred's face turned bright red beneath his untamed beard.

"Break out some of the good stuff, hon." Gloria rose from the creaking rocking chair before her shimmering wings fluttered to carry her across the kitchen and onto one of the high stools at the prep table. "I'll join you."

"Fine." Fred narrowed his eyes at the girls, then burst out laughing. "You know I can't say no to that."

He shook his head as he headed for the counter and the three different glass domes set over already baked and ready-to-eat pies.

Summer elbowed Amanda in the side and muttered, "What's the good stuff?"

The shifter girl shrugged. "I have no idea. It's gotta be good, right?"

Carlos hopped up onto his stool and slapped a hand down on the stainless-steel table. "That's the damn definition, isn't it?"

"Carlos." Gloria tossed a spray of multi-colored sparks in his face. The orange-haired pixie sputtered and reeled on the stool before waving away her warning magical slap. "We got kids in here. If you can't watch your mouth, I'll watch it for you."

"She called me glitterboy." He tossed a hand toward Summer. "Don't tell me those girls haven't heard their fair share of language."

"Sure. From *you*." Gloria waved the girls forward. "Come have a seat. We'll make it a party."

An urgent *thump* came from under the floor, and Summer nearly jumped out of her skin before she backed up into the metal shelving unit along the wall. "What the hell was that?"

"The bane of our existence." Carlos rolled his eyes, then shouted at the floor, "You coming up or what?"

"Bite me!" Greg shouted from below.

Carlos and Gloria broke into wild laughter as the girls climbed up onto the empty stools.

Chuckling, Fred returned with five plates of pie stacked in his massive arms. "Here we go. I finished these a few hours ago. No, I *won't* be serving half a pie for breakfast tomorrow. So don't even think about it."

The plates flew from his hands and settled perfectly in front of everyone at the table, followed by a barrage of silver forks flying from the open silverware drawer. Fred snapped his fingers, the drawer shut on its own, then he grunted and hefted himself up onto the empty stool beside Carlos.

Summer grinned as she picked up her fork and stared at the slice in front of her. "Is this—"

"Raspberry turtle cheesecake." Carlos kissed the tips of all five fingers, and a burst of purple light flew from his hand when he tossed it in the air.

"Now *that's* more like it." She barked out a laugh before digging in.

"Hear that, Fred?" Carlos waved his fork at the giant pixie. "This witch knows what she's talking about. Hey, Rainbow. You ever think about working in a kitchen?"

"Nice try, sprite," she said around her mouthful and didn't look away from her cheesecake.

Fred and Gloria cracked up laughing, and the others joined them when Greg pounded on the underside of the floor and let out an incomprehensible string of angry shouts.

CHAPTER FOURTEEN

The kitchen pixies extended the same invitation to Summer that they'd given Amanda first semester freshman year—to come back anytime she wanted, any time of night.

"Don't feel like you have to bring the other one," Carlos shouted through the open door as the girls headed outside into the night.

"Hey." Amanda spun with a laugh.

Fred grabbed the edge of the open door and scowled at the other pixie. "Listen, you winged barbarian. She has a name."

Carlos' fork whizzed through the air over Fred's head and clattered against the far wall.

"Now really, Carlos," Gloria chided. "If you wanted to start a food fight, you should've done that when we still had food."

"We *always* have food. Is that a challenge?"

With a snort, Fred returned his attention to the junior girls stepping carefully away from the kitchen. "You two have a nice night, you hear me? Door's always open. Well, figuratively."

"Bye, Amanda," Gloria called.

"Yeah, don't bring any more friends after this," Carlos added. "I know I'll be disappointed."

Summer laughed and turned away on her own to head across the edge of the training field. "Whatever, glitterboy."

Carlos and Gloria cracked up inside again. Fred smirked at Amanda and leaned down toward her, his shadow spreading far across the sliver of light spilling across the grass. "I'm guessing there's a reason you brought her here tonight, huh?"

Amanda glanced over her shoulder at Summer strolling away with her hands shoved into the pockets of her black hoodie. "Do I need more of a reason than good company and even better cheesecake?"

"Ha! Well, whatever you're up to, girl, don't stop. I meant it. Bring her anytime you want."

"Thanks, Fred. Have a good night."

"Stay out of trouble, Amanda," Carlos shouted before breaking into a high-pitched giggle. "Oh, wait! Never mind. I forgot who I was talking to."

"You hush," Gloria whispered.

Fred nodded one more time and slowly pulled the door all the way shut. Then Amanda hurried after Summer and caught up to her friend in the cool, humid night air to walk across the dew-covered grass.

"So."

"So." Summer smirked and shot her a sidelong glance. "Those are your midnight friends, huh?"

"I guess. You can't say they aren't a little awesome."

"Pixies." The witch shook her head. "Who knew they grew 'em as huge as mountains, huh?"

"With beards." Both girls laughed as they wandered in the swamp's general direction, away from the fields, the buildings, and the main part of campus.

Somewhere in the trees overhanging the water, an owl hooted. Something else splashed into the water. Amanda drew a deep breath of the cool air through her nose and sighed. "I love it here at night."

"Because of the pixies and free snacks? Yeah, I bet."

"No, I mean the Everglades. In the summer."

"It's not summer anymore, shifter girl. We're stuck here for the next four months because, *school*." Summer kicked a clod of dirt and waterlogged grass away from the edge of the river, and both girls watched it scatter and spray into the water like huge raindrops. Giant ripples moved away from them, and a small lizard scuttled off the bank before slipping into the swamp. "Don't think I don't know what you were trying to pull in there."

"With what? Pixies and free snacks?"

"Please." Summer rolled her eyes. Then they stood at the water's edge together in silence for a moment that felt like an hour.

I hope she doesn't turn around and tell me not to try it again.

Amanda bit her bottom lip and stared across the moonlit water shimmering with shadows and the movement of tiny swampy critters. "Did it work?"

The other girl shrugged. "I dunno. Maybe. Except now you got me hooked on pixie cheesecake. Why can't they serve that every day, huh?"

"I think they save it for me." A small laugh escaped the shifter girl before she slowly lowered herself onto the tall grasses at the edge of the swamp. "Us, now. Maybe."

"Well, don't expect me to come out here with you every single night. I got crap to do."

Risking a glance up at her friend, Amanda felt a large pebble beneath her hand and pulled it from beneath the wet grasses before tossing it into the swamp. "Still, that was better than sitting in your room and crying all night. Wasn't it?"

Summer stepped away and glared down at her. "I don't know what you're talking about."

"Come on, Summer." Amanda kept staring out across the water. "You're okay at hiding it from everyone else, but not me. I know something's wrong. I'm pretty sure Glasket knows too."

"What?"

"She found me in the greenhouse last weekend and asked a lot of…really weird questions. About you."

"Damnit." Summer ruffled her hair—each stripe of the rainbow rendered completely colorless in the dark—and let out a massive sigh. "She needs to keep her nose out of everyone's business."

"She's the principal."

"Yeah, not a counselor." Clicking her tongue, Summer shook her head and finally sat beside her friend. "So what did she ask about me?"

Amanda shrugged. "If I knew what was going on with you. She thinks you tell me everything."

"What an idiot." Summer found another stone and chucked it into the water with a loud *splash*. "I do one fun thing before classes start, and she gets all bent out of shape over a couple of customized fireworks. Like she thinks I'm acting out."

Amanda barked out a laugh. "You lit a giant middle finger in the air and, 'Summer, bitches!' What's she supposed to think?"

The witch snickered. "That was pretty freaking awesome."

They laughed, and Amanda glanced sidelong at her friend. *Guess I might as well bite the bullet and meet this head-on.*

"So are you?"

"Awesome? Damn straight I am, shifter girl. Don't you forget it."

"I mean acting out like Glasket thinks. Whatever *that's* supposed to mean."

Summer hissed out a sigh and leaned over her crossed legs. "I can't believe she tried to weasel info out of *you*. What'd you tell her?"

"Nothing."

"Oh, sure." The witch nudged Amanda's shoulder with a playful punch. "Clam up the second the spotlight turns on you. I get it."

"I'm serious. I didn't tell her anything. I mean, you didn't really tell me anything either, but—"

"You didn't tell her about my parents?"

Amanda slowly shook her head. "No. Only that something *might* be happening at home, but she'd already implied that."

"Yeah. She likes to do that." Summer snorted. "Principal Noseypants. I already told her what was going on, and she comes to *you* about it like she's a clueless freaking baby."

"Wait, you already talked to her?"

Summer stared up at the cloudless night sky and shrugged. "Saturday morning after the party. She thought she could get me to talk by being all nice and understanding. As if she thinks I need some kinda charity. Totally insincere."

"Well, what did you tell her?"

The other girl paused for a long time. "I told her what happened."

"So Glasket knows your parents are getting a divorce?"

"Yeah. Hey, and get this. She told me I could stay here over the summer next year with the rest of the upperclassmen urchins if I didn't have anywhere else to go. Can you believe that? Why the hell would I wanna stay here? *Here?*"

"I don't know. It's not so bad."

"Are you crazy? We're basically slaves—"

Amanda barked out a laugh and covered her mouth with a hand to keep it from getting louder.

"Something funny about that?"

"Summer, it's a school. We don't have security enchantments around the dorms at night anymore. We basically only have four classes this year now that we're only meeting with Petrov once a month."

"Best assignment he's ever given us."

"Ha. Probably. *And* we get to go to the kemana whenever we want, as long as we're not, like, skipping class to go down there."

"Stupid rule."

"It makes sense." Amanda brushed the dirt off her hands and shrugged. "Things are pretty good here."

"Yeah, says the shifter girl who can go home to her new bounty-hunter parents whenever she wants, and..." Summer's back grew rigid, and her hands clenched into fists in her lap.

Amanda frowned. "And what?"

"Nothing."

"You get to go home too. I know it sucks, but—"

"You don't know anything about it, shifter girl. So don't try to pretend you get how shitty things are for me."

"I would if you'd tell me."

"Really? You think that because you have a dead family and almost got sold to an asshole in a suit means you understand what I'm going through?" The echo of Summer's shout traveled across the water and into the trees.

Amanda blinked at the rippling surface of the river. "Wow."

"Shit. Amanda, I didn't mean it like that."

"Well, you meant *something*." The shifter girl turned toward her friend and spread her arms. "You're right, though. I know what it's like to have my family murdered in front of me, get kidnapped by a bunch of idiot criminals, and try to fight my way out of a shifter shock collar while I'm literally standing on an auction block."

"I didn't mean—"

"Everyone has their crap, Summer, okay? Mine's not worse than yours. It's not better, either. I'm here because I want to *do* something about turning what I've been through into an actual win."

Summer snorted. "They make a trophy for that kinda hell?"

"Oh, jeeze." Amanda rolled her eyes, and the girls shared a strained laugh. *I can't believe I think that's funny. If anyone else were listening to this conversation, they'd think we're completely insane.* "Tell me what's going on."

"I'm good."

139

"Obviously not. I still won't tell anyone. I won't, like, hold it over your head or anything either. Seriously, it wouldn't kill you to talk about—"

"She kicked me out of the goddamn house, okay? Marianne."

"What?"

"Yeah. Basically disowned me."

"That's..." Amanda blinked quickly. "I mean, that sucks."

"Ha. Yeah."

"She probably didn't mean it though, right? I mean, don't you guys fight all the time?"

Summer chucked a much bigger rock into the water. The splash made it back up to the bank, peppering the long grass in front of the girls. "She meant it this time."

"How do you know?"

"Huh. Besides the fact that she told me, 'I mean it this time, you little shit'? Let's see. Maybe it has something to do with Michael moving out to Baltimore without even saying goodbye. Or that Marianne was literally already in the process of selling her house and finding somewhere else to move before she even bothered to tell me about it."

"Whoa."

"Yeah. Wanna hear the best part?" Summer didn't wait for her friend to answer; she was on a roll now. "The best part is she had all my shit packed up and sitting out in the front yard the day she was supposed to take me to the stupid train station. Said she didn't care if I made it to school or dropped out, that I was on my own and she wouldn't bail me out this time, and that she never wanted to see me again."

"Damn." Amanda swallowed. "And... I mean, do you think she's serious about it?"

The other girl let out a bitter laugh. "She changed her cell number and never gave it to me. So yeah. I'm pretty sure it's a done fucking deal—" Summer's voice broke on the last word, and when Amanda finally looked at her again, she found tears shimmering in the witch's eyes and her friend's lower lip trembling.

"Summer..."

"Like, I *know* I'm a pain in the ass. I get it. I screw up more than I get things right. It's not like I don't *try*. But what kind of asshole gives up on their kid like that? Just— " she snapped her fingers and tossed her hand in the air "—one last straw, and that's it? I mean, shit. The police have never arrested me. I'm not, like, hooked on drugs or anything. Sometimes I blow things up, yeah, but I never *hurt* anybody."

"I'm—"

"You know what? I probably *am* adopted. Marianne and Michael Flannerty thought they could take in someone else's spawn and call it good. When the stupid baby didn't turn into the perfect little witch they expected, they didn't have the balls to stick it out. Screw them. I don't need shitty parents who don't love someone else's kids anyway." Summer sniffed and angrily wiped away her tears with the back of a hand. "I don't need anybody."

"Well, *that's* true." Amanda nodded slowly, forcing herself to keep looking out across the water despite how much she wanted to see Summer's face right now instead. *If I look at her, she can't keep pretending I don't know she's crying.* After drawing a deep breath, she added, "You're better than them, anyway."

Summer let out a bitter laugh and sniffed again. "I am, aren't I?"

"Most people don't get what it's like to be different. Yeah, it sucks when it's your parents. Maybe it sucks even more. Still, if your dad's gonna skip out and your mom's gonna make it impossible to find her, yeah. Screw them."

"Right?" The young witch cleared her throat and dashed the tears off her cheeks again. "I mean, I could find her if I wanted to."

"Do you want to?"

"Hell no. She can take her stupid amulets and her magical moron pills and grow old in a crappy trailer with no one around to love her, for all I care."

That's a little harsh, but okay. At least she's talking.

Amanda shrugged. "So what did you tell Glasket? You know, about staying here all through the summer."

"I told her I'd think about it." Summer shook her head. "I mean, at this point, whatever I do is gonna suck. It's not like a seventeen-year-old witch can find her own place with a summer job I'd have to leave again to come back here. But... The only real freedom I ever have is over the summer when I'm home. When those posers who call themselves my parents leave me alone all the time and I can do whatever I want. What am I gonna do if I stay here, huh? Do extra-credit projects with Blondie?"

With a soft chuckle, Amanda tossed another stone into the river. "I mean, you could always make more fireworks."

Summer kicked her legs out from under her and sent a landslide of dirt and waterlogged vegetation over the edge of the bank. "Yeah. And get kicked out of *this* place too. Life blows."

"Sometimes, yeah."

They sat there in silence for a while longer, listening to the nocturnal creatures flutter and scramble and splash into the water. The crickets and cicadas droned all around them, and Amanda thought about everything she'd been through and everything she had now.

My life sucked two years ago. Yeah, at least her parents are still alive, but they might as well be dead as far as she's concerned. Plus, she doesn't have Johnny and Lisa.

It didn't take a shifter's enhanced hearing to pick up on the shaky breaths escaping through Summer's nose beside her. Amanda didn't have to look at her friend to know there were even more tears now spilling down Summer's cheeks.

She has me, at least.

Without a word, Amanda scooted closer to the other girl until their shoulders touched. Summer didn't flinch or try to move away, and they sat like that for another five minutes. For now, at least, the conversation was over.

The shifter girl couldn't help a small smile as she stared at the rippling surface of the water under the stars and started to form a few new plans of her own.

She has me and this school and a bunch of other kids here who know how crappy life can be. I bet I can get Grace and the guys to help me out. A little 'make Summer feel better' surprise.

She opened her mouth to ask if Summer wanted to head out to the kemana next week for another adventure—sans crashing a magical mafia's "operation" or stealing anything from a Saithe crime boss—but Summer sucked in a sharp breath and leaned away.

"I wanna pass out. I'm not doing it here, shifter girl." She pushed herself to her feet. "You might be down with all the wilderness and stuff, but I'm not about to sleep on the ground like a wild animal."

"You think I *sleep* out here?"

Summer shot her a tiny smirk, her eyes puffy but completely dry now. "You would if you could. Don't try to deny it. I bet you dream about sleeping out here bare-ass naked and waking up to go hunt rabbits or whatever."

Amanda chuckled and stood, dusting off her pants. "Yep. You totally got me. Can't hide anything from you."

"I know. You're an open book, shifter girl. I see right through you." Summer bumped her shoulder against Amanda's, and they took off back down the water's edge to make their way toward the dorms. "Keep that in mind in case you feel like getting all share-y with anybody."

"What's that supposed to mean?"

"It means if you start talking about poor Summer who can't even keep her parents, I'll make you wish you'd never talked to me my first night freshman year."

Amanda laughed and ran a hand through her hair. "Trust me, that happened a long time ago."

"Fine. Then I'll simply kick your ass."

"Yeah, okay."

CHAPTER FIFTEEN

The next morning, Amanda couldn't help but wake up bright and early. Even after their midnight snack from the pixies, she was starving. Plus, the thought of her next impending trip off-campus with Fiona had kept her up a lot longer than it should have once she'd gotten back to her room the night before.

Fortunately, the kitchen pixies had set up an early breakfast in the outdoor cafeteria, but the line at six-thirty in the morning wasn't nearly as long as it usually was. Amanda stepped in line behind two seniors who barely acknowledged her and quickly loaded her plate with strips of bacon, plenty of sausage links, and two waffles dripping with butter, which she drowned even further in maple syrup. Then she poured herself a glass of orange juice and found her usual picnic table under the pavilion to start chowing down by herself.

Five minutes later, Grace shuffled into the outdoor cafeteria with a handful of junior and senior girls. Jackson and Alex fell into line with them, and before she knew it, Amanda was surrounded by her friends again bright and early on a Saturday morning.

"Man, I swear." Jackson shoveled biscuits and gravy into his mouth. "It's like those pixies can read minds or something."

"It *is* kinda weird they had breakfast out this early," Amanda added. "Did we miss some kind of memo about early weekend breakfasts?"

Grace yawned and picked at her bacon. "I wish they had coffee. I didn't even *try* to get up this early. Why am I up this early?"

"Habit," Alex muttered into his plastic cup of orange juice.

"Huh?"

He set his cup back down on the table and wiped off the orange mustache with the back of his hand. Grace snorted and handed him an extra napkin. "Anyone else notice who's *not* out here this early?"

"Yeah, dude. Like, half the school." Jackson shook his head. "They're seriously missing out."

"Oh my gosh." Grace studied the other students milling around the cafeteria and getting down to business with their breakfast. "He's right."

"Yeah, I am." The wizard held a fist toward her for a fist bump she didn't return.

"I was talking about Alex."

"Fine. Be that way." Jackson swung his fist toward Alex, and the Wood Elf bumped it without looking up from his plate.

"It's only upperclassmen out here." Grace's eyes widened. "Oh, no. They brainwashed us."

Amanda laughed and almost spewed chewed waffle all over the table. "What?"

"That's pretty much what I was thinking," Alex muttered with a shrug.

"Amanda, look." Grace gestured toward the sparsely occupied picnic tables. "It's only juniors and seniors out here. Because we're the only ones who've spent the last two years waking up this early day in and day out."

"Yeah, but there's no alarm on the weekends."

"That's the point! They've brainwashed us into waking up way earlier than we have to. The pixies *knew*. They already had breakfast out and ready. Nobody had to tell them. They're in on it."

"Wow." Jackson widened his eyes. "*Someone's* paranoid first thing in the morning."

"It's not paranoia if there's *proof*," Grace hissed.

"You know, I kinda like it," Amanda said.

"Of course you do. You can stay out all night as a girl or as a wolf." Grace slumped her chin into one hand and picked at her food with the other. "You get midnight snacks from the kitchens, and you *still* have more energy than the rest of us."

Amanda laughed. "Are you spying on me?"

"What?"

"Everyone knows you go out to the kitchens at night, Coulier." Jackson shrugged. "We pretty much covered that freshmen year."

"Huh. Like Alex said, right? Habit."

They don't know about last night. I'll have to figure out a way to get them on board with this surprise for Summer without telling them anything. If Grace wants to be friends with her, she'll have to deal with not knowing everything.

"Hey, guys—"

"Aren't you supposed to go off to your weird shifter internship today?" Jackson asked.

Grace smacked his arm with the back of a hand. "Don't call it that."

"What? That's what it is."

"It's not *weird*. She's worked hard for this."

"She has?"

"I have?" Amanda and Jackson looked at each other across the table. Despite the instant flush rose to the tips of his ears, he didn't look away and laughed with her.

"Of course you have," Grace added. "I mean, maybe not

completely on purpose. Still, you've been working with your magic for a long time, right? Trying to get to this point. It's not weird. It's just…with the Coalition."

"I think it's badass," Alex muttered.

"Thanks." Amanda raised her plastic cup toward him, and he lifted his in a toast before chugging down the rest of his juice.

"So does that work, then?" Grace asked.

"What, the internship?"

"Yeah. Like, what are you gonna be doing out there in the secret shifter research facility?"

Amanda laughed. "I literally have no idea. All I know is that I'm supposed to be out there every weekend. My guess is Dr. Caniss wants to *test* me some more. No clue why or what for. They already know about everything I've been doing."

"About that, Coulier." Jackson pointed at her with his fork. "How *did* you get your magic all up and running?"

"I'm…not exactly supposed to be talking about that. Still."

Jackson nodded at the entrance to the outdoor cafeteria. "Maybe *she'll* tell us?"

Amanda turned to look over her shoulder and found Fiona Damascus stalking across the field toward them. "What?"

"Wow." Grace shook her head. "Glasket needs to get on top of the security wards around campus. Apparently, anyone can walk right in."

"That's not anyone, Grace. That's Fiona."

"Oh."

Amanda went back to her breakfast, scowling at the rest of her waffle as she shoveled it into her mouth.

Fiona approached their table, ignoring all the curious glances the other juniors and seniors shot her way. When she stopped behind Amanda and folded her arms, a cold tingle rose on the back of the girl's neck. "Taking your own sweet time, I see."

"Hey." Amanda shot the shifter woman a glance. "I'm almost done."

"Well, you're gonna have to finish up right now, kid. Where are your bags?"

"My what?"

"Your things. Come on. You were supposed to have packed and been ready to go by now."

Amanda turned all the way around on the picnic bench to stare at her mentor. "Packed?"

"Boy, there's an echo out here, isn't there?" Fiona grinned at the other kids sitting around the table. "Morning."

"What's up?" Jackson grinned back at her and jerked his chin up in a quick nod.

Grace blinked drowsily at the redheaded shifter. "So *you're* the one who—"

"Look, as much as I'd love to stay and chat it up with a few teenagers, we gotta go, kid. We're late enough as it is."

"Don't you think telling me the time beforehand would've been a little helpful?" Amanda muttered as she stood to collect her trash. With a second glance at her plate, she grabbed the rest of her waffle and shoved it into her mouth.

"Would've been helpful for both of us, yeah. I just found out myself. Let's get moving."

"Oh, jeeze." Rolling her eyes, Amanda dumped her trash, stuck her cup in the bus bin, then raised a hand at her friends. "I'll see you guys later tonight—"

"Tomorrow night, actually," Fiona added quickly.

"Are you serious?"

"As a heart attack, kid. Which Dr. Caniss will have if we keep taking *forever* to get out there."

Great. There goes the entire weekend.

"Have fun," Grace called although she didn't sound very convinced that Amanda would have any fun at all.

"Yeah, I'll…see you later, then."

"Give 'em hell, Coulier!"

Fiona snorted and looked over her shoulder at Jackson. "He's spunky."

"What are you talking about?"

"The wizard. Got a nice smile too."

"Stop."

"Why? You don't agree?"

"I'm not talking to you about Jackson. Or any of my friends."

"Jackson, huh? Yeah, I like him. Does he always call you by your last name?"

Amanda shook her head and hurried toward the girls' dorm. Fiona stayed close on her heels the entire time, grinning and nodding and occasionally saying good morning to the groggy-eyed underclassmen girls starting to shuffle out of their dorm rooms.

"Hey, this is nice." Fiona looked around when they stopped at Amanda's door. "Right at the end of the hall. Not the first floor, but not at the top, either."

"The first floor is the common room," Amanda muttered as she unlocked her door.

"Oh, how very boarding-school."

"This *is* a boarding school. Kinda." She stepped into her room and tried to close the door behind her again, but Fiona barged right inside. "Hey, do you mind?"

"Not at all. I'm here for moral support. Chop, chop."

With a scowl, Amanda knelt beside her dresser to pack up an extra set of clothes for her impromptu weekend off campus. An entire weekend.

She kept sneaking glances up at her mentor as she withdrew her duffel bag from the bottom drawer and tried to shield her collection of student contraband from Fiona's view.

The redheaded shifter snorted. "Don't worry, kid. I'm not gonna tattle on you or anything."

"My room's supposed to be private."

"Sure. So is your little cubby in the greenhouse, right? I've seen *that*. Come on. What kinda mentor would I be if I kept the

Fatethistle a secret but ratted on you for..." Fiona leaned over the open drawer. "Ooh. Nice. Cell phone, knife, little black box. What does that last one do?"

"None of your business." Amanda slammed the drawer shut and didn't pay attention to what she was packing when she stuffed extra clothes into the duffel bag. "Anything else you forgot to tell me I need before we go?"

"You have the Shiverbloom and Blindman's...whatever ready to go, right?"

"I thought you said we were running late."

"We are! I think bringing the good ol' doc a peace offering with early harvests might make her, you know...less likely to kill us."

With a sigh, Amanda slung the strap of her duffel bag over her shoulder and headed for the door. "Yeah, I have some ready. Come on."

Fiona remained in the room for a moment longer, her arms folded as she looked around and nodded in approval. "I like it in here. Cozy."

"Fiona!"

"Yeah, yeah, I'm coming. Keep your fur on."

"Seriously?"

"What? You're not into shifter jokes? Ha. Trust me, kid. Spend enough time with the Coalition, and that'll all change."

The main building was empty when they made a brief stop at the greenhouse to grab the stems, leaves, and flowers of the Shiverbloom, Blindman's Bane, and Fool's Supper Amanda had already harvested. Fiona whipped three medium-sized burlap sacks out of nowhere and held them open as Amanda emptied the different five-gallon buckets into each. Then, with the sacks slung over her shoulder, Fiona led the way out of the greenhouse.

She waited for Amanda to lock up behind them before grabbing the girl's wrist and teleporting them right out of the main building's hallway.

The girl would have crushed her back against the bathroom counter in the Marco Island Starbucks if her duffel bag hadn't cushioned the landing. "The bathroom again? Really?"

"Where else am I supposed to pop us in, huh? In line behind the already scattered customers jonesing for their morning cup? That wouldn't go over too well."

"How about you teleport us into the lab?" Amanda caught the bathroom door before it swung shut and hurried after her mentor into the back hall.

"Why would I do that?"

"Because I'm sick of riding this stupid train."

"Trust me kid, I feel ya. You'll have to get used to this weekly trip. I'm sure it'll grow on you."

"Is this some kind of test too?" Amanda stepped into the supply closet after Fiona and waited for the woman to pull the elevator lever. The room dropped violently and shuddered to a halt who knew how far underground. She swallowed her breakfast threatening to come back up and sighed. "'Cause I'm okay with failing this one."

"Oh, come on. Where's the fun in teleporting us to the Rockies?"

Amanda fixed her with a deadpan glare.

"Ha. You'll come around. Besides, there's absolutely no fun at all when the wards placed around the Canisssphere will zap teleporting intruders to a crisp."

"Canisssphere?"

Fiona chuckled as the exterior doors to the Starbucks train slid open, and they stepped into the adjacent cabin. "Well, that's what we've been calling it. I'm sure it has an official name now that everything's up and running, but that one kinda stuck."

"Dr. Caniss is really in charge of the whole thing, isn't she?"

"One hundred percent, kid. Yes, she's also the one who put up the teleporter-zapping wards."

"So why doesn't someone update the wards to let in Coalition shifters teleporting into the..." Amanda snorted as they took their seats on the red upholstered benches. "Canisssphere?"

"There's only so much we can do, kid."

The train's exterior doors closed, and the robotic female voice declared the train would now be departing.

"Might wanna hold on this time," Fiona muttered. "We're back to epic—"

The train took off with an earsplitting *whine* and thrust Amanda against the back of her cushioned seat.

There's no way I'm keeping my breakfast after this.

Fortunately, after multiple abrupt starts and stops on the Starbucks train, one more teleport via Fiona's enhanced shifter skills, and another tingling walk through the illusion around the Coalition's Canissphere, Amanda didn't end up being sick at all. Her stomach had only started to settle when they reached the giant domed room serving as a combination of common area and conference room.

Bill—who Amanda still thought of as the zookeeper—and the doctor's assistant Lucy stood beside the closest table to greet them. Dr. Caniss was nowhere in sight.

"You're late." Lucy looked Fiona up and down with wide eyes.

The redhead woman thrust a finger in the air. "We're still here. With *three* big bags of—"

"I'll take those, thank you." Lucy lunged forward to snatch the sacks of harvested plants from Fiona's hands, then spun on her heels and hurried across the domed room. "Dr. Caniss will be with you shortly."

"Shortly, huh?" Fiona ran a hand through her fiery curls and laughed before noisily pulling out a chair for herself at the table. "I'll get comfy and wait, then."

Amanda started to do the same.

"Not you," Bill said with a warm smile.

She froze. "Not me what?"

"It's Amanda, right?"

"Yeah."

"Bill." He stuck out his hand, and she took it.

"Yeah, I remember."

"I bet. That was some pretty good work in the exam room last week."

"Would've been even better without you laughing at me."

"Hey, I was trying to give a few helpful hints. Still, seems like you figured it out on your own."

Amanda started to lower her duffel bag to the floor. "You missed the best part, too."

Bill chuckled and glanced at Fiona, who was busy picking dirt out from under her nails with the tip of a pocketknife. "That's what I heard. Hey, keep your bag with you, huh? I'll show you where to drop it when we finish."

"With what?"

"Your tour of Omega Industries—"

"Canissphere, Bill," Fiona muttered. "Yes, I already divulged that not-so-secret little secret."

"Ha. Okay. Let's get going then." He waved Amanda forward with him, then glanced around the dome and lowered his voice. "Don't let Dr. Caniss hear you call it that, huh?"

"Are there a lot of things we're not supposed to let Dr. Caniss hear us say?"

Bill snorted and nodded toward one of the hallways branching off from the main dome. "You'll learn as you go along."

Amanda hefted her bag over her shoulder again and looked at Fiona. "What about you?"

"I've already had the tour, kid."

"No, I mean are you—"

"I'll be here. Don't worry. Go get some learning in."

With a smirk, Amanda followed Bill toward the long, dimly hit hall that looked like all the others.

At least I get to tour the place with the only shifter here who isn't barking orders or staring blankly at me.

CHAPTER SIXTEEN

Bill led her first toward what he called "the labs"—a series of rooms connected by walls of windows where the shifters working in one could see their coworkers in every other room while running their tests in their private spaces. "Every new creature that comes in here provides a DNA sample, and we run it through the database of known Oriceran creatures. Which is fairly extensive, so finding genetic variations is pretty straightforward."

"Does it happen a lot?"

"What?"

"Finding unknown DNA from the creatures you bring in here."

He ran a hand through his dark hair. "Let me put it this way. The last guy who brought in a beastie that *didn't* end up being a divergent species got his severance package and a swift kick in the ass out the door—whoops. Gotta watch my language."

"I've heard worse." She stared at the shifters in white lab coats working diligently in the labs as they passed. One of them glanced up at her from behind his thick safety goggles and narrowed his eyes before returning to his work. "I'm guessing you guys don't see a lot of new faces around here."

"Nailed it." Bill turned down a corridor that seemed to stretch forever in front of them. "This place has only been here for… maybe three years. Most of us were handpicked by Dr. Caniss before they built Omega Industries. The higher-ups signed off on everything beforehand, although they didn't believe a word she said about mutating Oriceran species. No one did until the new little beasties started popping up more and more frequently last year. Your discovery of Subject UM-43562 last year got the ball rolling for all of us."

"The weird mermaid things, right?"

Bill chuckled. "Yep. Don't worry. You'll get used to the subject numbers eventually. I have a little cheat sheet for remembering them if you wanna take a look."

"Is this gonna be on the finals?"

He did a double-take and laughed when he saw Amanda smirking at him. "Funny. No. We won't grade you on your ability to memorize random numbers. However, it'll make things easier for you with Dr. Caniss if you nail down a few in the beginning."

"Then sure. I'll take your notes."

After the next turn in the hallway, they passed another long, wide room with the walls entirely made of glass, where several shifters were working diligently on a creature that looked like a feathered whale. Shimmering green blood poured from a wound in the magical animal's hide, and when it thumped around in pain, one shifter barked orders while the others scattered to fulfill them.

"Guess you could call that the hospital wing," Bill muttered.

Amanda stopped to watch the enormous magical animal struggling on the table. "What happened to it?"

"Probably got into a fight. Territory dispute, most likely. The Manahule tend to get a little ornery this time of year. Forget spring and summer. When fall rolls around, they're all business."

"How many Manahule do you guys have here?"

"So far? Eight, I think. As far as we know, their lifespans are as long as the original Oriceran whales, but they don't seem to breed nearly as often. And, of course, they have the added benefit of gliding."

"Gliding?"

"Yeah. The feathers on these aren't vestigial at all. Kinda like if a species of penguin suddenly evolved and gained the ability to fly."

Amanda stared at the bleeding Manahule, which seemed to have calmed down now, probably under some kind of anesthesia. "Those things can fly?"

"No, they're way too heavy for that. They do glide though. It's pretty cool to see. Come on."

They passed the hospital wing full of veterinarian shifters and two more branching hallways before Bill finally turned the corner on the right. "Back there, the hallways turn back into the storerooms. Food for the critters, medical supplies, and the testing facility that pumps out new rewards for us to test on the creatures."

"Wait, I thought this place was for studying the animals only. Nobody said anything about experiments."

"Behavioral only, Amanda. Relax." Bill shot her a flashing grin over his shoulder. "Nobody's getting tortured or picked apart or pumped full of magical drugs. I promise."

"You said rewards…"

"Yeah. Like dog treats for puppies." He laughed at her clueless expression. "Listen, we're trying to figure out everything we can about these divergent species. We study their behavior in close captivity for the first two weeks. You saw the initial examination rooms."

"Yep." She scratched her head and followed after him. "Honestly, I expected a bunch of newly captured creatures to be a lot more pissed off about being stuck in cages."

"Well, you got your first taste of that with the Harkliss, didn't you?" Bill opened a steel door at the end of the hall and headed up the enclosed staircase. Their footsteps echoed in the small space as the door *clanged* shut behind them. "Some of the more... feral creatures here definitely put up a fight. We have different exam rooms for those, of course."

"According to..." Amanda wrinkled her nose and tried to pull up Dr. Caniss's words again from memory. "'Similarity in temperament and dietary requirements,' right?"

Her guide burst out laughing. "That's one of the more impressive Caniss impersonations I've heard yet. That was right after Fiona called me the zookeeper, wasn't it?"

"I think so. I guess you have a better title, though."

"Not really. Subject Caretaker doesn't have the same ring to it. Honestly, I'll take Zookeeper over something that makes me sound like I'm working in a hospice or something. Zookeeper Bill."

They both laughed, and he opened the door at the top of the stairs to take them down yet another hallway that looked the same as every other hallway so far.

I'm never gonna be able to find my way around here on my own.

"So what do you do with the mean ones?"

"Ha. The animals with more vicious temperaments? We stick them in a different exam room for the first two weeks and let them rage it out all they want. We're not trying to train these things or subdue them into something they're not." He cupped a hand around his mouth and leaned toward her. "Still, when I'm trying to feed the ones with nasty teeth or poisonous spines, I've found a good pair of warded gloves goes a long way."

Amanda grinned at him. "Yeah, I know what you mean."

"I bet. Heard you're a whiz with magical plants too, huh?"

"I wouldn't say I'm a *whiz*. No training or anything—"

"Naw, that doesn't matter." Bill waved her off. "When you find something you're good at and enjoy at the same time, anyone who says you need a formal education can suck it."

She snorted.

"What?"

"You sound like one of my friends."

"So I sound like a seventeen-year-old." Bill shrugged. "That might be the highlight of my week."

I guess everyone here knows I'm a junior. No way am I gonna tell him I'm only fourteen.

As they approached another door at the end of the hall, a wild bellow from some animal below seeped through the walls. A tremor ran through the hallway floor, and Bill steadied himself with a hand on the wall with a small chuckle. "That'll be the Spinebacks. It's feeding time, and here I am giving you a tour. Don't get me wrong. I appreciate the change of scenery. We should probably get a move on so I can get back to my zookeeper duties though, or Caniss won't let me hear the end of it."

"You got randomly assigned to give the tour, huh?"

"Oh, no way. She asked me to show you around specifically."

"Then why would she get mad at you for not feeding the…animals?"

"You know what, Amanda?" He kept moving down the hall toward the door. "That's a question I've been asking myself since I got here. I've been here almost the whole three years. When it comes to Dr. Caniss, it's best to roll with it and not try to figure out why she does what she does. With pretty much everything. You can ask all the right questions at exactly the right time, and I swear, you'll never get an answer that makes sense."

A louder bellow seeped through the door at the end of the hall, followed by a *thump* and another shudder through the walls.

"Yeah, they're real hungry."

"The Spinebacks?"

"Yep. You saw one, didn't you? The giant purple rats with quills?"

"There are more of those things here?"

"Oh, yeah. Technically, the one we recently brought in would be the fourth. We lost one of the others when we mistakenly placed an evolved Heloton with the other herbivores."

"I have no idea what that is."

"Uh...basically a half-sized fire-breathing giraffe. With camouflage."

Amanda clapped a hand over her mouth to stifle a laugh.

"I know. Sounds hilarious, right? The original Oriceran Keloton uses camouflage in the traditional sense. You know, to hide from predators. Normal. Benign." Bill cleared his throat and opened the next door with a tight, sheepish smile. "Turns out the Heloton uses camouflage as a hunting strategy."

"Oh, no." Amanda blinked against the bright light spilling through the door when her guide opened it. "Nobody knew it was a carnivore?"

"Uh...no. The thing ate leaves and roots and grass like the rest of them. Turns out an omnivorous diet seems to have been part of the mutation. You can imagine how well *that* went over afterward."

"Sounds awful."

"Oh, it was bloody as hell. Animals freaking out, tossing weird magic all over the place. But hey, on the bright side, we got a heck of an opportunity to study how the herbivores react to danger. A few extra fights broke out. We're still analyzing most of the new abilities we saw that day, but it looks like a lot of these creatures have some hidden talents that only come out with the fight-or-flight response. It was chaos. And it was like Christmas around here."

"I don't get it." She followed him out onto a wide, open walk-way, trying so hard to wrap her head around his last statement that she hardly noticed the fresh breeze blowing across her face and the much thicker scent of greenery and animal musk in the air.

Bill grinned at her. "A bunch of scientists stumbling across data we would normally never have gotten without an accident like that? There's nothing in the world that can top that."

"If these mutated creatures are all in cages…"

"Ah. That's only for the first two weeks. After that, they get released into semi-captivity. For observation purposes, obviously." Bill turned toward the railing along the walkway and pointed down. "Separated, of course, according to similarity in temperament and dietary requirements." He chuckled. "We're a lot more careful now about testing which ones will eat plants when we're around but prefer to go after flesh on their own."

Amanda finally looked down over the railing, and her jaw dropped.

They stood two hundred feet above a massive wildlife enclosure she would never have seen the end of if it weren't for the flickering panels of yet another dome stretching across the space. Below them was short grass and a large pond that could almost have been a lake. A river cut across the domed enclosure and fed into the pond, and she followed it back across the open field toward a dense, lush forest taking up the far half of the dome. Some creature let out a sharp, echoing *yip* in the woods, and a massive bird launched up from the treetops before scattering into hundreds of much smaller, glittering blue birds swarming away to find another place to roost. At the tree line, the canopy trembled and rustled before a creature that resembled a cross between a grizzly bear and the Abominable Snowman burst through the foliage and stomped across the ground.

"Whoa…"

"Yeah." Bill readjusted his grip on the railing and gazed out with wide eyes and a huge grin. "Pretty incredible, right?"

"Yeah. How did all this even—never mind. Magic and science. I get it."

"Hey, now you're catching on."

"So where do you separate the predators from the prey? You

know, 'cause I'm assuming you want to keep them separate, right?"

"Obviously. This dome's only for the herbivores."

Amanda's eyes practically bulged from her head. "You mean…"

"Oh, yeah. We have three enclosures. Like a Venn diagram, almost. Carnivores on the far side of the facility, and omnivores between that one and this. You know, you'd *think* the dome filled with flesh-eaters would be the craziest one of all, but I'll tell you right now, we have the most trouble with the critters that like to sample a little bit of everything. That's where the Manahule came from. For the most part, meat-eaters and plant-lovers get along pretty well with 'their kind.' As long as we keep *them* separated, obviously."

"This is incredible. How many different animals do you guys have here?"

"Mm…almost fifty different species at this point. And counting, right?" He nudged his elbow against her arm. "I'm guessing that's part of why Dr. Caniss brought *you* in."

"To bring in more creatures," she whispered breathlessly. "Eventually. If she lets me get that far. They're *all* mutated?"

"Yep. Every single one."

"Okay, well, whoever doesn't believe Dr. Caniss about evolving Oriceran creatures needs to get out here and take a look at this place. I had no idea."

"That's the point, Amanda. No one else is supposed to know. Not yet."

"How come?"

Bill turned slowly toward her and fixed her with a concerned frown. "The world isn't even ready to know about *shifters* having magic. Everyone here has an affiliation with the Coalition in one way or another. We all have access to that knowledge. Still, it hasn't exactly been shouted from the rooftops yet. With good reason."

"Yeah. Nobody wants to believe we can do more than wolf-out and attack stuff."

"Ha. Wolf-out. I like it." He vigorously scratched his head and ruffled his dark hair before drawing a deep breath of the crisp air within the enclosure. "So I'm sure you can imagine how the rest of the world would react if they knew about divergent species of Oriceran creatures that have already been on this planet and in relative hiding for...who knows how long, really. The humans would freak out. Probably form some kind of military critter-response squad or something. The rest of the magical world—"

"Would want to pick all these animals apart," she whispered.

"Yeah, you know." Bill nodded sagely, though he couldn't quite hide the grimace spreading across his lips. "There are some real old Oriceran families who'd pay big money to get their hands on these creatures. Can you believe that?"

Amanda let out a long, slow sigh and nodded. "Not to mention all the criminals out there who'd kill to have a mutated pet on a leash who can do their dirty work for them without it being traced back to any other creature the rest of the world knows about."

"Wow." He chuckled wryly. "Not even out of that school yet, and you're already starting to think like a bounty hunter."

She wrinkled her nose and shrugged. "I live with two. Kinda runs in the family, I guess."

"Ha. Yeah, I can see that. You're Johnny Walker's kid, aren't you?"

"Great. Apparently, that's common knowledge all over the world at this point."

Bill drummed his fingers against the railing. "I mean, it's not like that dwarf does a lot to keep his work or his business a complete secret."

"Don't let *him* hear you say that."

Another wild bellow came from directly below them, followed by another tremble through the walls that felt a lot more violent out here on the elevated walkway. Amanda's hands clamped down around the railing, and Bill leaned almost over the bar to peer down at the culprits.

"Hey! Havalah! Maximus! Get down, huh? I'll be there in a second."

The larger Spineback peered up at him, sniffed once, then grunted and shoved itself away from the wall. The smaller creature—which still resembled a purple rat with quills, even from this height—let out a warbling groan and pawed at the enclosure wall.

"Oh, jeeze." Bill stepped away from the railing and ran a hand through his hair. "Listen, I gotta get down there before she loses it. You wouldn't think it by looking at them, but Spinebacks are prone to fits of depression."

"Um…" Amanda snorted out a laugh.

"I know, right? It might only be the female, at the very least. Who knows? Still, if she feels like I've abandoned her, I have my work cut out for me trying to bring her back from the edge."

"You named her Havalah?"

"Yeah." He shot her a crooked smile. "It kinda stuck."

The female Spineback whined again, and Bill leaned over the railing to point at her. "Havalah, you get those five-inch claws off the wall right now! I'm coming—"

The door at the entrance to the walkway shut with a loud *clang*, and Amanda spun to see Dr. Caniss striding purposefully toward them. "Bill, how many times do I have to remind you that these subjects are *not* pets?"

Bill whirled around, pressed his back against the railing, then ran a hand through his hair with a nervous chuckle. "Sorry, Dr. Caniss. Old habits."

"Yes, and I certainly hope you haven't made a habit of neglecting your responsibilities. Isn't it feeding time?"

"Dr. Caniss, Bill was giving me a—"

He stopped Amanda's attempted defense with a hand on her

shoulder and shook his head. "She's right, Amanda. Can't abandon my duties. I'll get right on it, doctor."

"By all means." The short-haired shifter biologist gestured toward the door and stared after Bill with a raised eyebrow until he disappeared inside. Then she turned back toward Amanda and cocked her head. "I assume the tour consisted of more than dangling over that railing like a couple of tourists."

"Yeah, it was...highly informative." Amanda readjusted the strap of her duffel bag over her shoulder. *She's pissed. And I sound like an idiot.* "Doctor."

The shifter woman looked her up and down, then passed Amanda with a quick stride and heading down the walkway toward another entrance door on the other side. "Keep up. I don't slow down, and I don't send search parties through my facility for teenage girls who can't focus on the task at hand."

"Yep. You made that clear last time," Amanda muttered under her breath.

"Then it shouldn't be hard for you this time," Dr. Caniss replied at full volume.

Crap. I seriously have to remember I'm in a giant lab base with nothing but shifters around me. And mutated Oriceran creatures. Amanda spared one more quick look at the herbivore enclosure. *At least if* they *hear me talking to myself, they won't talk back.*

CHAPTER SEVENTEEN

Dr. Caniss's brief and curt tour of the rest of the facility through which she led Amanda paled compared to Bill's. Mostly because the biologist didn't explain where they were. Instead, she barked short sentences and the names of the areas they passed as if Amanda was supposed to piece together the rest of the information herself.

"Medical bay. For us, not the subjects."

"Security."

"Communications and satellite monitoring."

"Waste disposal."

"Maintenance and repairs."

"Off-limits. No, I will not explain further."

Amanda snorted at that last one, but Bill's warning flashed through her head.

He's right. None of the answers she could give me about that one could possibly make sense.

They finally reached another large domed room that looked almost identical to the first one Amanda had seen in the facility. Instead of empty tables covered in tech equipment, computers, and paperwork, this one held couches, armchairs, and two pool tables beside a dartboard on the opposite end.

"This is the recreation room," Dr. Caniss explained dryly. "It also serves as the mess hall during mealtimes. The line forms over there. The snack station is open twenty-four hours, and every staff member is limited to no more than three snack items per diem. Don't try to sneak in any more than that, Amanda. I'll know if you do."

The girl tried to hide her smile and muttered, "So I'm a staff member now, huh?"

Dr. Caniss spun to face her, and Amanda almost walked right into her. "I left explicit instructions with the dean of your school to explain what this arrangement entails. All of them perfectly clear. This is not a paying—"

"I know. No pay. It's an internship." *Whatever that's supposed to mean in a place like this.*

The biologist narrowed her eyes, her nostrils flaring, and strode briskly across the rec room toward another branching hallway. "While you're inside my facility, you will be treated as a member of this staff in everything you do. I expect nothing less from you than to act accordingly."

Except for getting paid.

Amanda slowed to take in the giant domed room one more time. A small group of shifters in thick leather overalls sat at a table, eating quickly and not talking much at all. A woman with a pair of thick goggles pulled up onto the top of her head bit into a sandwich and met Amanda's gaze. A slow smile spread across her face as she chewed, and she nodded. The other shifters sitting with her turned to eye Amanda too, and one of them nodded toward Dr. Caniss quickly disappearing into the next hall.

"Crap." The girl spun to follow her second guide for the day, and the shifters at the table chuckled softly before returning to their meals.

"This is the wing for private living quarters," Caniss said.

"One magical per room, and that's a hard rule. I don't tolerate private fraternizing in this facility."

Amanda couldn't help a surprised laugh. "It's not like I'm bringing friends with me."

Caniss stopped abruptly and spun to look the girl up and down again. "A *hard* rule, Amanda. Here."

Amanda took the shiny, nearly transparent keycard from the biologist's hand and turned it over. "Um...thanks?"

"That's your room key. This is your room." Caniss snatched the key away again and flashed it across the panel over the door beside them before practically tossing it back at her new intern. Amanda fumbled to catch it as the door *hissed* open, then stuck the key in her pocket. "You are to keep that on you at all times while you're here. I have zero patience for lack of personal responsibility, and you will not be issued a new key if you happen to misplace that one. Enter."

Blinking quickly, Amanda sidled past the woman to enter her room. It was small—at least half the size of the waiting room she'd been locked in for two hours the weekend before. It held a twin-sized mattress built into a cubby in the curving back wall, a small single-user desk built into the wall beside the door, and a stainless-steel sink beside a stainless-steel toilet in the opposite corner.

Amanda tossed her duffel bag onto the floor and pressed her lips together.

This looks like a jail cell on a spaceship.

"Your rest hours are from eleven o'clock at night to five in the morning. I don't want to hear any complaints about the lack of sleep. Yes, I realize adolescents require more than six hours on average, but you can make up for the lost time when you return to the Academy. Understand?"

"No problem."

If she knew how late I stay up on campus, she wouldn't be giving me this lecture.

"And in the future, I expect you to arrive *on time* on Saturday mornings. Your tardiness today is unacceptable."

"What?"

"You were expected here at seven-thirty sharp. Don't be late again."

"That's not my fault," Amanda blurted. "Fiona didn't even pick me up until seven. If we need to be here earlier, you should talk to *her* about—"

"This internship does not belong to Fiona Damascus," Caniss snapped. "It belongs to *you*. I expect you to do whatever's necessary to abide by these requirements, Amanda. If that's not doable for you, don't bother returning next weekend."

"I—"

"Take some time to settle in. You'll shadow Dr. Ivory Blane for the remainder of the day. She'll come to fetch you when it's time." With that, Caniss grabbed the door and pulled it shut behind her. A small light on the key panel beside the door flashed green, then red, and Amanda was left on her own in this tiny pod of a room at Omega Industries.

"Thanks for the tour, doc."

Huffing out a disbelieving laugh, Amanda scanned her private room one more time, then noisily pulled the chair out from beneath the built-in desk and plopped into it.

Jeeze. I didn't think the Coalition would be way more militant than the Academy. Or maybe it's Dr. Caniss. She probably doesn't even know how to loosen up at the end of the day.

She stood again to test out the bed with its crisp, freshly washed sheets. The mattress was ridiculously firm, but at least the pillow was fluffy enough.

My room every weekend, huh? As long as I get to do something cool here, I guess it's fine for six hours at night.

Half an hour later, a brisk knock came at her door. "Amanda?"

She sat up quickly from where she'd been dozing on the bed and bumped her head against the concave ceiling of the little bed bubble around her. "Ow! Yeah?"

"It's Dr. Blane. Time to get started."

"Yeah, I'm coming." It took her a second to wake up completely as she rubbed her sore head. She finally straightened herself out and went to open the door.

On the other side of it, a shifter woman with jet-black hair pulled back into a long, straight ponytail offered a warm smile in greeting. "Nice to finally meet you."

"You too." Amanda shook the woman's hand, then gestured toward the bed cubby. "Does everyone here sleep in a box like that, or only me?"

"Hit your head on the ceiling, huh?" Dr. Blane chuckled. "It takes a little getting used to, but eventually you stop waking up thinking you have all the space in the world."

"Great. Is there, like, a scientific reason for building them like that, or..."

The woman laughed as they stepped into the hall and Amanda closed the door behind her. "I think there was a certain aesthetic in mind when they built this place. If you ask me..." The woman leaned conspiratorially toward Amanda and glanced up and down the hall to be sure the coast was clear. "I think Dr. Caniss's trying to train us all to avoid sleeping past our allotted shifts. You know, make sure we're always on our toes. The last thing you want when you first wake up is a nasty bump on the head like that."

"Yeah." Amanda grimaced. "Does she enjoy torturing all of you?"

"You know, we still haven't quite figured that out yet. There's a running betting pool on the eventual outcome. The pot's up to...five thousand, I think."

"Dollars?"

"No, meal credits." Dr. Blane laughed at the girl's expression of blank surprise. "I'm kidding. Yes, dollars. Real ones, too. Come on, let's get you geared up and ready to go for your first day, huh?"

Rubbing her still-tender head, Amanda hurried after yet another shifter doctor and cast wary glances around the hallway.

I thought the Academy was weird at first, but this place blows it out of the water.

When they reached one of the initial exam rooms—this one housing five different caged creatures that looked a lot more dangerous than the others she'd seen—Dr. Blane introduced Amanda to the other two shifters stationed here to observe the new subjects. "Dean and Antoinette. This is—"

"Amanda Coulier." Antoinette—a short shifter woman with spiky hair dyed a platinum-blonde—reached toward Amanda for a firm handshake and grinned. "It's great to meet you finally."

"Thanks."

"I tell you what," Dean added, reaching out to shake her hand next as he pushed his thick-rimmed glasses up the bridge of his nose with the other, "it was hard enough to wait all summer for you. You're gonna love this, I promise."

"Ivory, did you tell her about the bets?" Antoinette asked.

"Wait?" Amanda huffed out a laugh. "You mean there's more than one?"

"Uh…yeah?" Dr. Blane gave her a tight smile. "We can cover those later. Right now, we're here to work, and you're here to help us. So grab one of those aprons and face shields hanging on the wall over there. Oh, and a pair of gloves."

"Oh…" Amanda eyed the aforementioned gear and grimaced. "So I'm on cleanup duty."

"Not necessarily." Dean stuck his hands on his hips as Antoinette and Dr. Blane gloved up. "It's a precaution."

"For the Ripper," Antoinette added and jerked her gloved thumb toward a long, short cage on the far side of the room. "That one tends to spit."

Dr. Blane nodded and widened her eyes. "Acid."

All three scientists laughed, and Amanda backed away toward the wall to grab a large plastic apron for herself. She tied it on quickly, then snatched up a pair of gloves and shoved her hands inside. "Uh...what exactly are we gonna do with the Ripper, Dr. Blane?"

"Dr. Blane." Antoinette shot the other shifter woman an amused glance. "Aren't *we* getting fancy?"

"You can call me Ivory. It's easier to remember when everyone's first name isn't doctor, right?"

Dean snorted. "If you even *suspect* Dr. Caniss might be around, then we all have official titles."

Amanda nodded and slowly rejoined them. "She likes her rules, huh?"

"You have no idea. Granted, we appreciate rules too. It's not like we're always trying to break them." Antoinette grabbed a tablet off the desk at the back of the exam room.

"Gotta know the rules inside and out before you can effectively break 'em," Dean added.

Another small laugh escaped the shifter girl as she eyed the Ripper in the low cage. It mostly looked like a snake, but each of its glittering orange scales was at least five times larger than a normal snake's. It also had four stubby legs right behind its head and two larger ones almost at the end of its tail, which ended in a giant translucent bulb that glowed bright yellow. "You know, I wasn't sure about this place. But you guys seem all right."

"Ha. You hear that?" Dean finished putting on his gloves and slapped his hands together. "We're all right."

"You might want to hold off on the assessment of our characters until after we finish today." Antoinette's lips spread into a broad, crazed-looking grin as she widened her eyes. "Because you're in for a real treat."

"Yeah, good idea." Ivory gestured toward Amanda and shook her head. "Scare the poor girl out of her mind before we even get started."

"Please." Dean waved her off. "Amanda's not some fragile, squeamish teenage girl who can't handle a few curveballs, are you, kid?"

"Um…I don't think so."

The scientists cracked up again. Then Ivory gestured toward one of the stainless-steel instrument carts at the far end of the room. "Grab that cart and wheel it over here, Amanda. We've been trying to get that Ripper to liven up a little."

"I thought this was for, you know…observation."

"It is. We simply haven't figured out yet if the acid-spitting is a defense mechanism or a symptom."

"Of what?"

"Could be anything, really." Antoinette shrugged. "A species-specific illness. Hunger. Lethargy. The little stinker is trying to mess with us."

"Little. Right." Amanda eyed the Ripper one more time and swallowed when it lifted its bulbous tail and shook it like it a rattle on a rattlesnake. The yellow glow intensified, and the creature opened its mouth to shoot out not one but three forked black tongues and mewled like a cat.

That thing's staring at me. I know it.

"The cart, Amanda." Ivory grinned at her. "I know it's all pretty overwhelming, but we do have a lot of work to get done here."

"Yeah. Right." She hurried toward the cart as the scientists chuckled and tossed around observations.

Some internship. I'll probably get blasted with glowing-snake acid, and after that, they'll give me their coffee orders.

CHAPTER EIGHTEEN

When Fiona dropped her off on school grounds that Sunday night after dark, Amanda wasn't sure she'd be able to wake up at all the next morning, even after sleeping in her bed again. However, the obnoxiously loud blaring of the Commodores' *Brick House* through the campus-wide speakers made sleeping in impossible.

So Amanda shuffled out of the dorm with the rest of the girls to head out to breakfast. Grace caught up to her before they'd made it halfway to the outdoor cafeteria. "Amanda! Hey! How was—whoa. You look..."

"That bad, huh?" Amanda blinked heavily and grabbed the straps of her backpack just to keep her arms from feeling like they were going to fall off.

"I mean, a little...tired, maybe."

"Just a little, yeah."

"They worked you hard out in the lab, huh?"

"If you can even call it work."

"Coulier!" Jackson raced toward them, and they fell into line behind the buffet table for breakfast—this time with the entire student body on a Monday instead of only the upperclassmen hitting up the early-bird special on the weekends. "So? Spill it."

"Nothing to spill," Amanda muttered, staring in a daze at the back of the kid's head in front of her.

"Aw, come on." He bumped his shoulder against hers, and she staggered sideways before catching herself. "Whoa. Must've been some kinda monster-hunting, huh?"

"I didn't hunt any monsters, Jackson. Only helped a bunch of weirdo scientists do their weirdo science."

"Huh." The wizard scratched his head. "That sounds boring."

"It wasn't that bad. Only, I didn't think I'd be doing *that* for eighteen hours a day."

Grace's eyes widened. "They have you working *eighteen hours?*"

"No. I mean, I get breaks. But apparently I'm supposed to be shadowing these shifters 'at all waking hours.' Unless I'm eating, sleeping, or on the toilet."

"Not, like, manual labor, right?"

Amanda gave her friend a deadpan stare. "I spent all day yesterday studying tiny Oriceran new-things and writing down my observations of living rocks."

Jackson laughed, then quickly covered it up when she turned her stare onto him. "Oh. Oh, that wasn't a joke?"

"Nope."

"Well, what does the Coalition say about those weird mermaid things living here last year?" Grace asked as they moved up the line.

"They're a *divergent species.*"

"Yeah, but what about all the other evolved creatures out there? Do they think there's a threat of more…divergent species showing up like the mermaids did? Like, wreaking havoc on schools and businesses or whatever—"

"Grace." Amanda let out a heavy sigh and tried to smile at the witch. "Can we keep the questions to, like, one every ten minutes? I'm pretty sure I'm too tired to remember how to hold a plate."

"Hey, don't worry," Jackson said. "I got you, Coulier. You tell me what you want, and I'll load it up." He grabbed two plates from the stack at the end of the table and grinned.

"That was sarcasm." She took one plate from him and tried to laugh. "But thanks."

"Okay, fine." Grace moved down the table beside her, filling up a paper bowl of oatmeal before grabbing a banana and two strips of bacon. "How about you answer my last question. About the threat."

Amanda shrugged. "Well, if there *is* a threat, it's obviously not that big of a deal. I'm not doing any monster-hunting."

"You're at least learning stuff that'll help you with that, right?" Jackson asked as he crammed a strip of bacon into his mouth and dropped another handful onto his plate.

"I don't think analyzing Keloton urine samples is gonna help me fight anything."

"Ew." Grace grimaced at her plate. "Can we *not* go there before breakfast?"

Amanda shrugged. "He asked."

"Well, I guess that's what internships are about, right?" Grace stopped at the drink stand to pour herself a tall glass of orange juice. "You work a bunch for free, find out everything there is to know about what goes on behind the scenes, then you work your way up."

"I don't think it's supposed to work that way when they're the ones who wanted *me* there," Amanda muttered. "Maybe if I was dying to get a job and wanted to get in however I could. That's not what happened though..." She stopped feet from their usual table and blinked wearily at Summer and Alex already sitting there together and munching happily away on their breakfast. "How long have you guys been out here?"

"Longer than you, shifter girl." Summer ripped a big bite out of her cinnamon roll. "You look like crap."

"Thanks."

"Fight any monsters?" Alex asked, his voice echoing up from his plastic cup before he chugged his juice.

"No. No monsters. No fighting. No energy for Twenty Questions, okay?" Amanda sighed and poked at her eggs scrambled with the perfect amount of cheese. "I can't believe I agreed to this."

"Don't worry." Grace grinned at her. "I'm sure it'll get better."

"Or worse," Summer added with a snort.

"Not helping." Amanda took a sip of her orange juice and somehow managed to spill more of it down the front of her shirt than she got in her mouth. "Aw, *man…*"

"Wow." Summer popped a grape into her mouth and stared at her friend with wide eyes. "They did work you hard."

Everyone else around the table laughed, and Amanda couldn't help but join them as Grace offered her a handful of extra napkins to clean herself up.

The next few weeks flew by in a blur. Amanda could hardly keep her head on straight between classes and long weekends spent in the Canissphere. It didn't help that she'd learned everything there was to learn about the Spinebacks' mating rituals and the exact temperatures required at every minute of every day to ensure the Harkliss didn't molt prematurely. Somehow, she still slid by with passing grades in her classes, and the DarkSkull and Angler's Root were growing nicely in the greenhouse. Every weekend, she filled another few burlap sacks with the harvest from the plants the Coalition had specifically requested. Sometimes, Fiona handed them off to Lucy when they got to the lab. Other times, she took the bags with her after wishing Amanda good luck for two long days of being an overnight intern. At least the shifter woman got them into the dome on time every Saturday morning after the first weekend of *unacceptable tardiness*.

When it came time for the first round of Petrov's Bag the Bounty to end, Amanda had forgotten about the assignment altogether. Grace had to explain it all on their way to the training building in a low voice. "Don't worry about it. It's taken care of."

"We didn't get the keychain."

The blonde witch waggled her eyebrows. "Oh yeah, we did. You simply weren't with us when it happened."

Three of the four teams managed to apprehend their target and retrieve the artifact on their assignment sheet.

"Points all around," Petrov said blandly, twirling an unenthusiastic finger in the air before pointing at Team Two. "Except for you guys. At least you're still at zero. Better luck this time."

Team Two groaned, then Petrov went around the mats to deliver the next assignments for the game.

Amanda didn't even try to read the information on their sheet before the teacher burned it for them. She could hardly stay on her feet.

If they need my help, Grace'll tell me what to do. Maybe they won't need me at all.

The Saturday morning before Homecoming week, Amanda wasn't even thinking about the dance until Grace brought it up at breakfast. "They're not gonna make you work next weekend, right?"

"Why?"

"Um...Homecoming? The dance? An integral part of the high school experience?"

Summer snorted. "If you're into that kinda thing."

Grace tossed a grape at the other witch's forehead, and they both laughed when it bounced back down onto Summer's plate. She picked it up and popped it into her mouth.

"I *am* into that kinda thing," Grace said. "You guys are too. I thought Glasket said this internship thing wouldn't interfere with school."

"She said it wouldn't interfere with classes."

"Well, she should include school dances on that list." Grace folded her arms. "It's not fair to you to make you miss out on it. Especially if they're not paying you to do a bunch of menial work you shouldn't have to do in the first place."

As it turned out, Amanda got a surprise visit in the greenhouse that week from Fiona, who laughed when she took in the sight of the shifter girl's shirt covered in dirt, with larger clumps of earth and a few plant clippings clinging to her hair. "Fell asleep in the garden, huh?"

"What?" Amanda brushed off herself off as best she could, then finally gave up. "I was taking a little nap."

"Uh-huh. I hope it was by these DarkSkull and not the Underweaver."

"I'm tired, Fiona. Not completely stupid."

"Well, buck up, buttercup." The red-haired woman clapped her hands together, then shot Amanda the guns with both pointer fingers. "You're getting a break."

"Right."

"No, I'm serious. Dr. Caniss doesn't want you killing yourself for this internship, and I might've heard a little birdie talking about how your principal insisted you got to go to this Homecoming dance. So you're free for a weekend. Tada!"

Amanda perked up although she still frowned at her mentor. "I can't tell if you're serious or messing with me."

"Aw, come on. I'm looking out for you too, kid. No jokes. No pranks. Enjoy your weekend off." Without another word, Fiona slipped into the hallway and disappeared.

Amanda grinned.

I can't believe I'm this excited about a school dance. I won't have to wear gloves or aprons or write down scientist notes with the stub of a pencil. Even when they have tablets lying around everywhere...

The entire student body buzzed with excitement the morning of the Homecoming Louper game that Friday. The last thing Amanda wanted to do with her first real Friday of freedom—and no internship the next day—was to sit around with a bunch of screaming students to watch a game she wanted to play but couldn't. So she found Summer after dinner and figured that was the best place to start. "Hey. You busy?"

Summer kicked herself away from the outer wall of the girl's dorm and spread her arms. "What does it look like?"

"Honestly, it looks like you've been standing against that wall since you left the cafeteria. Did I interrupt some serious thinking?"

The witch snorted. "Come on, shifter girl. You know I don't do that."

"Right. You do first, then *maybe* think about it later." Amanda laughed and nodded toward the northeast edge of campus. "Wanna go to the kemana?"

"And listen to you complain the whole time about how tired you'll be in the morning before going to scientist school? No thanks."

"Well, good thing I can promise that won't happen." Amanda grinned. "I have the weekend off."

"No kidding."

"Yeah. Grace was right, apparently. Nobody wants me to miss out on an *integral part of the high school experience.*"

Shoving her hands into the pockets of her hoodie, Summer smirked at the other girl and headed toward the edge of campus where they'd find the airboats. "Well lucky you."

MARTHA CARR & MICHAEL ANDERLE

"Yeah, I guess. Hey, let's pretend I don't have anything to do with the Coalition or scientists or that I ever leave campus for anything else, okay? If I'm not going out to the Canissphere for a whole weekend, I don't even wanna *hear* the word intern—"

"Canissphere?"

"Oh. Yeah, they call it that. You know, behind Dr. Caniss' back."

Summer burst out laughing. "You have some seriously weird friends, shifter girl."

"They're not really friends. I mean, some of them are cool. At least the ones I work with. Half the shifters there don't pay attention to me at all. The other half... I don't know. It feels like they think I shouldn't be there. Maybe it's because they keep making jokes about how young I am when they think I can't hear."

"Ha. Screw them. It's not like you've never been made fun of before."

"Yeah, thanks. A couple of school bullies and grown adults making fun of me are totally the same things."

Summer raised an eyebrow. "I thought you didn't wanna talk about your non-paying job."

"Right. No, I definitely don't. Feel free to hit me if I bring it up again, okay?"

"Ooh, yeah. I'm *really* gonna hold you to that one, shifter girl."

The following morning, the excitement levels for the Homecoming dance had skyrocketed. Everyone seemed to feel it except for Grace. She stalked across the outdoor cafeteria during breakfast and didn't bother getting in line before heading right toward their usual table.

"Uh-oh." Jackson hunched his shoulders and stared at the angry blonde witch coming their way. "Somebody's gonna get it."

"What'd you do, Rainbow?" Alex muttered.

"You know, you're the second person to call me that." Summer grinned at him. "I kinda like it. Maybe I won't change my hair again."

"Cool." He returned nonchalantly to his pancakes.

"Seriously, though," Jackson whispered. "What did you *do?*"

"Nothing." Summer laughed at him. "Why does it always have to be me?"

"Hey, Grace." Amanda plastered on a huge smile. "Excited for the dance?"

The blonde witch stopped in front of the table and folded her arms. "I don't wanna talk about that right now."

"So...maybe you don't wanna talk at all?" Jackson muttered, shrinking away from her despite her glare targeting Summer and Amanda. "It's totally cool if—"

"Can I talk to you guys for a minute?"

Amanda and Summer exchanged a curious glance. "Sure. What's up?"

"No, I mean the two of you. Alone. Real quick."

Summer clicked her tongue through a mocking grimace. "I dunno, Blondie. Your face right now doesn't say, 'This'll be a fun chat.'"

"That's because this is important, okay?" Grace spat. "Come on." She spun and headed for the edge of the cafeteria.

"You should go talk to her," Jackson said. "It'll get worse if you don't."

"Yeah." Amanda stood. "Come on, Summer."

"What? I'm still eating."

"You can finish after we hear whatever she has to say." Amanda grabbed her friend's arm and hauled her away from the picnic bench.

"Aw, come on. I'll lose my appetite." Laughing, Summer let Amanda drag her away and pointed at the guys. "Either of you touches my food, I'll take your hand off."

Jackson lifted both hands in concession.

Alex reached across the table and took a strip of bacon from her plate.

"Hey! You don't think I'll do it—"

"Get more later," Amanda whispered and tugged Summer's arm again. "I'm a little more worried about Grace right now than how much bacon you did or didn't get to eat."

"Ugh."

They reached Grace, who still stood with her arms folded as she tapped a toe against the grass.

Summer looked down at the other witch's foot and smirked. "Feelin' a little antsy?"

"Where were you two last night?"

"Uh…what?"

Amanda shrugged. "What happened?"

"I couldn't find you anywhere. That's what happened. Jenny Tanden said she saw you guys by the dorms, but you weren't there. Trust me. I looked *all over campus*."

"Whoa, Grace. Okay." Amanda tried to smile, but it was way too hard with the blonde witch scowling at them like that. "We went to the kemana."

"Really?" Grace stared at Summer. "Is that where you went?"

"Like she said, Blondie. Kemana time." Summer crossed her finger over her heart in an X. "No, we didn't blow anything up or steal anything or get kicked out of anywhere. Promise."

Grace's jaw clenched furiously over and over, and her foot wouldn't stop tapping. "So you guys decided to have a girls' night out without me, huh?"

Summer laughed and rolled her eyes. "*That's* what this is about? You didn't get invited on the airboat, so you have to call a meeting about it?"

"No. This isn't a meeting." The blonde witch tightly shook her head and blinked in surprise. "This is… This is me telling you guys that next time you go, I wanna come with you. To hang out. You know, have fun or whatever."

"Uh-huh." Summer pointed at her. "You wanna get your hands on more of that HardPull. I see what your game is—"

"Stop." Grace smacked her hand away, then stared at it like she couldn't believe what she'd done. "Sorry."

"Hey, it's cool, Blondie. Honestly, I didn't think you had it in you. You hit harder than I thought."

"Thanks. I guess." Grace's scowl finally softened into a timid smile. "Yeah. Fine. I wanna hang out with you guys in the kemana and maybe drink a whole case of HardPull, okay? So...don't leave me out next time."

"Sorry, Grace." Amanda shrugged. "I assumed you wouldn't want to come with us."

"Well it's a good thing I'm telling you now. So we're all on the same page."

"Yeah." Summer looked incredibly confused as she eyed Grace up and down. "Yeah, we'll tell you next time. Hey, if you can hit like that again, maybe you should—"

"I'm not hitting anybody else simply because you think it's funny," Grace snapped. Then her smile widened a little, and she added, "Only you."

Summer burst out laughing and tossed the other witch a middle finger as she headed back toward the table to finish her breakfast.

Amanda expected another fight to break out after that, but Grace surprised her by laughing too. "Huh. You guys seem to be...friendlier."

"Yeah, well, with you gone every weekend, I've been stuck here with Summer."

"You have lots of other friends."

Grace quickly looked away from the shifter girl and folded her arms again. "I'm doing what you said, Amanda, okay? I'm making an effort."

Amanda grinned. "Looks like it's paying off."

"Maybe. Jury's still out on that one. Hey, do you have something to wear for the dance?"

"Yeah." Amanda gestured with both hands toward her clothes. "Probably something like this."

Grace looked her up and down, and her nostrils flared. "Again? You're joking, right?"

CHAPTER NINETEEN

The Academy faculty didn't disappoint with this year's Home-coming dance. When the shimmering veil beneath the archway finally opened to allow the students through, Amanda could have sworn she was walking into a different world.

An impressive light show cast glittering orbs all over the dancefloor, making them race across the stand-in "ceiling" where more of the same spheres floated in the skylight glowing bubbles. Tall standing mirrors—the kind that floated two inches above the ground without needing a stand— bordered all the edges of the dancefloor. With the lifelike tree props placed in front of every mirror, it looked like the students had stepped into a clearing in the middle of woods somewhere. Purple mist curled across the ground from at least six different fake hedges scattered around the dancefloor, and every time a spinning bubble of light crossed the fog, it left a trail of bright yellow in its wake.

"This is definitely something different," Grace muttered as they passed the tables inside the archway, which had been laid out with a swath of masquerade masks all made to look like different animals.

"Totally cool," Amanda whispered, then saw the masks and

pointed at the table. "Except for those. I've seen way too many animals in the last month. I'm over their faces."

"Even if it's your friend's face?"

The girls leapt away from Jackson, who'd already put on one of the glittering, stylized bear masks and had snuck up behind them.

"Jackson!" Grace punched him in the shoulder, then instantly looked horrified. "Wait, you *are* Jackson, right?"

He laughed and peeled the mask up over his face to waggle his eyebrows. "I like this thing. You couldn't even tell it was me."

"She would've punched you anyway," Summer said as she studied a bird-shaped mask. "If you ask me, Blondie should hit people more often. Get out all that pent-up frustration."

"Yeah, well, nobody asked you."

"You're cooler after you hit somebody, though." Summer strapped on the bird mask, cocked her head, then squawked madly and flapped her arms as she raced toward Amanda and her friends.

Grace shrieked and stepped out of the way before shoving Summer in the back. The other witch stumbled forward and spun with her bird-mask askew. Amanda and Jackson cracked up.

"Come on, Blondie! Is that the best you've got?"

"Hey, I already knocked your head sideways. You don't want me to take it *off*."

Summer pulled up her mask and grinned. "I'd like to see you try."

"'Sup?" Everyone turned to see a frog mask with comically huge eyes staring at them.

Amanda tilted her head and glimpsed a long dark ponytail dangling behind the mask. "Alex?"

"Ribbit."

"Dude." Jackson snorted out a laugh and punched the Wood

Elf in the arm. "You get one ribbit all night. Anything after that is just asking for it."

"Ribbit." Alex took off running across the dancefloor as Jackson lunged after him, both of them laughing like idiots until they got to the refreshments table.

"Juniors." Grace shook her head. "We're *juniors*. How have they not matured at all since freshman year?"

"Blame the Y chromosome, Blondie." Summer handed Grace a butterfly mask.

"Actually, that's… Yeah, that's exactly why."

"Oh, shit! Check it out!" Summer grabbed another mask and headed toward Amanda. "Whoever made these things has a serious sense of humor."

Amanda took the mask and turned it over to study the swirling lines of gold and silver across the wolf face. "Very funny. Now I won't be the only wolf tonight."

Grace backed away from two more kids in frog masks—who were immediately recognizable as Tommy Brunsen and Evan Hutchinson when they both squatted in the grass and started a game of actual leapfrog across the dancefloor guffawing the whole time. "Okay, I have to remind myself not to hit *every* bear thinking it's Jackson."

"No, that's the hilarious part." Summer pointed at the table. "Only one wolf."

"Seriously?" Amanda scanned the table, which had zero other wolf masks, and didn't see a single one that matched hers on the faces of the other students milling around. "Oh, come on. I'm not wearing the only one."

"Cool. I'll take it." Summer ripped off her bird mask and held it out for a swap.

"Okay… Just be careful." Amanda laughed and strapped on the bird mask as Summer fumbled with the wolf. "Everyone's gonna think you're me."

"You think I wouldn't switch places with you for a day, shifter girl?"

Grace barked out a laugh. "I *know* you wouldn't."

"Hey…"

"Nothing against you, Amanda." The blonde witch batted her eyelashes from behind the glittering blue butterfly mask. "Summer's too in love with herself."

"You're funny." Summer pointed at Grace and tilted her wolfy head. "Not, like, hilarious. But decently funny."

"Yeah, yeah."

Glasket took the stage, dressed up in a ballgown of light green at the top that blended into blue, then purple, then dark indigo at the bottom. Before she said anything into the floating microphone by her face, she slipped on her mask and spread her arms to address the student body. "Welcome to your Homecoming dance!"

The kids on the dancefloor cheered.

Summer snickered and elbowed Amanda in the ribs. "Hey, check out Principal Peacock."

"At least *she* had a chance to match her outfit to her mask," Grace muttered.

"Only you would be disappointed by that, Blondie."

"Tonight," Glasket continued, "we're celebrating our Louper team and their win by a landslide against the Philadelphia Coyotes last night."

"Gators! Gators! Gators!"

The chant picked up for ten seconds but slowly died again.

"Yes, the Florida Gators are moving up on the Louper roster. We might have a shot at winning the championship this year."

"Not if we don't make it that far," someone shouted.

Glasket cleared her throat as the kids up front by the stage broke into laughter. "I hope the rest of you aren't as pessimistic as Mr. Harland. Tonight, though, I hope you all enjoy yourselves. A special thank you to Mr. Frederick for making these incredible masquerade masks."

She gestured toward the group of teachers beside the stage, each of whom wore a different mask as well. Next to them, the slightly hunched man in a dress suit and wearing a comically elongated alligator mask pressed a hand against his heart and looked up at the principal as all the students clapped and cheered. When he removed the mask, everyone saw Shep's humble, gap-toothed grin clear across the dancefloor.

"Mr. Frederick made these?" Grace said through a laugh. "Wow. Who knew he liked arts and crafts?"

Amanda turned toward Summer. "Well, now I know why there's only one wolf mask. Give it."

"No way, shifter girl."

"Summer, come on. That one's obviously mine."

The witch in the wolf mask leapt away, throwing up both hands in the shape of claws. "I'm keeping it. Don't make me tear you apart!"

"Hey!" Amanda lunged after her friend, but Summer darted off into the crowd with a wild cackle. The students closer to her spun and quickly backed away to let her through.

"Oh my God." Grace shook her head. "Maybe she *would* trade places with you for a day."

"Yeah, only to get me into as much trouble as possible before leaving me to clean up the mess." They laughed, then Annabelle and Margaret shouted Grace's name and headed toward her, waving their hands.

"I'm gonna go get some snacks, I guess." Amanda headed toward the refreshments table. "You want anything?"

"Maybe later."

As Grace and the other junior girls fawned over Shep's masks and the real dance music finally started, Amanda bobbed and danced her way to the refreshments table. The kitchen pixies had added to the school spirit in perfect form—they'd even shaped the desserts like wild animals.

She laughed and grabbed a frosted cookie shaped like a wild boar before crunching into it. On the dancefloor, the kids moved around in a blur of sparkling masks and streams of yellow light across the purple mist. Half of them danced to the music, while the other half messed around and acted like the animal portrayed by their mask.

"Talk about party animals, right?" Jackson asked.

Amanda laughed, completely thrown off-guard when she looked up to see a sequined bear mask instead of his face. "Totally."

The current song ended, and something a lot slower and more suggestive for partnered dancing took its place. A group of freshmen boys groaned, but most of the upperclassmen paired off for slow dances. Amanda lifted her bird mask to shove the rest of the cookie into her mouth and didn't look at Jackson again.

He leaned toward her and cleared his throat. "Think she'd say yes this time?"

"Uh…who?"

"Come on, Summer. Just give it to me straight. I'm dying over here."

She froze. *Did he call me Summer? Oh, no. We switched masks.*

"Hello?" He waved a hand in front of her face and let out a nervous laugh. "Don't be like that. I know you don't wanna hear it, but I'm kinda—"

"Jackson, stop." Grimacing, Amanda whipped off the bird mask and looked up at him.

He lowered his hand immediately and stepped away, standing rigidly behind the refreshments table. All she could see of him were his wide eyes behind the bear mask, but she had no problem imagining the deep flush that had no doubt taken over his entire face by now.

"What…"

She shrugged. "Summer wanted to be a wolf for a night. Didn't think it would confuse anybody."

"Oh, man…"

"Sorry."

"For what? I'm the idiot over here." Jackson tugged off his mask and tossed it onto the refreshment table. It landed in the punchbowl filled with HardPull, and she couldn't help but laugh as he jumped to retrieve it and shake off the school-sanctioned drink. "See what I mean? Complete idiot. Don't tell Mr. Frederick I drowned his bear in the punch, okay?"

"Honestly, I think he'd appreciate the artistic license." They both studied the bear mask beaded with drops of HardPull; the lines that made it look like a bear in the first place were now blurred and smudged, drooping down toward the bottom edge.

"I think my mask had a stroke." With a nervous laugh, Jackson chucked the thing over his shoulder onto the grass, then ran a hand through his hair. "So, uh… You know, normally, I'd say—"

"Just forget about it, right?" Amanda shrugged and looked away at the sea of students slow-dancing in couples. "Yeah, already done. I didn't hear a thing."

"Actually, I—" He cleared his throat. "I was gonna say screw it and ask you to dance with me anyway."

When he didn't say anything else, Amanda slowly looked up at him and found a sheepish smile on the wizard's face despite what probably was his telltale blush. "For real?"

"Yeah. I mean, unless you think it's the worst idea I've ever had. Then again, even if you did, I'd probably still ask you."

"Um…okay."

"Yeah? Really?" He laughed at himself and puffed out a sigh. "I'm gonna stop talking so we can…you know…"

She froze when he slowly took her hand, but she didn't pull away. In fact, she let him pull her toward the dance floor, her legs feeling suddenly numb and her gut clenching in a way she wished more than anything would stop already.

I can't believe I said I'd dance with him. What am I doing? This is Jackson, and he doesn't... Does he? Do I?

Amanda shook her head when they stopped on the dance-floor, and Jackson wrinkled his nose above another sheepish smile.

"Everything okay?"

"What? Yeah. Fine. We're dancing. At a dance. With other people dancing."

He stepped toward her but didn't start the dancing part. "You don't have to stay stuff like that to make me feel better. I'm already bad at this."

"Psst." Amanda looked over her shoulder to see Grace with her butterfly mask up, her arms resting over the shoulders of some kid with a frog mask. The blonde witch grinned, then shot a pointed look at her arms.

Yeah, Grace. I know how this works, thanks.

"Who's that?" Amanda asked instead.

"Ribbit."

"Dude." Jackson punched Alex in the shoulder as he and Grace laughed and danced away. "We got a serious frog problem, huh?"

"You know, some birds eat frogs." Amanda slid the bird mask down over her face. "Want me to kick his—"

"Don't." He lifted her mask again, then tossed it like a frisbee toward the refreshments table, barely missing the head of a kid standing there in a gopher mask. Then he set his hands on Amanda's hips and gently pulled her closer. "I kinda just wanna dance with you. Not a bird. You know, if it's all the same to you."

"Well, I don't have a mask anymore so... Right. Yeah." For a minute, she'd completely forgotten what she was supposed to do with her hands. Then she spotted Grace and a masked Alex over Jackson's shoulder, and her friend gave her another wide-eyed reminder. Amanda looked quickly away and reached up to drape her arms over Jackson's shoulders.

So weird, so weird, so weird. What am I doing?

He laughed and leaned closer as they swayed back and forth. "You sure you're okay? Like, we can stop if you—"

"No, I'm good," she blurted and instantly wished she hadn't.

Now he's gonna think I want to dance with him. Like this. And I'm not even sure I don't.

When she looked up at him again, Jackson was grinning.

"Okay."

"Okay." She nodded and tried to look everywhere but at his face.

I have no idea what I'm doing.

Summer's wild laugh came from their right, followed by a curdling howl as the witch spread her arms and tossed her head back to aim her awful impersonation at the moon.

"Summer, cut it out!" Grace hissed, slapping the other witch's arm.

"Hey, I'm getting in touch with my wild side." Summer let out another warbling howl, and the kids around them laughed and joined in.

Jackson raised his eyebrows in question, and when Amanda didn't do or say anything, he released her to throw his head back too and join in the noise.

The absence of his hands on her hips made her pause because she couldn't quite wrap her head around the idea that she didn't necessarily want him to let go.

"Hey, shifter girl, check it out." Summer elbowed her in the ribs and laughed. "Guess you're not the only wolf at the party after all."

Amanda shoved her friend away, then tossed her head back and howled with the other kids around her.

At least I don't have to pretend to be a bird.

CHAPTER TWENTY

Amanda didn't precisely avoid Jackson for the rest of the weekend and into the following week, but she didn't go out of her way to talk to him, either. By Wednesday, she was starting to feel like she'd lost her mind.

Apparently, everyone noticed.

"Okay, what crawled up *your* butt?" Summer asked as they headed away from the outdoor cafeteria after dinner.

"Dunno." Amanda glared at her. "I'm not really in the habit of checking. Could be anything."

Summer cracked up and shook her head. "You got it bad, shifter girl."

"What? Unknown-butt syndrome?" Amanda couldn't help but laugh at that.

"So you danced with Romeo for half a song. Big deal."

"No, that's not—"

"Not gonna fly with me, shifter girl. You're freaking out about it, and you aren't exactly great at hiding, like, any of your emotions."

"Oh, because you *are*?"

Summer rolled her eyes. "Look. If you don't quit acting like he has cooties, I'm gonna lock you two up in a room together and force you to figure it out, okay?"

"That's the last thing I need."

"Well, I obviously won't be doing it for *you*." Summer glanced over her shoulder, but Grace and the guys were still sitting at the table finishing their dinner. "Seriously. It's been nonstop with that guy for the last four days. He keeps asking me if you've said anything about him, blah, blah, blah. So my options here are either lock you guys in a room or knock his mouth off his face so he'll stop *talking* about it."

"Wait, he's talking about me?"

"It's nothing new, shifter girl. Two whole years of this already, and you still haven't noticed?"

"He's been talking to *you* about *me* since freshman year?"

"Okay. You know, for a shifter, you have a serious lack of awareness about this. Are you telling me you can't smell it on him?"

"*What?*"

Summer clamped her hands together under her chin and leaned toward Amanda, grinning and batting her lashes like a lunatic. "Love, shifter girl."

"Don't." Amanda shoved her away and tucked her hair behind one ear.

"Or whatever he wants to call it. So you gotta do something about it."

"What am I supposed to do, huh? I don't even know—"

"Look, you only have two options. One, admit you like him and tell him. Then he can talk to *you* about it, and I won't feel like I wanna cut my ears off all the time. Or two, put him out of his misery. Either way has the same effect."

Amanda stopped and stared at her friend. "No. Those two things definitely do *not* have the same outcome."

"Yeah, I meant for me. For the love of...of... Shit, shifter girl.

Don't leave everybody in this limbo, okay? I can't take it anymore."

"For the love of—"

"Yeah, I couldn't think of anything to say."

Amanda snorted. "I'm not gonna make a decision about Jackson because you want me to. There isn't even a decision to make. And don't say I'm leaving *everybody* in limbo. That's not even real."

Summer raised an eyebrow. "Wanna bet?"

"It has nothing to do with anyone else."

"Hmm. Maybe talk to Blondie and Woody about it. Tell them to be *really* honest with you. If they tell you Romeo's pining for you isn't affecting their quality of life, I'll dance on the freaking table. In front of everyone."

"Okay, stop."

"As long as you hurry up and do something."

"There's nothing to *do*, Summer!" Amanda tried to smile at the freshmen passing them in the central field and shooting her weird looks, and she lowered her voice. "Like you said. It was a dance at a dance. Or whatever. Not a big deal. So drop it, okay?"

Summer shrugged. "If you say so. Clock's ticking, though."

"Oh, yeah? Ticking down to what?"

"Somebody jumping your loverboy 'cause he won't *shut up* about you."

Amanda shoved the other girl away with both arms, and Summer stumbled wildly sideways across the grass with one of her off-putting cackles. "Change the subject."

"Yeah, yeah, fine. Okay. So when's the wedding?"

"Summer!"

The witch leapt away fast enough this time to avoid being pushed by a tiny shifter girl who was way stronger than she looked. "Okay. I'm done, I'm done."

"You better be."

"Hey, Scout's honor." Summer gave her a thumbs-up. "So, wanna go back to the kemana this weekend?"

"Can't." Amanda pulled her hair back into a ponytail and tied it off with the hair tie around her wrist. "I'm going back to Omega Industries."

"Really? One weekend's all you get?"

"Apparently, yeah." She shrugged. "So unless there's another dance or super important *school function*, and there's not, my weekends are gone again."

"Bummer." Summer bit her lip and frowned at the grass as they walked aimlessly across the field. "Hey, you think Blondie would go with me?"

"As long as you don't try to steal anything, blow anything up, or get kicked out of at least one shop, then yeah. Probably. Oh, hey. You guys could have a *girl's night out* for the two of you."

The witch wrinkled her nose. "I'm really glad I cut off all my hair."

Amanda laughed. "What?"

"She'd probably wanna braid it next. Ugh."

That night, Amanda was once again unable to get to sleep. So she snuck out of the girls' dorm and figured a regular walk on two legs would do her some good. By the time she got out to the tall stand of cattails where she usually hid her clothes after a shift, going for a run on four legs seemed like a much better idea.

Run it all off. That's what I need. Forget about Jackson and school and the Canissphere. Let it all—

A loud cry of surprise came from behind the boys' dorm before it cut off abruptly.

Amanda turned to scan the dark campus, sniffed the air, and took another minute to listen. The only sounds came from the crickets and buzzing cicadas, plus the occasional *plop* in the water as the swamp's nocturnal wildlife moved around. Then she heard another strangled cry, this one muffled but definitely from the same voice.

That doesn't sound good.

She headed away from the cattails, moving silently across the grass toward the boys' dorm on the other side of the girls'. The sounds of a struggle grew clearer and louder. Then low voices reached her across the open campus grounds.

"Shh! Hold him down already."

"I *can't*. He's—ow! Hey, man. It's not personal or anything."

"You think I'm gonna let you take it? Get off."

"Get—stop *fighting*. This is how it's supposed to go. We caught you, okay? So give it up, and I'll get off your back!"

Amanda picked up the pace and darted around the back of the boys' dorm. There was no one there, but the voices, grunting, and the sound of a body hitting the grass came from the other side of the building. She sprinted around the next corner and stopped when she saw four junior boys crowded around a body in the grass. "Hey!"

Evan shrieked and leapt away. When he saw it was her, he heaved a sigh of relief and rolled his eyes. "Jesus, Amanda. You almost made me crap my pants."

"Get off him." She tried to see who they'd pinned down on the ground, but Brandon Everly had his knee on the other kid's lower back, and the rest of the Crystal's huge body blocked whoever it was from view. "Right now."

"Get lost," Jack snapped. "It's none of your business—"

"I said get *off* him." Amanda charged forward and shoved Brandon in the shoulder with both hands. He flew sideways and landed on his opposite shoulder with a *thump*.

"What the hell was *that* for?"

"Yeah, you're not even on our team," Evan hissed.

"I don't know what the hell you're talking about," she snarled, her skin prickling with the tingle of her magic before a shift, "but

I'm pretty sure four against one is a good enough reason for me to step in."

"Here, man." With a grunt, the kid who Brandon's weight had almost squashed pushed himself calmly to his feet and held out a large gold coin toward Jack. "Take it. You would've gotten it anyway."

"Alex?" Amanda stepped back and frowned. "What—"

"Naw, dude." Jack waved away the coin in the Wood Elf's hand. "We're supposed to *get* it from you."

"Yeah, well, if you kept trying to pat me down for it, she would've ripped your head off." He nodded toward Amanda and shook the coin. "Take it."

"Fine." Jack snatched it up and stuck it in his pocket.

"What's going on?" Amanda asked, only now realizing she'd been clenching her hands into fists. She slowly released them but eyed each of the boys throwing her dirty looks.

With a sigh, Alex offered Brandon a hand up, which the Crystal kid took without a word. "It's for the Bag the Bounty, Amanda. I had the artifact, and they found me."

"Yeah, and we would've gotten it from him too," Evan added. "I think. Dude, you're way stronger than you look."

Alex nodded at the kid and shoved his hands into the pockets of his jeans. "Word."

Amanda finally realized nothing was going on here that anyone needed to stop in the first place, and she shook her head. "Sorry. I just... I mean, I heard yelling, and it sounded like someone was getting beaten up, so I—"

"You thought you'd come in and save the day, huh? Yeah, we get it." Evan snickered. "Of course it'd be *you* finding us out here."

"I wasn't gonna hurt him," Brandon said.

"Yeah. No, I realize that."

Tony stepped toward her with a scowl and didn't stop until he only two feet away. "You better not tell anyone about this."

She laughed. "What?"

"You know the rules. If Petrov finds out you saw us, we get negative points. If *that* happens, we'll know who ratted us out."

Folding her arms, Amanda plastered a grin on her face and leaned toward him. "I'm not gonna tell. I get how the game works, Tony."

"You better not." He pointed at her face. "Or you'll be sorry."

Alex snickered and shook his head as he smoothed his long hair away from his face after the short-lived scuffle. "Dude, you're an idiot."

"I'm just saying—"

"Threatening the shifter girl? Really? What makes you think that'll work?"

Tony's eyes widened, and he stepped slowly backward away from Amanda, still pointing at her. "It's not a threat. But if you tell anyone, I'll know—"

"I literally have no reason to tell anyone." She smirked. "You guys are losing anyway."

"Not after this round."

"Not ever if you keep making so much noise about it."

"Yeah, she's right, dude." Evan thumped Tony on the back and peered around the corner of the boys' dorm. "We got the coin. Time to split."

"Right. Back inside." As the four boys from Team Two headed toward the back door of the dorms, Tony turned to glare at Amanda again, stuck two fingers toward his own eyes, then pointed at her. "I'm watching you."

She laughed and spread her arms. "Great. Have fun."

He looked at Alex, jerked his chin up at the Wood Elf, then slipped through the back door of the boys' dorm before it closed completely.

"Total idiot," Alex muttered, swiping grass and dirt off his clothes. "Even if you hadn't shown up, he still would've botched the whole thing."

"You okay?"

"All good." He swiped his foot across the patch of grass where Brandon had taken him to the ground. Now that she was looking at it, Amanda saw the very Alex-shaped outline in the smooshed grass and even the dirt beneath it. "They thought they were all badass. I learned this spell that makes the ground all soft, though. Kinda like putty. It was actually pretty comfy."

She laughed and folded her arms. "It sounded like they were hurting you."

"Yeah, well, they're losing. Figured I'd at least help them *feel* like they earned it, you know? I'm good." Alex shot her two thumbs-up and nodded. "Now I'm going to bed."

"Wait, did you come out here so they could—"

He snickered. "Yeah. Literally walked right past Tony's door about twenty minutes ago. They were talking about how they were gonna jump me tomorrow morning after breakfast. So I made sure they saw me come outside. I wanted to get it over and done with, you know? Good night."

"'Night, Alex." She forced back another laugh as the Wood Elf slipped through the back door of the dorms after his Bag the Bounty attackers and shook her head.

Is that what I do? Try to step in and save the day all the time?

Turning slowly around to head back across the field, she shoved her hands in the pockets of her black zip-up hoodie and huffed out a laugh.

I guess it is. I'd take a fake fight over a real one any day, though.

CHAPTER TWENTY-ONE

Fiona showed up in the outdoor cafeteria bright and early that Saturday morning. Amanda was one of four upperclassmen who'd made it out to the picnic tables before 6:30 a.m., and she was ready to go with a new batch of harvested magical plants for the Coalition, and her duffel bag packed and beside her.

"Looks like a week off did you some good, kid."

"I guess." Amanda handed the sacks over to her mentor, then slung her duffel bag over her shoulder. "I mean, not that I don't appreciate the weekend off. It just...wasn't exactly what I expected."

"Oh, yeah?" Fiona eyed the other upperclassmen staring at their breakfasts far more than actually eating it and chuckled. "How so?"

"It was Homecoming. What do *you* think?"

The shifter woman grabbed her arm and teleported them right out of the outdoor cafeteria without the other students noticing a thing.

Amanda sucked in a sharp breath when they landed in the Starbucks bathroom, but she'd been through this enough times by now to finally *not* fall over afterward.

"Ah." Fiona nodded as she headed for the bathroom door, continuing their conversation as if they hadn't made a forty-five-minute trip in half a second. "You hoped someone would ask you to the dance, and no one did. Yeah, that's a pretty normal let-down, kid. Sorry to hear it. You'll get your moment, though. Don't worry."

The girl stared at her mentor until the *squeak* of the bathroom door swinging shut snapped her out of her surprise. Then she hurried after Fiona and found her in front of the supply closet. "No, that's definitely not it."

"You don't have to pretend with me, kid. I remember what it's like to be in high school. Not exactly the best feeling when you get turned down for a dance."

"No, it was…kinda the opposite, actually."

They stepped into the supply closet, and Fiona shot her an amused look. "Oh, yeah? So you got asked by one of the nerdy kids, huh? Not really your type?"

Before Amanda could answer, the shifter woman jerked down on the brass lever, and the elevator dropped like a stone.

Bracing herself against the wall when they ground to a halt, Amanda puffed out a sigh and readjusted the strap of her duffel bag. "Wrong again."

"Well, then, enlighten me, huh? There are only so many depressing options I can run through before there's nothing…" Fiona stepped through the doors into the train car, paused, then turned with a grin. "Wait a minute. That wizard with the goofy smile asked you to the dance, didn't he?"

"Jackson. No, he didn't exactly—"

"Ha! I didn't think the little dude had it in him. How'd he do it? Was it super embarrassing?" Fiona sat on the red-upholstered bench and crossed one ankle over the opposite knee, gazing up at the ceiling in contemplation. "I kinda picture him as the bumbling type. You know, stumbling all over his words. It's pretty cute, actually."

"Nobody asked me to the dance," Amanda muttered as she plopped down on the opposite bench in the cabin. "He only asked me *to* dance."

"Huh. Okay. So let me guess. You said no, broke his heart, and now you wish you'd given him three minutes and forty-seven seconds of awkward swaying so you wouldn't have to see the damage on his face every time you close your eyes. Yeah, that's a whole different level of—"

"Fiona."

"Yeah."

"Just stop." Amanda gave her a grimacing smile and shook her head. "You're making it worse."

"Oh." The woman pursed her lips in mock surprise. "Sorry. I nailed it with that last guess, right? That's what happened?"

"Nope." Amanda closed her eyes and dropped her head back against the seat. "Forget I even said anything."

"Yeah, okay. Still, if you ever wanna talk about it, I'm here."

"And play 'guess Amanda's worst problems' again? No thanks."

Fiona chuckled. "Don't worry about it, kid. Whatever it is, you'll forget the whole thing once you get to work in..." She checked her watch and let out a satisfied hum. "About ten minutes. Good thing you have such a good distraction, huh?"

"Right. What would I ever *do* without the best internship in the world," Amanda replied flatly. When she opened her eyes again, the subdued smile on her mentor's face made her laugh. Then the overhead lights flickered, and the little *ding* filled the cabin before the robotic female voice.

Fiona waggled her eyebrows and grabbed on tight to the edge of the seat beneath her. "Here we go."

Fiona didn't stay long at the Canissphere after dropping Amanda off for the next two days. For the first time since she'd started this internship with the Coalition's best shifter scientists, Dr. Caniss summoned the girl into her office for a meeting.

The summons came through the woman's assistant Lucy, who knocked briskly on the door of the DNA analysis labs where Amanda was shadowing a gruff, silent shifter named Dr. Skeiner. He didn't say a word when he noticed Lucy but instead grunted at Amanda and nodded toward the assistant out in the hall.

"Yep." Amanda set down her safety goggles and took off her apron before hurrying out of the labs.

I'm glad he doesn't talk. Pretty sure the guy hates my guts, and I'd hate anything he had to say anyway.

"Hey, Lucy." She closed the door behind her and glanced up and down the hall. "What's going on?"

"I'm here to take you to Dr. Caniss' office. Right now."

"Okay, um… Does *he* know that?"

"All you need to worry about is following me closely, thank you." The woman turned sharply with a flick of her hair and walked purposefully down the hall.

Can't say no to that, can I?

As it turned out, Dr. Caniss' office was in the same hallway as the first room in which she'd locked Amanda for two hours for her first "test." Amanda chuckled when she glanced through the waiting room's open door and recognized it instantly. Her smile immediately faded when Lucy turned with a disapproving glance. "Sorry. Just…memories. You know?"

The woman blinked and knocked on the door three rooms down and across the hall.

"Enter," Dr. Caniss barked.

Lucy opened the door and stepped aside for Amanda to enter. She said nothing and hardly waited for the girl to step into the room before shutting the door again behind her.

Amanda stumbled forward and frowned over her shoulder at the door. "Thanks…"

"Have a seat, Amanda." Still poring over the papers scattered across her desk, Caniss gestured toward the area in front of her.

Amanda smirked. "I would, Dr. Caniss, but…there's nowhere to sit."

The biologist glanced sharply up at her, then down at the floor in front of her desk completely bereft of chairs, and finally straightened to sit back in her seat. "Then feel free to keep standing. I have some questions for you."

"Okay."

I guess she doesn't pull that many people into her office for a private chat. Lucky me.

"You've done exceptionally well over the last few months here. As a student, of course. I wouldn't dare compare you to the rest of the staff."

Amanda wrinkled her nose and decided against any kind of response to that.

"I find your one-on-one work with the subjects themselves impressive on a rudimentary level. They seem to respond well to your presence. What do you think?"

The girl shrugged. "I'm…doing my job, I guess."

"Yes. Would you say you've gotten to know these subjects fairly well?"

"I mean, sure. If they had names, we'd probably be on a first-name basis."

Dr. Caniss blinked and slowly removed her silver-framed glasses to set them on the desk.

Okay. Mental note—don't make jokes with the bigwig doctor in charge. Got it.

Amanda cleared her throat.

"I have to ask you now why you're doing this," Dr. Caniss said dryly.

"Why I'm doing what?"

"All this." The woman gestured around her office. "Why you're here. What you hope to achieve after learning everything there is to learn about what we do here at Omega Industries and why."

"Um…" Amanda frowned and huffed out an unsure laugh. "I'm here for this internship. Because the Coalition wants me on your team. Maybe *you* want me on your team, although that could go either way at this point."

Caniss looked her up and down. "Let me phrase this differently, Amanda. What motivates you to keep going and work these long days as a fourteen-year-old girl missing out on an entire high school experience? You clearly want something more out of this and aren't getting it. So *why* are you still here?"

The girl drew a deep breath and thought carefully about her next words.

This is one of those 'spill your guts' talks, isn't it? Just like Fiona wanted to drag the truth out of me last year.

"I'm here for the same reason I'm at the Academy," she finally replied.

"Hmm. Except we don't train bounty hunters here, and the Coalition of Shifters has no say in who the Academy's students become. I'm talking about all your work with us. With the Coalition. With Ms. Damascus. You grew a fully mature Fatethistle plant in less than half the natural timeline. Over the last year, you've pushed yourself to activate and gain mastery of your magic as a shifter. Now you're by far the youngest shifter employed at this facility. I believe someone twice your age previously held that position. I want to know what, in your mind, carries so much urgency. Why the rush?"

Amanda blinked. "I guess I'm impatient."

The biologist stared at her expressionlessly.

While she wondered whether or not Caniss would explode on her as she'd seen a handful of times over the last few weeks, the back of her mind picked up the very faint sounds of some creature struggling in a cage at least three corridors down from this one.

Doesn't matter. Someone else will handle it while she's interrogating me.

Caniss inhaled a sharp breath, returned to her work, and slid her glasses back on. "If you're going to give me nonsensical answers, Amanda, I see no reason to keep you here any longer. You've obviously finished."

A prickle of apprehension crept up the girl's spine—not from the doctor's words but something else. Something she could feel in the air.

Whatever that is, it's not right.

She strained to listen more intently to the snorting, snuffling noises of some angry mutated creature working itself up in one of the exam rooms. At least ten seconds must have gone by before Caniss cleared her throat and ripped Amanda from her concentration.

"I assume you're still here because you have something to say."

"Sorry. What was the question?"

"I asked you why you're in such a hurry to achieve all these things in record time, Amanda. If you have a different answer this time—a *genuine* answer—by all means, speak frankly. Otherwise, I'm quite finished with you."

How am I supposed to focus on this conversation when something's not right out there?

She balled her hands into fists and tried to drown out the sound from the exam room that would have taken her at least ten minutes to get to on foot. Caniss stared at her blankly and raised her eyebrows.

"You look ill." The woman straightened in her chair and tilted her head. "Are you ill? Honestly, it's so much easier to read a subject's levels of discomfort without all the nuances of facial expressions—"

"Someone murdered my whole family," Amanda said in a flat,

emotionless tone. "Right in front of me before they kidnapped me to sell as a kid-shifter slave. No one knows who did it. Still. That's the rush."

"Ah." Caniss sat fully back in her chair again and for the first time smiled fully at the young intern. "Now we're getting to the *real* heart of the matter. I'm aware of your past. I believe your future—"

A massive *crash* of heavy steel across the linoleum floor of the exam room filled the air, followed by an agonized scream that came from a shifter's mouth. Shifters also shouted and ran around outside in all three hallways between Caniss' office and the exam room in question. Amanda had no idea how she knew all of that at once, but she knew. She could feel it.

She didn't wait for Caniss to say anything else on the subject. The woman could have kept talking without hearing a thing for all she knew. It didn't matter.

Amanda's magic reacted on its own, without her having to think about it. The next thing she knew, she was running through the office wall, straight across three corridors, one right after the other, and into the exam room where the howling, screeching creature in question was officially out of control.

The thing was massive, the three straight vertical spikes at the top of its head scraping against the ceiling as it thrashed this way and that.

"How did it do that?" someone shouted.

"How the hell should *I* know? It's completely new."

"Great, we can add spontaneous tenfold growth to the list of new subject attributes *after* we get this thing contained."

Amanda and her ghost-wolf skidded to a halt on the linoleum floor so they could get a good look at the creature stomping around the room, crashing into the desks and the shelving units and the other cages as the creatures inside those squawked and growled and yapped in excitement.

Not excitement. They're as terrified as this other... What is that thing?

The massive creature bucking and thrashing around the room, stomping and snorting when any of the shifters got too close, looked like someone had spliced a squirrel and a rhino together and had spray-painted it blue.

"Hey!" One of the scientists reached out toward the creature with a long pole. A corded metal leash like animal control used to catch stray dogs dangled at its end. "Someone help me calm this thing down!"

"Oh, sure, Jim. As if we weren't already all thinking the same thing!"

"Just get it to stop—look out!"

The rhino-squirrel charged the shifter with the loop on a stick, and the guy threw himself against the wall to get out of the way.

They're scientists for crying out loud! They should be smarter than this!

With a silent snarl, Amanda scurried around the stampeding creature to get a better look at the damage it had already left behind. There was the broken cage where they'd held the thing before it ballooned into a giant and broke right through. The bars were bent and crooked, and the screws holding the cage together had completely stripped before toppling out of their places.

Lying at the bottom of the cage was a small nest made of rag strips, dried grass, and—strangely enough—the blue ribbon whoever did the laundry around here used to tie up the clean loads before delivering them to their final destination.

That's it.

Amanda and her ghost-wolf leapt toward the nest to take a quick sniff. The stench of fear and rage was overwhelming and would have stung her nostrils if she'd smelled it with an actual nose—wolf or girl. Beneath all that was another odor that took her a second to place.

There was an egg here? That thing lays eggs?

As soon as she had the thought, the rhino-squirrel thing crashed against the wall and almost knocked another creature's cage on its side before it turned to face her. When the thing's massive, bright-red eyes—normally beady and a dull crimson at the creature's regular and innocuously small size—fixed on the white ghost-wolf standing beside the broken cage and the empty nest, everything changed.

The creature let out a guttural roar that rattled the cages and sent the desperate scientists staggering across the room trembling beneath them. Those three vertical horns on its squirrel-shaped face crashed into the ceiling when the creature threw its head up and tried to rear back on its hind legs. Plaster rained down all around the beast, ripped wires in the ceiling threw hissing sparks all over the floor, and the rhino-squirrel finally ripped its head free before dipping it low and charging straight for Amanda.

"I know it's against protocol," one of the scientists shouted, "but maybe we should—"

"No! Stop it before it—"

The rampaging beast had no luck tossing Amanda's ghost-wolf across the room but instead stomped right *through* her before crashing against the back wall. The desk there exploded into fragments of wood and crushed computer components. The creature bellowed and pulled itself away from the giant dent in the crumbling wall, shaking its head and staggering under the blow.

"Hey. Hey!" Another scientist pointed at the white ghost-wolf leaping across the exam room. "She shouldn't be in here."

"Get out of here, girl. We'll handle it!"

Amanda ignored them all as she dodged the furious beast still trying to swat her away with its giant front hooves and scraping its head across the floor to catch her on its horns. Instead, it only managed to hook its horns through the bars of its ruptured cage, and now the *clang* of metal on horns and against the walls filled the room with the scientists' panicked shouts.

Where is it? Jeeze, you'd think it wouldn't be that hard to realize what's going on here. Come on...

The ghost-wolf leapt right through another cage in her way, startling the yellow tortoise-thing with long rabbit ears and whiskers, but she was following the scent. Then she found it.

Dropping to their belly, Amanda and her ghost-wolf stretched out their neck and gently grasped the small, bright-purple egg the size of an almond in their jaws. The long-eared tortoise growled when she half-phased through its cage again before leaping across the room in a long arc toward the rhino-squirrel's open and empty nest.

Oh, sure. Out of everything that gets smashed to bits in this place, the nest *is still in one piece.*

She dropped the tiny egg into the circle of rags and grass and ribbon, then lunged for the destructive beast still too furious and terrified to pay attention.

The ghost-wolf snapped at the creature's ankles and snarled, darting back and forth to get the thing's attention.

She won't even know I'm here if she can't feel it.

With a little more focus on her intention, Amanda felt herself solidifying for a split second. She felt the cool floor beneath her ghostly paws and the rhino-squirrel's hot, panicked breath rippling across her fur. She felt fully, one hundred percent *there*.

It worked.

Of course, at first, the maddened creature was ripped out of its panic by pain and surprise. It let out a bugling cry when it finally felt the ghost-wolf's teeth clamping down around its ankles and on the end of one of its tails.

Yes! Come on!

Amanda raced back toward the nest, and when the angry beastie she thought of as a protective mother—but it could have literally been anything—charged after her again, the creature's bright-red eyes fell on the purple egg inside the tiny nest. It stopped in its tracks with a curious snuffle, grunted, then decided to charge toward the ghost-wolf anyway.

"Get out!" a scientist roared.

Before Amanda knew what was happening, another ghost-wolf leapt toward her from the side of the room.

She didn't have time to avoid both the charging rhino-squirrel and the scientist's anger-propelled magic. Right before the massive creature—which seemed to be shrinking again by the second—could reach her, she was knocked aside by a much larger and much stronger specter of another shifter's magical power and right back into her body in Dr. Caniss' office.

CHAPTER TWENTY-TWO

The first thing she noticed when her awareness flooded back into her body was the creak of Caniss' office chair, and the woman's sharp inhale. Then the biologist chuckled. "Well. If you can't tell me unequivocally that you enjoyed that little adventure, I'd say you're rather in the wrong line of work."

Amanda grunted, her cheek smashed against the tile floor of the doctor's office. When she pushed herself up, a string of drool connected the corner of her mouth to the tile for a moment longer, and she quickly wiped it away with the back of a hand. "What?"

"That was excellent work."

The girl paused for a moment to assess whatever damage might have occurred during her impromptu and highly unintentional fight with a rabid rhino-squirrel—at least in the beginning —but no. Amanda's real body was perfectly fine.

Except for my head. I bet that hit the floor first.

"You were...watching?" Finally, she got up onto all fours, then pushed herself slowly to her feet.

"I had to follow you, didn't I? No time for racing down hallways when one can simply leap *through* the walls." Caniss leaned forward in her chair and studied Amanda over the edge of her desk. "I'll speak to the staff. I don't doubt they'll have an insurmountable number of questions and an equally large array of complaints. But *you*, Amanda, have done quite well."

"I—"

"You are relieved of your duties for the remainder of the day. Eat something. And feel free to take an extra snack if you're still hungry." Caniss gestured toward her office door and chuckled again. "You've earned it."

"Um…thanks." Amanda turned jerkily toward the door, cast the doctor a final dubious glance, then shuffled into the hall and closed the door slowly behind her.

I fought a rampaging and overprotective beast parent with my magic from three corridors down, and I deserve an extra snack?

Stretching out her aching jaw from her sudden crash-landing on the floor when she'd left her body with her magic, she snorted and headed toward the wing of the Canissphere she probably knew how to find blindfolded now—the living quarters.

Forget food. That bed's calling my name. Those scientists probably are too, and not in a good way. They were pissed.

Thirty seconds after she flopped down on the firm mattress within the curved pod of her private room in the facility, she fell asleep. She didn't wake up until a brisk knock came at the door.

"Amanda?"

She tried to mutter a reply, but it came out as a garbled moan through a dry, sticky mouth.

"It's Dr. Blane. I can hear you in there, so feel free to peel yourself out of bed. We need to talk."

Great. Everyone knows about my little 'save the day' stunt now, and the one scientist I liked the most is stopping by to lecture me on knowing my place.

Amanda pulled herself off the mattress and almost slithered onto the floor like a limp noodle before her legs finally decided to start working again. Blinking heavily, she shuffled toward the door, slammed her hand against it to keep herself from falling forward, then found the doorknob.

"Listen, Ivory—"

"Better stick with Dr. Blane for now." The woman smirked, then she darted a glance down the hall. "May I come in?"

Amanda stepped back and gestured for her visitor to enter, not bothering to shut the door again. It took everything she had to keep her eyes open. However, the low, constant drone of dozens of voices from somewhere down the hall—most likely the rec-area dome—tickled her ears.

Why does that sound so weird?

"What's going on?" she muttered.

"Oh, you know." Ivory reached into the pocket of her lab coat. "Some teenage girl deployed highly advanced magic to help with a little behavioral snafu. Subject UM-48713, to be exact."

"Huh?"

"Everyone's talking about it."

Amanda stared through the open doorway and swayed a little.

That's what's not right. I've never heard every shifter in this place talking all at once.

Ivory dipped her head to enter the girl's line of vision and chuckled. "Have you eaten anything?"

"No. Just…sleep."

"That's what I thought. Here."

Amanda almost fell backward over her own feet when she leaned away, trying to focus on the cellophane-wrapped package the scientist extended toward her in one hand. The red silhouette of a chicken took up the front of the wrapper. "What?"

"It's a protein bar. Not the sweet kind, so don't expect chocolate or peanut butter flavor before you bite into it." When Amanda didn't move to take the snack, Ivory laughed and peeled open the package for her before handing it over again. "Seriously. Eat that now, and you'll feel like a new shifter."

The scent of chicken and black pepper overwhelmed Amanda's senses. Before she knew what she was doing, the cellophane wrapper was on the floor, the savory protein bar was gone, and she was licking the last bits of greasy leftovers off her fingers. "Oh, man. I definitely should've eaten first. Got any more of those?"

"Not on me. The mess hall's still open though."

"Great." Amanda started to head for the door, but Ivory stepped into her path to cut her off.

"Hold on a second. I have something else for you too." From the same pocket, the woman withdrew a small, shiny cell phone in a sleek silver case and offered it to the groggy intern. "This is yours."

"Um…" Amanda cracked a crooked smile. "It's not. My phone doesn't look like that."

"Now you have two phones."

Slowly taking the device, the girl frowned. "Why, exactly?"

"The Coalition wants a better way to contact you. Directly. And yes, the…" Ivory lowered her voice. "The *board* heard about what you did this morning. Impressive stuff. I heard it even caught Connor Slate's attention."

"Awesome. Last time I caught his attention, he almost ripped my best friend to pieces." Amanda looked up quickly to find the scientist staring at her with a playful frown. "Long story. Doesn't matter."

"Fair enough. Make sure you keep that phone on you all the time, okay?"

"Yeah, I *would*… Except I'm not supposed to have a phone on campus. You know, contraband and everything."

"Right." Ivory grinned and nudged the girl good-naturedly in the shoulder with her fist. "That never stopped you before, did it? No reason for the rules to stop you now, either. Seriously. On you at all times. Whatever messages you get—calls, texts, voicemails, anything else that phone's capable of—answer them as soon as you can. If someone's trying to get hold of you on that thing, it's important."

"Okay." Amanda hefted the slender device in her hand, then her curiosity won out, and she thumbed the wake button to bring up the home screen.

"Now you can grab some more grub." The scientist winked at her, stepped through the doorway, then paused. "Oh, yeah. Best part about this kind of gift. It already has the shifter app downloaded onto it, so feel free to use that whenever. It usually comes in handy."

"Wait, *shifter* app?"

"Yeah. It's in the Productivity group, I think." Ivory gave her another playfully surprised frown. "It's the network. The Coalition's the central hub, of course, but that app is how the rest of us get connected. Perks of the job, right?" She laughed and headed into the hall. "If I don't see you tomorrow, Amanda, have a good week. And you didn't hear it from me, but I'm pretty sure you can expect a change of pace around here when you come back next weekend."

"Okay..."

The scientist had already disappeared down the hall. Amanda was no longer paying attention—not to Dr. Ivory Blane, not to her pounding headache or her fiercely growling stomach, not even to the unusually chaotic rumble coming from dozens of shifters' voices echoing from the rec dome at the end of the hall.

Shifter app. That would've been nice to know, like, as soon as Johnny bought me a phone.

She scrolled across the home screen's multiple pages before she found the app grouping labeled 'Productivity,' snorted, and opened it.

There was only one app in there, and she would never have recognized it for what it was if Ivory hadn't explained it first. The app was covertly and still accurately called Global Shift.

Yeah, I'm definitely gonna check this out. Later. If I don't get more food right now, I'll end up eating one of the subjects. Or two.

Shoving the new phone into her back pocket, she locked up her private sleeping pod and headed down the hall. The second she entered the rec dome, the loud conversation cut off abruptly. Someone sniffed, another shifter coughed twice, but that was it.

Every single staff member working and living together at Omega Industries stared right at the shifter girl.

Good thing I'm used to this.

The smile she put on just for fun felt tight and haggard, and she nodded to the closest shifters before turning toward the meal window and what was essentially a lunch line for adults stretching away from it.

"Amanda." Dominique—the middle-aged shifter woman with a gap-toothed smile and a single long, dark hair sprouting from a mole above the corner of her mouth—leaned forward through the meal window and waved at the shifter girl. "Get up here."

"No, that's okay." Amanda raised a hand in greeting, then pointed at the end of the line. "I can wait."

"But you won't. Get up here, or I'm stepping out to serve you myself."

A collective groan rose from the staff standing in line before the adults broke into good-natured laughter. The shifter at the end of the line—she only knew him as Jones and was pretty sure he worked maintenance—grabbed her wrist and hauled her toward the meal window. "Hurry up. We're all hungry."

"Yeah, don't take too long."

"Get up to the front and get something to eat, kid. This doesn't happen every day."

One by one, the shifters in line nudged her forward toward

the next, and Amanda couldn't help but laugh as she stumbled up to the meal window. "Okay, okay. Thanks."

"What'll it be, girl?" Dominique grinned her gap-toothed grin.

"Whatever's fastest."

The rec dome exploded with laughter, and Omega Industries' resident lunch lady set a steaming tray of meatloaf, mashed potatoes, green beans, and a mouth-wateringly fresh biscuit on the counter at the window. "Now go sit before these drooling clods stage a coup."

"Thanks, Dominique." Amanda grabbed the tray and turned to look for an open table. The dozens of eyes all settling on her face was intensely distracting. "And everyone else. I'll just…"

Someone gave her an approving pat on the back, and she staggered forward before slowly moving toward the round tables taking up the center of the dome.

The conversation erupted again as if it had never stopped. Amanda breathed in the steamy aromas flaring up into her face from the plate, and as she sat at the closest empty table, she felt a different kind of stare flickering across her skin. The hair on the back of her neck stood on end.

That doesn't feel like a go-get-'em kinda stare.

All she had to do was look up and straight ahead across two other empty tables to see the four scientists who'd been working in the examination room that morning. They all stared at her too, but none of them graced her with the smiles and accepting nods the rest of the staff had so effortlessly sent her way.

One woman at that table offered a quick and highly unconvincing smile—merely a twitch at the corner of her mouth—before she dipped her head and focused on her meal. It took Amanda a few seconds longer than it should have to recognize the tall, broad-shouldered shifter man blatantly scowling at her.

He's the one who told me to get out. I wonder if Dr. Caniss saw him attack me in there too. Probably. I bet that's why he looks ready to do it again.

Without even thinking about it, she flashed the angry scientist a wide grin—complete with a thumbs-up—before she snatched up her fork and dug into the meatloaf.

It's not Darlene's, but it's close enough to perfect.

CHAPTER TWENTY-THREE

As exhausted as she was after her scuffle with Subject UM-48713, Amanda finished off the rest of her work that weekend feeling like she was on top of the world. None of the staff at the Canissphere brought up her escapade again, though she noticed the perturbed scientists who'd failed to contain the raging beast still shooting her dirty looks whenever she saw them in the hallways.

It's not like I'm here to take their *jobs.* The thought alone made her swallow. *That better not be what this turns into.*

She didn't see Dr. Caniss again either before Fiona arrived to cart her back to the Academy with the Starbucks train ride sandwiched between two teleport jumps. However, the redhead shifter woman wouldn't let Amanda hear the end of it.

"So imagine my surprise when I got a call from Connor himself. Can you guess what he had to say?"

"I honestly have no idea," Amanda muttered as she munched down the last of the extra protein bar Dominique had snuck her before she left.

"Oh, come on, kid. Take a guess."

"He told you about the phone."

"Nope. He—" Fiona's smile faded. "Wait, how did you know about that?"

"I didn't. You told me to guess."

"Okay, I'll forget about your eerie mind-reading skills for the moment. Yes, he told me about the phone. Which, by the way, I highly recommend—"

"Keeping on me at all times and quickly answering any message I get on it. Voicemail, text, or other."

Fiona snorted. "Am I gonna get two words in edgewise here, or should I let you talk for me?"

Cramming the last of the protein bar into her mouth, Amanda gestured with a sweeping hand for her mentor to continue.

"He called to congratulate me." The woman grinned. "I know, I know, the win's all yours. You did all the work. Honestly though, I thought I'd screwed up all my chances with the board after our last interaction."

"You haven't seen them since then?"

"Then, as in the time I stuck my neck out to get you an in-person meeting, and your devious little witch friend crashed the party?" Fiona clicked her tongue. "No, I might not be *on* the board—not yet, at least—but believe it or not, kid, I see them on an annoyingly regular basis. It just gets harder and harder each time to keep proving I'm worth keeping around." The shifter woman sniffed the air in their late-night train cabin, then looked her mentee up and down. "You got any more of those?"

"Nope. Only the one. You ever have one of these?"

"They're good, right?" Fiona sniffed again, licked her lips, then sat back against the cushioned bench and folded her arms. "Who would've thought grinding up a bunch of chicken and jamming it into a gelatinous brick would be so damn tasty?"

"The people who did it."

"Obviously."

That Monday morning, Amanda was ready to face the world. She probably got more of a kick out of relaying the entire rhino-squirrel-debacle story to her friends than they got out of listening to it, but she had to talk to *someone* about it. Specifically, someone who wasn't involved with the Coalition of Shifters, Omega Industries, or Dr. Caniss.

"That's freaking nuts!" Jackson exclaimed through his mouthful of eggs. "Wait. You can't, like, get any diseases if those things bite you or something, right?"

Alex snorted. "You worried about contracting something, dude?"

"Shut up."

"I can't believe she followed you and *watched*," Grace added, slowly shaking her head. "Without even trying to step in. That's a gross abuse of power. You're a minor. They should have safety precautions in place."

"Ha!" Summer slapped the picnic table and almost knocked over her glass of orange juice. "Forget safety precautions. As if those would mean anything to our shifter girl anyway, am I right? How about the fact that all you got was a pat on the back and an *extra snack*? Like, what is this? *The Hunger Games*?"

"What?" Grace frowned at the other witch.

"It's a cool movie, Blondie." Summer waved her off. "You wouldn't get it."

"Ivory said things were gonna change when I go back next weekend." Amanda spooned up a mouthful of highly brown-sugared oatmeal and couldn't stop grinning. "Like, I might start hunting. Not to kill, obviously. Only to bring back to Omega Industries, but still. It's better than staring at giant slugs all day or retyping the notes the scientists had me take down by hand first."

"You were the *only* one who thought to look for the egg?" Grace uttered a sharp laugh. "I thought these shifters were supposed to be the best of the best."

Amanda shrugged. "I don't know. I mean, yeah, they're

supposed to be. Still, it's not like anyone has all the answers for how to deal with these mutated species. They figure it out by trial and error."

"Yeah, and having you do all the work *for* them." Summer clamped a hand on Amanda's shoulder and gave her a little shake. "You really stuck it to 'em, shifter girl."

"No, she—" Grace laughed and covered her mouth with a hand. "I'd call what she did *helping*."

Summer smirked at the other witch and spread her arms. "Same thing."

———

That week flew by in a blaze of Amanda's growing pride in her accomplishments—both within the classroom and at the Canissphere.

They finally finished their mid-semester assignments for LeFor in Applied Tech, which included the alchemized magic they'd created in Advanced Alchemy. She and Jackson had the bright idea to concoct a concentrated solution of *his* alchemized magic, the best of which came in the form of his illumination orbs that he could change colors at will. LeFor had partnered them up with Blake and Jasmine, who'd created some kind of shimmery, sparkly thing the purpose of which neither one of them could accurately explain.

"We gotta find a way to make this badass," Jackson had muttered in Applied Tech when their assigned teams were left alone to devise the practical application of their soon-to-be-built projects. "I can do lights. But glitter?" He dragged his hands down the sides of his face and fixed Amanda with a miserable stare. "What were they thinking?"

That was when the lightbulb went off in Amanda's head.

"Emergency lights."

"Huh?"

"That's it."

"You're not making any sense," Jasmine muttered as she picked at her fingernails.

"It's cool. I don't have to. Jackson, help me get the pieces we need. I know exactly how to put it all together."

Even then, by the end of the week, they still hadn't finished constructing the device that had appeared in Amanda's head with perfect clarity.

"You sure this is gonna work?" Jackson grimaced at the half-built piece of machinery on the worktable in front of them.

"Hey. You trust me, right?"

"I mean, for a lot of things, yeah." He scratched his head. "I'm not sure tech-assembly is one of those."

Amanda grabbed his arm and gave it a reassuring squeeze. "Well, trust me. It's gonna be awesome."

The wizard stared at her hand on his arm, flushed a dark red again without looking at her, and she immediately let go of him before hopping off the tall bistro chair. "I'm gonna get another pair of pliers. Someone has to wrap those wires, or we'll blow our heads off when we use this thing."

Plus I need to stop touching Jackson during class projects. Or at all. What am I doing?

When it came time to get back to the Canissphere, she hadn't fully prepared for what awaited her. Knowing Dr. Caniss and how she ran things in the facility, she hadn't exactly gotten her hopes up that the changes Ivory had mentioned would be drastic or even exciting. At least she was wrong about that part.

Bill was the one who greeted her in the main dome when Fiona dropped her off with another shipment of harvested plant material from the Academy's greenhouse. "You're with me today."

The girl's excited grin disappeared, and she wrinkled her nose. "Lemme guess. You get the bucket. I get the shovel."

The creature caretaker laughed and waved her forward before leading her across the dome toward one of the many branching hallways. "I see how you might think that, but I'm pretty sure this will be much more fun. Unless, of course, you'd *rather* muck out some cages and a few habitats?"

"Nope. I'm good."

As it turned out, Amanda's internship "promotion" now meant she was shadowing Bill, but not in the exam rooms or even with feeding time for the evolved magical creatures. Instead, he took her right out into the herbivore enclosure and gave her the simplest set of instructions she'd received yet.

"Get on out there. Make yourself familiar with as many of these critters as you can. Hell, if you can make a few friends, even better."

"Won't they, like…get spooked?"

Bill grinned. "Not if you don't get too close. I'm pretty sure you can figure out how to make that happen."

It took her a minute to fully feel comfortable roaming around the enclosed habitat for generally nonconfrontational creatures. Then Bill left her out there all on her own, and she stopped worrying about what anyone would think when they saw her stretching her abilities to do as he said.

Mingle with the beasties, huh? Yeah, I can do that. They won't even smell me coming.

She sat against the outer wall over the enclosure—right below where Bill had shown her the place for the first time from the walkway above—and didn't have to close her eyes before her magic reacted precisely the way she wanted.

For the next two days, she roamed the herbivore enclosure with her ghost-wolf, leaping across the field, darting through the thick woods on the far side, running across the surface of the river. Together, they watched, smelled, and listened to more magical creatures than she'd expected to find here despite knowing how many divergent species the Coalition had already brought into the facility.

Most of them didn't seem to notice the ghost-wolf's presence among them at all. Or if they did, they didn't mind it nearly as much as they would have objected to the physical presence of an actual wolf.

They can tell I'm not here to hunt them.

The thought came to her so intensely that she knew it was true. That made studying these new magical creatures in their mostly natural habitats that much more incredible.

Only once that first weekend in the enclosure did she come across the Harkliss again, which stalked along the riverbank on its three long longs and stretched its head out over the water, searching for fish. The Harkliss recognized Amanda and her ghost-wolf, and when it lifted its head to fix her with beady eyes, she prepared herself for another magic-to-magic battle.

Instead, the silver and red mutated bird spread its shimmering wings, dipped them behind its fluffy-feathered body, and draped its head to the ground in a surprisingly graceful bow. Not once did it look away from the ghost-wolf standing on the other side of the river. Mesmerized, Amanda found herself sitting back on her ethereal haunches to watch the creature. Eventually, the Harkliss resumed its hunt for food in the river, completely at peace in the presence of a teenage shifter's magic.

Maybe this is what I should be doing. Not hunting these creatures. Simply sitting here to watch them.

As she mulled over the idea, she knew it wasn't true. The Coalition needed skilled operatives out there in the world who could track, at least partially identify, and peacefully apprehend the divergent species growing more numerous by the day all over Earth.

As Bill pointed out later when she asked him why she was

doing this, "I'm sure you've heard *someone* in your life talking about thinking like a criminal to catch one, right?"

"Yeah, something along those lines."

"Well, same thing goes for these creatures. If you can adapt to think like any of them out here, at a moment's notice, you'll have no problem finding the ones out there. Even the ones causing more trouble than any of these guys." Bill grinned and handed her a bucket of reeking Heloton feed. "I have a feeling you might even be one of the best."

Her weeks moved fluidly like this over the semester—new ideas and a renewed enthusiasm for her classes, interspersed with long days of seeing through the eyes of her magic to explore the herbivore enclosures on the weekends. She couldn't remember a time when she'd been anywhere near as happy.

The week before Halloween, the junior class met for the third time in the training building to receive their Bag the Bounty assignments for round three. Amanda balked when she found her name at the bottom of the paper marking her as this round's target and artifact-keeper. "Um...Mr. Petrov?"

"What is it, Coulier?"

"I don't think this is gonna work." She pointed at the paper, but the teacher merely stared at her with a deadpan expression.

"Nice try. These assignments are in stone." To prove his point, he snatched the paper from her and ignited it in a burst of purple flame. "Good luck."

She had to wait until after the rest of the class had filtered outside onto the training field to approach him about it again.

"I don't see what the problem is, Coulier. Don't tell me you don't think you can handle another team ganging up on you to snatch your artifact."

"No, I can handle that no problem," she blurted, trying to get to her point instead of paying attention to how that sounded.

Petrov raised an eyebrow and snorted. "Someone's getting a little cocky."

"No, I mean... I'm not here on the weekends. Isn't it kind of unfair to Team One if they have fewer days to find me and my artifact? Every other team has seven days a week. They'd only get five."

The bald teacher narrowed his eyes. "Surprising rationale, actually. But clever. Trying to get out of a little extra work by saying it's unfair to everyone *else*."

"I'm not trying to—"

"Tough nuggets, Coulier. You're the keeper. If Team One hasn't figured out by now that you're gone every weekend and can't plan accordingly, they don't deserve the extra points in the first place. No handouts. Now get out."

Well, when he puts it like that, I guess it's not so bad.

That night, she found the aforementioned artifact on the floor of her dorm room. Petrov had stuffed it into an enchanted manilla envelope that prevented anyone else from opening it, which they wouldn't have been able to do anyway since it was already in her room by the time she turned in for the night.

Shaking her head, she opened the envelope, poured out the black lanyard with the Florida Gators' mascot embroidered on it, and unfolded the accompanying note.

On you at all times. Negative points for your team if you forget.

"Awesome." Without knowing why, she strung the lanyard over her neck and let the metal clip at the end *thump* against her chest. A sharp laugh burst out of her, and she whipped it off again.

Everyone's gonna know what this is the second they see it on me. Who would even wear one of these?

She stuffed it into the side pocket of her backpack instead, then pulled out the sleek silver phone Ivory had given her by order of the Coalition's board members.

Perusing the shifter app had become a part of her nightly ritual, and she didn't mind that it seemed to have replaced her runs out in the swamp a few times a week.

I spend enough time as a wolf on the weekends anyway. Kind of. This is totally new.

The app was insanely easy to navigate. All she had to do was type in a zip code, city, state, or even a specific address, and a comprehensive list of all the "registered shifters" in the immediate vicinity pulled up instantly, complete with a map. Seeing all those tiny red dots in every area she searched blew her mind every single time.

There are so many of us out there. And they're all right here at my fingertips.

The app had a chat feature as well—navigable via subject matter, thread topic, or geographic location—but Amanda hadn't used it yet. Shifters already surrounded her every weekend, and it hadn't felt like the right time yet to reach out to any of the others through the app. She did scour the community threads and read the conversations about everyday, mundane shifter things.

At least I know I'm not entirely alone. This will definitely come in useful someday.

She and her team had finally finished their project for LeFor's class. That Thursday in Applied Tech—twelve hours before the Halloween party was scheduled to kick off in true Academy fashion—the juniors got to showcase what they'd been working on all semester.

Grace and her partners had taken alchemized Light Elf magic and combined it with some of Brandon's. They made a point of explaining the Crystal kid had given his full permission to alchemize and use his magic for their device. Grace gave an impressive demonstration of what turned out to be an unpatented medical device.

"For treating burns mostly," she added as she finished activating the magitech on Tommy, who'd willingly volunteered. The boy shuddered as a burst of icy hair washed over his bare arm, followed by a glow of golden light that made him sigh. "At least, we're pretty sure it would work for that. Can't really test out its ability to heal when we weren't allowed to burn someone first."

Summer burst out laughing.

LeFor pressed his lips together and nodded. "Still an impressive application. Mind if I take this to Nurse Aiken so she can look it over?"

Grace grinned, although her three partners seemed unaware of the subtle compliment. "Totally. Yeah. I'll have to ask her what she thinks."

"Great. Miss Coulier, Mr. Pris, Miss McVar, and Miss Lamar." LeFor pointed at their table.

Amanda held their finished device out toward Jackson. "You wanna do it?"

"No. No, you're the brains behind the thing. Go ahead."

"You sure?"

"Yeah. Honestly?" He leaned toward her to whisper, "I'm still a little afraid of how it's gonna pan out. Feels like something's missing."

"No way. We'll be fine."

"We're waiting, Miss Coulier," LeFor interjected. "Let's see it."

"Sure." She slid off the tall chair with what looked very much like a miniature bazooka in her hands and nodded at the door. "Can I turn off the lights? Kinda part of the show."

With a dubious frown, LeFor pointed at the light switch, which pulsed with a green light before clicking off all on its own and enveloping the workshop in complete darkness.

"Nobody move," Tommy shouted.

His friends snickered, and Evan added, "This is not a drill. I repeat, this is not—"

"Brunsen! Hutchinson!" LeFor barked. "Just because we can't see you doesn't mean your voices are not still completely recognizable."

"Aw, man…"

"Anytime now, Miss Coulier."

"Yeah." She felt around on the device for the trigger and drew a deep breath. "Here we go."

She aimed their invention straight up at the ceiling and pulled the trigger. A bright burst of light erupted from the barrel with a loud *crack*, and the blindingly white ball of light shooting toward the ceiling broke off into four smaller pieces before zipping right up into the dark lightbulbs. The room illuminated again, the magical lights flickered from white to blue to green, then they all popped in quick succession and sent a rain of pink and gold glitter showering down like sparks around the students.

The junior class erupted into a mix of helpless laughter and applause.

Amanda spun toward Jackson and their team at the table. The wizard held out his hands and stared in horror at the glitter raining down around him. Jasmine and Anabelle smiled.

"All right, that's enough." LeFor snapped his fingers, and the actual lightbulbs flicked back on with a stuttering flicker before the glitter and the green lights disappeared. Then he stomped toward Amanda and held out his hand. "Let me see that."

"Sure." She handed it over, and the red-haired teacher's eyes widened as he turned the small magical firearm over a few times.

"What, exactly, do you call this?"

Amanda shrugged. "A flashlight. With…glitter."

Half the class burst out laughing again.

"Witty." LeFor wasn't smiling. "You know what I call it?"

"Nope."

"A gun." He shook the device at her, then pointed toward her teammates at the table before realizing he'd aimed a weapon-ish device at four of his students. Then he raised his voice to address the entire class. "In case the rest of you had any doubts, let me make this clear. Weapons are not toys."

"Wait, we could've built *toys*?" Brandon shouted through his laughter.

LeFor ignored him. "Weapons most certainly should not be the focus of *schoolwork*."

Amanda huffed out a laugh. "It's not a gun, Mr. LeFor. It's a light...thing."

"The practical application is admirable, Miss Coulier, but I can think of at least four different shapes right now off the top of my head that would have been way more appropriate for the classroom. Not a...baby bazooka."

Snickers and forced coughs to cover them up filled the workshop.

"I better not see anything else in my class that even remotely resembles a weapon, understood? You build only useful gadgets in here. *Without* the ability to seriously maim your fellow students."

"You know, I'm not even sure it works if you point it at anything but the lightbulbs anyway," Amanda muttered.

The teacher raised an eyebrow at her and hefted the gun-like device in his hand. "What's the glitter for?"

"Ooh." Jasmine finally looked up from her nails and raised her hand without waiting to be called on. "Because it's pretty."

Amanda wrinkled her nose, Jackson dropped his head into his hands, and the class enjoyed another round of wild laughter.

Turning away from her, LeFor strode across the workshop to drop her team's assignment into the top drawer of his desk and muttered, "At least it did what they created it to do."

CHAPTER TWENTY-FOUR

The entire campus buzzed with excitement that night as the student body waited for the veil covering the archway into the central field to let them enter for the Halloween party. Some of the students had kept their animal masks from the Homecoming dance and now incorporated them into costumes for tonight's festivities.

Amanda laughed when she headed down the hall in the girl's dorm and found Summer wearing the wolf mask. Only this time, the girl had added a bunch of black-dyed feathers and long artificial black braids all around the edges of it. "You look like a psycho."

"Hey, good guess, shifter girl." Summer lifted the mask to flash her friend an exaggerated grin with wide eyes. "That's exactly what I am."

"Way to ruin a perfectly good mask."

"Yeah, well, this time, Romeo won't mistake me for you. How 'bout that?"

"Stop." They headed down the hall with the rest of the girls, most of whom had put a lot more effort into creating decent costumes using whatever they had to work with.

MARTHA CARR & MICHAEL ANDERLE

"I'm looking out for your best interest, okay?" Summer bumped Amanda with her shoulder. "Good thing Halloween isn't a dance, right?"

"Hey, guys." Grace caught up to them, her hair spray-painted with shimmering silver sparkles and her face painted.

Summer pulled her wolf mask down over her face and lurched toward the other witch. "Boo!"

Grace looked her up and down. "I think you're the only kid on both planets who gets a ghost and a wolf confused."

"Hey, no way!" Summer cackled and pointed at Amanda. "Ghost-wolf!"

"Oh…" Grace burst out laughing with her as they hurried down the staircase. "I guess I was wrong."

"No problem." Amanda tugged on one of the fake braids fastened securely to the wolf mask, and Summer stumbled sideways with a laughing growl. "Mine's a lot more realistic."

"I guess we *kinda* had the same idea about the masks, huh?" Grace pointed at Summer, then at her face.

"Uh…I'm a wolf, Blondie. You're only blue."

"No, I painted my actual *face* like a butterfly. That just so happens to be blue. Why am I even trying to explain this to you?"

"Because you know I'm messing with you, and I can't stand the thought of actually being cool with it." Summer's snort was as muffled as her voice behind the mask. "You do that paint job yourself?"

"Yeah."

"It's decent." Summer scurried across the common room toward the front door of the dorms and let out a wild howl. The girls closest to the door jumped against each other and screamed before shoving each other through the door and out into the field. Summer laughed behind them and took off running.

"Why do I get the feeling she *would* be a wolf if she could?" Grace muttered as they followed the other mostly costumed girls outside.

"I don't know. Take away the mask, and what's left?"

"A feral beast with no regard for rules, personal safety, or acting on anything but base instinct."

They burst out laughing.

"You guys seem to be doing pretty okay lately." Amanda nodded toward Summer, who prowled along the outskirts of the closed-off central field in her wolf mask and jumped out at incoming freshmen to make them scatter. "You and Summer. You know, the whole being-friends thing."

"I mean, yeah. Maybe." Grace delicately tucked her glittery hair behind one ear, then smoothed the front of her bright blue dress that matched the shades of her face paint. "She's cool. I mean, she's definitely been less of a jerk lately."

"Oh, yeah? So it's all 'cause Summer decided to change, huh?"

Grace playfully rolled her eyes. "Okay, fine. Maybe *I'm* not so much of an uptight—"

"Know-it-all?" Alex muttered behind them.

Grace shrieked and scuttled forward across the grass. Amanda stepped away from him and looked the Wood Elf up and down with a laugh. "Whoa."

"Alex!" Grace spread her arms. "You can't keep sneaking up on people like that. Especially not wearing that... Is that the same mask from Homecoming?"

"As far as I know, yeah."

"Wait... What *are* you?"

Both girls tried to hold back their laughter as they took in the sight of the tall, skinny Wood Elf dressed up in a green button-up shirt, green corduroy pants, and a shimmery green bowtie that matched what must have been the green spray paint he'd also used to cover his shoes.

Alex's dark eyes darted back and forth behind the holes in his frog mask. "Take a guess."

"Hey, what's up, Kermit?" Summer shouted as she rejoined

them, the black braids on her wolf mask flying comically around her head.

"Whoa. Dude." Jackson joined them and clapped a hand on Alex's shoulder. "What's this? The Frog Butler?"

"Frog Prince, man," Alex muttered, his shoulders slumping. "*Prince.*"

"You're, uh…" Summer pointed at his head. "You're missing a crown there, man."

"That comes after the frog's not a frog anymore—Seriously? None of you know this?"

Grace tilted her head and looked him up and down. "So you're waiting for a princess to kiss you then, is that it?"

"Finally." The Wood Elf let out a massive sigh. "Thank you."

"Oh. No, I—" Grace clapped a hand over her mouth but failed to cover up her laughter. "No, I wasn't *volunteering.*"

"You sure?" He sidled up to her and stuck his froggy mask in her face, batting his eyelashes furiously behind the eyeholes. "Ribbit?"

Laughing, she shoved him away, and the group made their way toward the veiled archway as it lit up to signal the Samhain festivities had begun.

"Hey, you guys heard anything else about that *guru* Calsgrave said she got to come out here this year?" Jackson asked as they stepped through the veil.

"You mean the séance lady?" Summer snorted. "I'll be fine if we don't hear anything else about her ever. I've had enough dead people in my life as it is. Oh, hey." She elbowed Amanda and slipped the mask up over her face to reveal a surprisingly sympathetic frown. "No offense. I wasn't—"

"It's cool, Summer. Trust me. I'm past seeing real ghosts too."

"Wow." Grace gazed around the field with wide eyes. "They really went all out."

Alex nodded slowly. "Jack-O-Lanterns. Floating candles.

Desserts shaped like severed body parts on a creepy blood-stained tablecloth. All I need now is a princess."

"Dude, you don't really think your frog look is gonna get anyone to kiss you tonight, do you?"

The Wood Elf shrugged. "You never know, man."

"Hey, check it." Summer thumped his chest with the back of a hand, then pointed across the field. "Skeleton princess counts, right?"

The whole group studied Candace Jones' getup from afar—the senior girl wore a skin-tight black outfit on which she'd painted a skeleton.

"Wow." Grace sighed. "Whoever did her makeup for that is good."

"Yeah, I dunno…" No one could see Alex grimacing beneath his mask, but it was clear enough in his voice. "I'm not trying to catch something."

Amanda laughed. "Like *what?*"

"I don't know." He shrugged. "I heard someone talking about her bad breath."

Jackson burst out laughing and headed toward the refreshments table. "I'm gonna grab some chocolate-covered fingers. Anybody want something?"

"Ooh, yeah." Summer took off with him. "I think I saw some shredded gummy ears."

"I'm gonna try the tarot readings again this year." Grace offered a sheepish smile. "For fun."

Then it was only Amanda and Alex standing there in a sea of students running around in costume. She was about to head off for the snack table too but stopped when her back pocket buzzed.

Crap.

Alex stood there beside her, drumming his fingers against his thighs and bobbing his head to the spooky Halloween music that didn't have an actual beat. "So…"

"Yeah. Halloween, right?"

"Ribbit."

She choked on her laugh when the phone buzzed again.

Seriously? Right now? I can't answer my secret shifter phone in the middle of a party.

The Frog Prince had to turn his whole body toward her to look at her through the mask. "You okay?"

"Totally. I just—" Amanda jumped sideways at the third buzz in her back pocket. "I'll be right back."

"Yep." Alex turned to watch a group of freshmen dressed as bedsheet ghosts walk by, and she booked it across the central field toward the veiled archway.

This is the worst timing ever. What's so important the Coalition needs to get hold of me on Halloween?

She paused briefly on the other side of the veil when the most outrageous answer popped into her head.

No. I am not *leaving a party to go fight off some kind of mutated creature spirit. Not tonight. If that's even a thing.*

The shifter phone went off again in her pocket, and she jerked her hand back toward it before stopping herself. She at least had to get away from the entire student body, plus all the faculty gathered behind her if she was going to answer the thing.

So she stalked off toward the girls' dorm with the full intention of slipping behind the building for a little more privacy.

Only when she stopped and thought to look over her shoulder did she hear the quick, muffled footsteps through the grass heading right toward her. Before she *could* turn around, warm hands grabbed her roughly by the wrist and jerked her hand away from her back pocket. The shifter phone flew from her hand and toppled into the grass.

"What—"

"Gotcha." A tall kid with his face painted up like some kind of bloody goblin grabbed her other wrist and grinned in her face. "Give it up."

"Get off me."

"Arms *behind* her back, Ricky." Blake panted as she jogged toward them. "Or she'll throw you off—"

With a snarl, Amanda whipped her wrist out of Tony's grasp, then shoved the goblin kid—who she now recognized as Mark—roughly away from her. "Whatever the hell this is, you better cut it—"

A small but incredibly compact weight barreled into her from behind and sent her sprawling forward across the grass.

"Holy crap, Blake!" Mark shouted. "You just rammed her to the ground."

"Sorry," Blake whispered in Amanda's ear before grabbing the shifter girl's arm and twisting it backward in a painful armlock.

Amanda snarled louder in pain and knew she couldn't struggle out of something like that without dislocating her arm. "What the hell?"

"You have the lanyard on you, right?" Blake said breathlessly.

"Jeeze, you're a lot heavier when you're on my *back*, you know that?"

"We got you fair and square," Ricky said. "So tell us where you're keeping it, then you can go back to—"

Amanda bucked off the ground enough to make Blake catch a few inches of air off her back. She rolled sideways and brought her elbow up into the smaller girl's shoulder to knock her even more off-center before snatching her arm away and leaping to her feet. "You're gonna have to do a lot better than that. Right now, I seriously don't have the time to fight all three of you. I have to handle something."

"What about all four of us?" Breathing heavily and eyes wide, Blake stuck her thumb behind her, and Jackson rounded the corner at the same second.

"Oh, jeeze. Come on, Team One. I get it. You want the—"

"Get her!" Mark leapt at Amanda again, and she ducked his

wild swing that was probably supposed to hit her in the face before she brought a knee up into his gut.

"I said not now!" she snarled and spun to look for the dropped shifter phone in the grass.

"Dude, what are you *doing?*" Jackson hissed.

"Apprehending the..." Mark held himself around the middle and grunted. "Target."

"You can't punch someone in the face."

"He didn't, did he?" Blake lunged toward the shifter girl and tried to wrap her up in another debilitating hold.

Amanda stepped aside at the last second and shoved the smaller girl in the back, letting Blake's momentum take her down almost all on its own.

The once-mousey girl immediately rolled over onto her back and scrambled backward before rising again. "Give us the lanyard, Amanda. Then we're done. Unless you *want* a fight."

"No, I—hey!" Amanda pointed at Jackson, who'd somehow found her phone and now held it in front of him, staring at it with wide eyes. "Don't touch that."

"What is it?" Ricky asked.

"A phone." Jackson looked up and met her gaze. "Is this—"

"It's not for you." She stormed toward him, and Blake took it as a perfect opportunity to rush the shifter girl from behind again.

The rest of it didn't exactly play out with any kind of rational action. Amanda simply reacted. The guys shouted and cheered Blake on, Jackson shouted and tried to pry the tiny, intensely motivated girl away from Amanda, and Amanda only tried to get to the stupid shifter phone.

"Hey, hey! Blake!" Jackson reached for her, but she ducked under his arm and tried to sweep Amanda's legs out from under her. "We can't—"

With a growl, Amanda slapped her hands onto Blake's arms,

now trying to find a hold around her neck from behind, and tossed the girl over her shoulder with a *thump*.

"Jesus, Amanda, it's only a—"

"Give me the damn phone!" She spun toward Jackson and meant to snatch the phone away from where she'd last seen him holding it out of reach of the fighting. He was much closer than she expected though, and her elbow whipped up to jab against the side of his throat instead.

Jackson grunted, coughed, and staggered backward as he clutched his throat with both hands. The phone fell to the grass again. Blake moaned. Ricky and Mark stared in mute horror.

"It's a freaking *game*," Ricky muttered. "You don't have to break his windpipe."

"Not..." Jackson coughed. "Not broken."

Amanda stared at him, her gut churning. "Jackson..."

"Just give me...a minute." He took a few searing breaths, and she glanced down at the glinting silver phone on the ground by his feet.

"I didn't mean to do that," she muttered. "I'm sorry. Are you okay?"

When she stepped toward him, he quickly stepped away and lifted a hand to stop her. "Don't."

"Seriously, I didn't—"

He coughed again, and when he looked up at her, she found the creases of physical pain lining his eyes, plus anger and disbelief and what looked a lot like sadness.

Oh, man. This was not *supposed to happen.*

Jamming her hand into the front pocket of her jeans, she fumbled to close her fingers around the lanyard and yanked it free. Then she hurried toward the shifter phone, quickly snatched it up, and met Jackson's gaze again. "Here."

The lanyard landed on the grass between them.

"Sorry. I gotta..." She spun and raced off toward the back of the boys' dorm instead, unable to look at him any longer.

That's the worst look I've seen on anyone's face. Ever. Petrov's an idiot for pitting us all against each other like that.

Blinking back what felt like oncoming tears that never really appeared, Amanda rounded the back of the boys' dorm and thumped her back against the wall. Then she looked down at all the notifications—two missed calls from an unknown number and five texts that all said the same thing.

Immediate response required. Check in to this number.

"Crap." Her fingers slipped on the screen, but she finally managed to hit the return-call button and practically slapped the phone to her ear.

The line rang once before a bland, flat male voice answered.

"Identify yourself."

"Uh…Amanda. Coulier."

"Confirmed. Dr. Caniss requested your presence at the Omega Industries facility in Colorado. Immediately."

"What?" She glanced around the dark grounds and lowered her voice, but there was no one there. "I don't… I mean, I'm at *school* right now—"

"The Starbucks train runs at all hours, Miss Coulier."

"Yeah, but I don't have a way to get to the station."

"Do what you have to do. Dr. Caniss expects your assistance with an urgent matter at the facility. This is not a drill. Understand?"

"Yeah, but—"

The line went dead, and Amanda stared at the dark grass in disbelief.

"Hello? Are you there?" She jerked the phone away from her ear and stared at the backlit home screen. "Crap!"

CHAPTER TWENTY-FIVE

"How the heck am I supposed to get out there when I don't have a redhead shifter to teleport me to the stupid—"

"Hey." Jackson stepped around the corner of the building with his hands buried deep in his pockets.

Amanda whipped the phone behind her back and quickly shoved it into her back pocket. "Hey. Listen, about what happened—"

"I'm pretty sure I'll live." He gave her a weak smile and slowly approached where she leaned against the building. "Everything okay?"

"Yeah. Of course." When she met his gaze and concerned frown as he looked her over, she puffed out a sigh and shook her head. "No. Not really. I'm kinda screwed, actually. I think."

"If you're worried about Glasket finding out you have a phone, don't be."

"What?"

"The rest of Team One doesn't give a crap about anything but that stupid lanyard. Um..." He scrunched up his face. "I told them it was a bad idea to follow you away from the party, but they didn't exactly listen."

"Oh. No, that's okay. I mean, find the artifact or have to take Petrov's final, right? I'd do the same thing." She scratched her head and nervously scanned the grass as Jackson stopped and leaned back beside her against the wall.

Worried about Glasket finding out? She wouldn't even care. It's part of her Coalition deal, which I'm about to blow if I don't figure out how to get my ass onto the train.

"Did…" Jackson sniffed and looked up at the black sky. "Did something happen between the Halloween kickoff and us ambushing you?"

Amanda huffed out a wry laugh and shrugged. "I mean, yeah. It's not—"

"Did *I* do something?"

"No. No, definitely not. I just…" She exhaled deeply and turned to face him. "Okay. The Coalition gave me a cell phone after I fought the brooding mama rhino-squirrel."

He smirked.

"Yeah, we need a better name for that one. They told me to keep this phone on me all the time in case they needed me for something. Like, I have a whole bunch of other responsibilities, and nobody told me what those are supposed to be. Everything was fine until the thing started going off in my pocket in the field. I have to answer it, too, by the way."

"That's why you left." Jackson hissed out a sigh and dropped his head back against the wall. "We sabotaged your internship for a stupid lanyard."

"I mean, it's an enchanted lanyard, but yeah. You guys didn't sabotage my internship. I called the number back." Amanda pulled the phone from her pocket again and wiggled it in her hand. "Dr. Caniss wants me at Omega Industries, like, right now, and even though I could get most of the way there on the train, I have no idea how to get *on* the train because I've always had—"

A muted flash of blue light appeared in front of them, then Fiona Damascus stood there in all her unusually furious glory.

"Ah!" Jackson plastered himself against the brick wall and stared at her. "What... Did you just..."

Fiona looked Amanda up and down, saw the shifter phone in her hand, then flicked her gaze toward Jackson with wide eyes. "What the hell do you think you're doing?"

"Yeah, nice to see you too. I guess you know about the bajillion phone calls I just—"

"Jackson, right?" The shifter woman pointed at him with a tense and slightly crooked finger.

"Y-yeah..."

"Get lost."

"Amanda, what's—"

"I said *scram*, wizard!" Fiona snarled at him, her eyes flashing dangerously silver as she lunged toward him.

Jackson slid along the wall, tripped over his feet, and booked it across the grass.

"Hey, what's wrong with you?" Amanda snapped. "He didn't do anything."

"No, you can take all the credit for this epic screwup, Amanda."

"Wait, what?"

"Come on." The shifter woman glared at Jackson quickly backed across the grass as he watched them with wide and terrified eyes. She sneered at him as she clamped a hand on Amanda's shoulder, and both shifters disappeared in another muted burst of blue light.

"Oh, shit." Jackson spun in the damp grass, slipped again, and saw absolutely nothing around him but dark shadows and starlight. "No, no, no..."

He raced across the grounds, passed the girls' dorm, and booked it toward the central field where the creepy Halloween music and the occasional spooky laugh did absolutely nothing to dampen the knot tightening in his gut.

The veil whipped aside as he shoved his way through the

crowd of students and into the central field.

Not good. Nothing about that could ever be good. How did she do that?

He almost overlooked the girl in the wolf mask standing next to the girl with the blue face on the other side of the refreshments table before remembering those were the exact two girls he was trying to find. Pushing his way through costumes and fluttery things that only served as more distractions, Jackson hurried toward the table and scrambled around it before skidding to a stop beside Summer.

"Guys—"

"'Sup, Romeo?" Summer lifted her wolf mask to bite into a caramel apple. "What happened to you?"

"Guys, it's bad. I mean, I think it's bad. It didn't look good. It's—"

"Whoa, okay." Grace stepped around Summer so she could put a hand on his shoulder.

He tried to shrug it off but couldn't quite figure out how to move his shoulder the way he wanted.

"Ate too much Halloween candy, huh?" Summer asked with a smirk before taking another crunching bite.

"You wanna sit or something?" Grace peered closer. "You look like you're gonna be sick."

"No, I don't wanna—listen!" Jackson puffed out a sigh. "You know that redhead who comes to get Amanda on Saturdays?"

"Amanda, huh?" Summer shrugged. "Must be serious."

Grace shot her a warning glare. "Fiona. Yeah. What about her?"

"She...she showed up out of nowhere." He ran a hand through his hair. "We were out behind the dorms, and that lady just *appeared*—"

"Wow, Romeo. You and the shifter girl behind the dorms, huh?" Summer offered him a second caramel apple and grinned. "Didn't think you had it in you."

"What? No. It wasn't—Guys, she was pissed. She tried to *attack* me, and I think... I think she kidnapped Amanda."

The witches slowly looked at each other, and the second their gazes met, they burst out laughing.

"What?" Jackson stepped away from them and looked back and forth from one girl to the other. "Why's that funny? Jesus Christ, they *disappeared*!"

"Don't worry about it, Romeo." Summer waved the uneaten caramel apple at him again as Grace tried to pull herself together.

"Don't worry? How can you say that? We need to tell somebody—"

"No way. Let them handle it." Summer snorted. "It's a shifter thing."

"A what?"

"They teleported, Jackson." Grace carefully wiped the tears away from her eyes, making sure not to smudge her butterfly makeup. "That's a thing Fiona does. If Amanda went with Fiona, she's fine."

"But...she..."

"You need to relax." Summer shoved the apple at him one more time. "This'll help. Oh, hey. They broke out the HardPull tonight too."

Grace rubbed her hands together. "Ooh, yeah. That'll *definitely* help."

"You talking about him or you, Blondie?"

"Both. Let's go get some."

The girls hurried down the side of the table toward the giant punchbowl filled to the brim with spiced HardPull and left Jackson standing there with a caramel apple he had no intention of eating.

He looked up across the central field toward the dorm buildings he would have seen if they weren't blocked from view by the entrance arch and the shimmering veil.

Shifters can teleport *now too?*

MARTHA CARR & MICHAEL ANDERLE

"Dude." Alex stopped beside him and clapped a hand on his shoulder. "You gonna eat that?"

Jackson stared blankly at the Samhain party, seeing none of it, and slowly lifted the apple on a stick toward the Wood Elf. "Take it."

"Sweet."

CHAPTER TWENTY-SIX

"I can't believe you did that," Amanda muttered as she folded her arms on the upholstered bench of the Starbucks train.

"You can't believe what *I* did?" Fiona glanced into the aisle through the open cabin doors, then leaned forward and hissed, "*You're* the one who had a little private meeting with your boyfriend so you could spill top-secret Coalition affairs."

"That's not—"

"I get it, Amanda. It's hard to carry around so many secrets with you, but you can't open your mouth to anyone who looks like they might be trustworthy."

"I didn't tell him any top-secret anything—"

"You had the phone in your *hand*!" Fiona cleared her throat as the train's exterior doors closed. "You expect me to believe you two were behind that building taking selfies together?"

"What?"

"Serious mistake on your part. If anyone finds out about this—"

"Fiona, my friends already know about the internship. It's not like I have a bunch of secrets passwords to share with them. I'm not spreading Coalition knowledge all over the place. Jackson saw me leave our Halloween party so I could reply to all the messages blowing up that stupid phone *in private—*"

"*This train is now departing. Please remain seated. Thank you.*"

The Starbucks train lurched forward. Somehow, Amanda's anger made it more possible than ever to withstand the incredibly high G-force that would have smashed her back against her seat otherwise. Then the train screeched to a halt, and she continued.

"He wanted to make sure I was okay."

"I don't care who asks you what. You don't tell anybody about what we're doing, and you certainly don't show them the *phone* you're not even supposed to have."

Amanda slumped back against the cushion. "You're pissed that someone called you to get me on this train, aren't you?"

"We're not talking about me."

"That's why you're such a jerk."

Fiona hissed, then bit down on her bottom lip and shot her mentee a warning sidelong glance. "Don't go there."

"Really? Because I haven't done anything wrong. I could've stayed there at the party and ignored *all* the calls, but I didn't. I answered. Besides, I thought this whole internship wasn't supposed to interfere with my classes."

"You weren't in class, Amanda."

"It's Thursday."

"The parameters have been stretched a little, okay? So you'll have to—"

"*This train is now departing. Please remain seated. Thank you.*"

Fiona growled. "I'm gonna rip those speakers out of the ceiling if I have to listen to that one more time!"

Amanda's sneaker tapped up and down on the floor of the cabin. "Good thing we're getting off at the next stop."

"Yeah. I'm overjoyed."

Neither of their moods had improved when they showed up at the Canissphere ten minutes later. For just after 9:00 p.m. on a Thursday, the facility's main dome was unusually busy, and that only made Fiona even more agitated.

"Did anyone tell you why my *presence* is requested so *immediately?*" Amanda asked.

"No. Cut it out with the attitude, huh? If we both got called in, it's a big deal. It's hard enough for me to keep the sarcasm out of my voice when it's so poignantly oozing from yours."

"They're here!" Lucy shouted as she shoved through the crowd of shifters gathered in the dome. "They're here. Excuse me. *Move*, Bradley. Excuse me." When she stumbled to a halt in front of Amanda and Fiona, she looked them both up and down and clutched her tablet tighter against her chest. "You're here."

"Yes, we've established that," Fiona growled.

"Come with me." Dr. Caniss' assistant said nothing else as she led them down corridors and two steep staircases Amanda hadn't seen before. The light was dim at the bottom of the stairs, but as soon as they exited the hall, Amanda blinked against the bright glare of a work light aimed right at the staircase entrance.

"That's them," Dr. Caniss muttered, her voice coming from seemingly everywhere at once.

Nope. That's only an insane echo.

"Rick, turn off the light."

The bright light clicked off, and Amanda's vision adjusted quickly to the dark.

They stood on a circular walkway surrounding an incredibly wide pool of dark water. Another set of stairs on the right led down to the edge of the pool, where Dr. Caniss stood with four other shifter scientists beside a massive metal rectangular box covered in sporadically blinking lights and standing seven feet tall.

"Why would they put that so close to the water?" Amanda whispered.

"Shh." Fiona shot her a sidelong glance and shook her head. "Keep it to yourself."

Okay, it's bad if she won't even joke about it with me.

"Amanda." Dr. Caniss waved her forward from the bottom landing. "Down here, please. Ms. Damascus, I'll have to ask you to stand back."

"Sure." Fiona nudged her mentee toward the side staircase. "Go ahead. I'm staying right here."

Frowning, Amanda paced toward the stairs, her footsteps echoing in the massive underground chamber filled with water in the center. When she reached the bottom, she saw one more shifter she didn't recognize sitting back in a metal folding chair against the half wall. His eyes were closed, and he looked like he could have been sleeping if it wasn't for the giant, heavy-looking metal helmet resting on his head and connected to the massive box of blinking lights beside him.

She pointed at the machine. "You build a computer or something?"

"Or something," a shifter man muttered. One glance at the nametag on his lab coat told her this was Rick. He folded his arms and stared at the sleeping shifter in the sci-fi helmet.

"What's going—"

"Shh." He lifted a finger to stop her but didn't look away from the guy hooked up to the machine. "Wait 'til Mel comes back."

"Um… Where did he go?"

"Silence, please," Caniss muttered.

The wait felt like it took forever, and Amanda turned slowly to eye the massive pool. The water wasn't completely dark after all. A faint turquoise glow came from somewhere very far down —so far, she didn't think she could see the bottom even if she leaned over the edge. She was about to test that theory when the shifter in the chair sucked in a sharp breath and salt bolt upright.

"There he is." Caniss nodded.

Mel slowly removed the helmet and blinked heavily before looking up at the shifters crowding around him. "They're ready."

"Excellent. Dr. Han, please outfit Amanda for—"

"No." Mel shook his head. "Sorry to interrupt, Dr. Caniss. They were clear about wanting to meet with her in a specific way. I tried to explain, but there's still a rather frustrating language barrier, as you can imagine."

"Of course." Caniss narrowed her eyes, then gestured toward Amanda. "Tell her, then."

"Wait a minute." Amanda shook her head. "*Who* wants to meet with me?"

"Subject UM-43562," Mel said as he handed the wired helmet over to another scientist and slowly stood from the chair. "You're familiar?"

She darted a glance at the dark body of water. *No way...*

"You mean the...divergent mermaids? They're *here*?"

"Right in that very water." Caniss nodded. "So far, the underground lake has managed to sustain their immediate needs. Until a few hours ago, when they refused to speak to any of our staff. And requested an audience with you specifically."

"You're kidding."

"I can't say I am."

"Well... I mean, how am I supposed to talk to those things? Even the *mermaids* can't understand them. What do they want from me?"

"That we don't know." Caniss tilted her head and gave the shifter girl a single stern nod. "We hope you'll find out."

"I don't—"

"One of our colleagues was injured earlier this evening," Rick added, scratching his chin. "We would've written it off as an accident, but the representative for this divergent species made it clear they'd manipulated us into something of a hostage situation."

"Hey, listen, if those dragged him down to the bottom of that lake, or whatever, there's nothing *I* can do to help him." Amanda shrugged. "He's probably not even—"

"He's currently in critical condition in our medical wing," Caniss cut in. "So no, diving for injured colleagues is not our to-do list tonight."

"Okay." Amanda glanced from one shifter to the next, unable to put any of the pieces together. "Why am I here?"

"Because during Mel's attempts to reason with the Subject UM-43562 representative, to discover why they injected one of our fellow shifters with an unknown and as yet unstudied neuro-toxin with no conceivable explanation, their representative mentioned you."

"They want to talk to you," Mel added. "I couldn't get anything more out of them than that."

"Why?" Amanda almost laughed but forced it back down again. "It's not exactly like we're best friends or anything. I *fought* them."

"We're as perplexed by this as you are, Amanda," Caniss said.

"I doubt that."

"One of ours is lying in a hospital bed upstairs with his life on the line. We'll do whatever we must to ensure he pulls through, and that means bringing you here to commune with the representative who requested you specifically."

"By name?" Fiona asked from the top walkway, her voice echoing across the water.

Mel shook his head. "Wolf-girl from the swamp. That's the clearest translation I could get. So unless there's another shifter girl at your school, we have to assume they meant you."

"Yeah, that's probably me." Amanda pointed at the metal helmet. "That's how you talk to them?"

"It connects to a device we installed at the bottom of the lake. Even with all the improvements, the translations are rudimentary at best. You won't be using this." Mel cocked his head and studied her face for a moment before adding, "They said they want to speak with you again in the same way as before, only beneath the surface this time. Does that mean anything to you?"

"I didn't…" Amanda blinked quickly when the only possibility popped into her head.

That's insane. I saw them with my ghost-wolf that one time in the swamp. When they were in the giant cage. Still, we didn't exactly talk.

Then again, she'd come a long way with her magic since then.

"Okay." She nodded and looked out over the dark water with the faint turquoise glow blooming up from the depths. "Yeah, I'll give it a try."

"Your best effort," Caniss added. "Preferably not an attempt at all but a conversation that produces actual results."

Amanda swallowed. "Well, trying is pretty much all I can promise at this point."

"Understood."

"What do you need?" Mel asked.

"Um…just that chair." The shifter stepped aside to let her pass, and she sat in the metal folding chair before looking up at all of them with wide eyes. "Maybe someone to catch me. You know, in case I start to fall over. I'm sick of waking up on the floor."

Rick smirked. "No one's going anywhere. We'll make sure you stay put."

"Thanks." Amanda craned her neck to look up at the elevated walkway, where Fiona now stood along the railing, and looked down at her with wide eyes.

Her mentor nodded. "You got this, kid. Piece of cake."

"Right." Closing her eyes, Amanda let herself settle back in the cold, hard chair and drew a deep breath. "They won't come up to the surface for this?"

"That's what I understand," Mel replied.

"Then I guess I'm going in."

CHAPTER TWENTY-SEVEN

Fortunately, Amanda's apprehension about slipping out of her physical body right here beside the not-mermaids' underground lake didn't have any effect on her ability to call out her ghost-wolf. The second she saw the surface of the water much closer to her face instead of the dark backs of her eyelids, she knew she was ready.

"We'll pull you back if there's a need." Rick nodded. "Try to get as much as you can as quickly as possible."

Oh, sure. I'll tell the mutant creatures who put your guy in a neuro-toxin coma that they need to hurry up with their hostage terms.

She looked up at the other shifters gazing down at her from far more than a foot away, then turned toward the water.

Really glad nobody can hear me.

Amanda and her ghost-wolf padded toward the pool's edge and gazed down at their reflection rippling across the surface.

Déjà vu so hardcore right now. Doesn't even matter. We're going down. Good thing magic doesn't need to breathe underwater.

Fully intending to *not* walk across the surface of the pool, Amanda stepped one smoky-white paw off the edge of the pool, and it phased right through. So she leapt, and down they went without a splash, running through the briny water as if it were nothing more than an incredibly steep downhill slope.

The turquoise glow at the bottom drew closer and closer, but she still couldn't see the bottom of the underground lake even when she swam beneath the edge of the chamber.

The underground lake was massive, stretching out in every direction around her. Long strands of kelp rose from the lakebed too far below in the darkness to gauge. Something that almost sounded like music echoed all around her, and the ghost-wolf pricked her ears.

Okay, mermaid...creatures. I'm here. Time to talk.

The sensation of moving around in whichever direction she wanted—including straight up and straight down—without physically having to move legs she still couldn't completely feel was disorienting, to say the least. She somehow felt the current of much cooler water brushing past her from behind.

A mere thought directed her magic and her ghost-wolf toward the source of the dropping temperature. Then she was face-to-face with one sneering, razor-toothed, turquoise-scaled divergent mermaid.

Yeah, that's not creepy.

It was impossible to tell the gender of the magical in front of her, even with its long, seaweed-green hair fanning out around its face in all directions. Beady black eyes stared right at her, and Amanda didn't move.

Not sure this is gonna work, but apparently, you wanted to talk. So I'm here to...talk.

The mermaid-thing darted closer and extended a claw-tipped finger toward her.

Amanda backed away through the water as if caught on the end of a fishing line, but the divergent mermaid widened its eyes and reached out again, slower this time.

When that tip barely brushed against the center of the ghost-wolf's forehead, a burst of startling cold flared behind Amanda's eyes—or the ghost-wolf's eyes or maybe both. She was still there afterward, floating as an actual specter in the water in front of this creature who'd attacked her school and Rob Mackey and now one of the Coalition's top scientists.

What do you want?

"We offer an exchange."

In no way had Amanda expected to hear a voice in her mind, let alone dozens of them all at once. They were neither male nor female, but as she stared into the divergent mermaid's beady black eyes, she knew exactly who the voice belonged to.

Wow. Okay. Um, an exchange for what?

"The wolf-man above. We can restore him."

The one you poisoned to get this meeting in the first place, right?

"He lives. The others above do not understand. You do. We wished to speak with you, wolf-girl. Now we offer an exchange."

Yeah, you said that. What do you want?

"Our…" A loud, blaring screech filled Amanda's ears, and thousands of tiny bubbles burst from the creature's open mouth lined with razor-sharp teeth. "It was stolen. We want it returned."

I…didn't catch that first part. She studied the creature floating there among the ridiculously long kelp. *Weirdest conversation I've ever had, and I should probably stop having thoughts at all if it can hear me.*

"You will see." The divergent mermaid reached out one more time and tapped the center of the ghost-wolf's forehead with a black-tipped claw.

Amanda did see. Without words, she saw an entire sequence of events straight from the creature's mind—or maybe its finger. When it was over, she and her ghost-wolf drifted backward through the water one more time to collect themselves.

So where's the one who took it?

"That, we do not see." The creature tipped back its head to look up toward the surface and slowly pointed that way with the same clawed finger. "You will find the thief. You will retrieve what is ours.

Then we will restore the wolf-man who sleeps with our blood in his veins."

Your blood? Wait, is it poison or—

The creature let out another grating screech with those thousands of tiny bubbles. Then it whipped its powerful tail with the sideways fin and darted away into the dark underbelly of the lake.

Um...hello?

Amanda searched the water, but she no longer felt the cold temperatures, and nothing else moved but the thick strands of kelp and a single slow pulse of turquoise light from the lakebed far below.

Guess we're done.

Two seconds later, Amanda jolted forward on the metal folding chair, and Rick steadied her with both hands on her shoulders. "Whoa. There you go."

She puffed out a sigh and blinked quickly in the darkness before looking up at Dr. Caniss and all her hand-selected scientists for this particular pickle in which they'd found themselves.

"Did you speak to them?" Caniss asked.

"Kinda, yeah."

"You either did or did not, Amanda."

The girl pushed herself to her feet. "Did you see my mouth moving when I passed out in the chair?"

The other scientists stared at her in mute shock.

Dr. Caniss bit her bottom lip and squinted at Amanda, and for a moment, it seemed as if the girl was about to get her ear chewed off by the head biologist who no one spoke to that way in the least. Instead, the woman finally nodded once. "I see."

"What did they tell you?" Mel asked softly, darting glances toward Caniss as if he thought she'd lash out at him instead.

"They hurt your other scientist to get your attention," Amanda replied. "I think. So they could get you to get me to talk to them. Which doesn't even make sense. It's not like I have a super-strong connection with those creatures. One of you didn't try the whole 'send your magic down into the lake' thing first?"

The scientists exchanged knowing glances, and Dr. Caniss steepled her fingers, tapping them slowly together. "As far as we know, you're one of the very few shifters who've managed to get that far with the advanced use of their magic. And the only shifter approved by the Coalition at this facility."

Amanda spun to look up at Fiona, who gave her a sheepish smile and shrugged. "Okay, I definitely wasn't expecting that."

"What did they tell you, Amanda?"

"Right. There's a… I guess it's some kind of power source for them. Like a life…cell or something. It was stolen."

"Well, we certainly didn't take it," Rick muttered.

"No, I know. They know that too." The girl nodded toward the pool. "They know who did take it. It's more like a *what*, actually—"

"Speak some sense, girl!" Caniss barked.

"Hey, I just got a creature's entire thought process blasted into my head through pictures because it didn't have the words," Amanda shot back. "So, can I get a minute?"

Her voice echoed through the underground cavern, disturbed only by an abrupt snort up above from Fiona.

"Sorry."

"Take your time," Caniss muttered before spinning away to pace the length of the ledge beside the pool.

"It's another divergent species," Amanda finally said, piecing everything together as mermaid translator. "I'd call this one a monster. So, we might wanna get on that. Oh, yeah. Because they'll heal the shifter who's knocked out in the med wing after we return their stolen power whatever."

Caniss hissed and stormed back toward her. "Can you give an accurate description of this new species?"

"Yeah."

"Did Subject UM-43562 give you any information as to how we can track down the creature in question?"

"Yeah."

"Then we'll take you to the operations unit, and you'll work with them from here on out." Caniss glanced at each of her scientists and nodded. "We can't wait that long."

"Dr. Caniss, no offense, but we have to get this thing back," Amanda said. "To heal the—"

"We will do it anyway, whether or not those creatures down in that lake adhere to their end of a bargain that's precarious at best." The woman nodded. "Until then, we can work faster with producing our antidote and hopefully find at least a semi-effective solution before this new *monster* of yours is apprehended."

"It's not *mine*—"

"Plus, we'll need you to work on a new plant in your greenhouse."

"Wait, what?"

Mel nodded. "That should work. I'll have Calvin put together a list."

"No, hold on." Amanda held up her hands. "I don't have time to grow a bunch of plants. We should be out there going after this monster thing so the mermaid-things can help your guy."

"You have plenty of time, Amanda." Caniss glanced up at Fiona without expression, then nodded at the intern. "You have a knack with these things, demonstrated particularly well with your shortened timespan for growing Fatethistle. You'll take the seeds and instructions from Calvin, and you'll grow these too."

"I don't have any more of the—" Amanda gritted her teeth. "I don't have what I had last time to grow the Fatethistle. It's all gone."

"Then you'd best figure out a way to make more or get more. I don't care how you have to do it. If you can grow these plants before the end of the year, even better. Until then, we'll work on forming a team to take you with them to find this monster eventually."

"Did they give you a timeline?" Rick asked. "For returning their stolen item before they keep up their end of the agreement?"

"No." Amanda shook her head. "They said he was sleeping with their blood in his veins."

"Hmm." Mel stroked his hairless chin. "Sounds like an induced stasis."

Caniss clapped a hand on Amanda's shoulder and nodded. "Then it seems we're at the mercy of *your* timeline. Your top priority for the rest of the school year is to grow the plants we need to attempt healing this stasis on our own. By the time you finish the semester, we'll be ready to launch a campaign for this stolen power source. See you at Christmas."

"What?"

Amanda spun to stare after the shifters as they all followed Dr. Caniss out of the chamber. Finally, only she and Fiona remained, so she stared at her mentor in disbelief instead.

"What just happened?"

Fiona gave her a tight smile. "That, kid, was you getting your first real job. I'll talk to Glasket. Make sure she knows what's going on. Looks like you got a lot of work to do."

With a humorless laugh, Amanda blinked and stared at the wall beside the giant semi-useful translating computer.

I'm gonna be hunting monsters. Over Christmas.

Get sneak peeks, exclusive giveaways, behind the scenes content, and more. PLUS you'll be notified of special **one day only fan pricing** on new releases.

Sign up today to get free stories.

Visit: https://marthacarr.com/read-free-stories/

April was an interesting month. Let's just say I went in for a regular physical – you know, quarantine was ending, and it was time to get some of those regular chores done that had been put off – and I came out the other side with cancer. My 5th turn around the dance floor with melanoma.

Fun fact – melanoma is a tricky little bastard and doesn't always appear in the same way. It's rare, but it happens. That means that the way a tumor appears doesn't really help the oncologist know much. Well, I've also had three variants and this particular one looked like it might finally be curtains for me.

Or at least a good fight on our hands. Just to make things more exciting, the PET scan, which would reveal all, was delayed and delayed and delayed. About halfway through the long wait, I realized I was either going to give in and relax, no matter the outcome, or I wasn't going to be able to have much of a life.

I made peace with the possibility that my life may be shorter than I expected. After all, death is not a tragedy. The way we die sometimes is, but not that we some day shrug off this identity.

Inch by inch, I was letting go of the fear – not completely, but just enough.

By the way, to end the insurance stalemate on the PET scan I finally paid for it myself. That actually added to my gratitude that I was able to do this for myself (and that has a lot to do with all of you – so Big Thank You for reading all of these books).

Two more days after the PET scan and a long wait in the doctor's office and he finally broke the news. No sign of cancer anywhere else despite the way this cancer presented. He looked a little confused and surprised and relieved. I could relate.

Somehow, I had once again whistled past the cemetery.

(By the way, as I write this, I'm awaiting surgery in two days to become cancer-free again. It's a strange thing to walk around with cancer, waiting on everyone's schedule.)

What to do with this newly found peace? That question was already swirling around in my head after a year of Covid and 2020 and masks and spending so much time alone. Everything had been wiped away and I am left with a blank slate to create whatever I want.

A very unique gift.

How can I use this to my benefit, to be of service to others? To be a part of building a better community? And to have more fun – a lot more fun.

Right off the bat, I know I need to slow down and become more aware of the world around me. Helps that a massive garden is being laid out in my backyard as I write this. Soon, I will be able to sit in my backyard and just be. Not every hour, but more.

Small changes add up to a different life.

I'm also going to be more deliberate about making new connections and strengthening the ones I have. Little things like sending postcards and remembering birthdays with more than a post on Facebook, or making actual phone calls to people and not just a quick text. And, now that I'm vaccinated, getting together for coffee or meeting up for a walk around the lake.

Old me would have squeezed in some of those things around book deadlines and marketing. If I got to them, great! But there was a good chance I would have squeezed in so many books that there wasn't a lot of time left over.

I've decided to change the question I ask myself from – can I fit in one more? Instead to – what would make a great balance and leave time for a life?

I still have a year of monthly immunotherapy injections to go, just to be sure. But that will only be a very small part of a bigger – and fun – life. More adventures to follow.

AUTHOR NOTES - MICHAEL ANDERLE

MAY 18, 2021

Thank you for not only reading this story but here to the author notes as well.

Martha has been one of my collaborators from the beginning. I met her in July of 2016, and we released our first series in July of 2017.

In that time, I have witnessed her many battles with cancer and am amazed at her calm disposition each and every time she goes through the challenge of dealing with it.

I also talk about how she "author blocks" me with her amazing story about the latest challenge where whatever I write about is going to pale in comparison to her story. Mind you, if the option is to go through a cancer scare to "win," I'm good, thanks.

During these five years come July, we have released a massive amount of titles with either both of our names on the cover or our joint pen name, Judith Berens.

Martha was a published author for decades before I even tried to write my first book. Like most authors, she had her ups and downs with the Trade publishers (the big 5.) I like to say they had

273

a bestselling author but failed to understand what genre to ask her to write in.

I can't say it was with wisdom and authority that I chose Urban Fantasy as the genre she would excel in. The reality is I just asked and was too ignorant to know any better. She liked stories in Urban Fantasy and could write. What else was there to know?

Many stories later, my collaborator still cracks me up with the funniest quips and memes. I'm glad her ugly stalker is being taken off tomorrow and that her future is looking so bright, we all need to wear shades.

Until the next book!

Ad Aeternitatem,

Michael Anderle

Solve a murder, save her mother, and stop the apocalypse?

What would you do when elves ask you to investigate a prince's murder and you didn't even know elves, or magic, was real?

Meet Leira Berens, Austin homicide detective who's good at what she does – track down the bad guys and lock them away.

Which is why the elves want her to solve this murder – fast. It's not just about tracking down the killer and bringing them to justice. It's about saving the world!

If you're looking for a heroine who prefers fighting to flirting, check out The Leira Chronicles today!

<u>AVAILABLE ON AMAZON AND IN KINDLE UNLIMITED!</u>

CONNECT WITH THE AUTHORS

Martha Carr Social

Website: http://www.marthacarr.com

Facebook: https://www.facebook.com/groups/MarthaCarrFans/

Michael Anderle Social

Website: http://lmbpn.com

Email List: http://lmbpn.com/email/

Social Media:

https://www.facebook.com/LMBPNPublishing

https://twitter.com/MichaelAnderle

https://www.instagram.com/lmbpn_publishing/

https://www.bookbub.com/authors/michael-anderle

Made in the USA
Las Vegas, NV
01 March 2024